MIDWE$T GUNNAZ

J. MONEY

SetBack Press

Midwe$t Gunnaz
All Rights Reserved.
Copyright © 2015 J. Money
v5.0

SetBack Press

ISBN: 978-0-578-16279-9

PRINTED IN THE UNITED STATES OF AMERICA

Chapter 1

Knock, knock.

"Who is it?"

"It's me, Ma."

"Me who?"

"Jay."

The door swings open. Mom is standing there, smiling from ear to ear. "Will, why didn't you tell me he was coming, boy?"

"Ma, I wanted to surprise you," I say.

"Come in, Jay, out of the cold, so I can shut that damn door. When did you get up here?"

"About twenty minutes ago. It's colder than a motherfucker up here."

"I know that, Jay. And watch your mouth in my house, boy."

"Okay, Ma. My bad. Where's Pops at?"

"In the back, sleeping. I was just about to lay down myself, but since you're home now, I can wait to lay down."

"What you cook, Ma?"

"Oh, boy. Some mac-n-cheese, greens and cornbread. And some pork chops. You ate yet?"

"No, Will just came and picked me up from the bus station."

"Well, eat up, son. It's more than enough to eat."

"Yeah, Jay, let's eat," my brother says.

"So how has things been going for you, Jay?"

"Things are okay. I'm just tired of Little Rock. You know, it's only so much a young goon can do there. Plus, I missed my family, too, Ma.

I felt alone those few years without you guys."

Ring, ring, ring. Mom walks over to the phone on the wall and answers it.

"Hello. Ghost, your little brother is here."

"Is he? When he get there? I'm on my way. Me and Shaunna."

"Okay. That was Ghost. Jay, he's on his way to see you with his girlfriend, Shaunna."

"Cool. I've not talked to him in years, either."

"Boy, you're so skinny. Have you been eating right?"

"Yeah, Ma. I sure can't gain weight fast."

"You need to slow down and take care of yourself, Jay."

"I do, Ma."

"No, you don't," Mom says, crossing her arms. "You smoke them damn blunts and shit all day. You think I don't know what you've been doing down there? Boy, I talk to Annie and Fred every week. And Keith tells them how you act out."

Shit, I'm going to have to have a real talk with his ass about that shit.

"That's cool, Ma. They don't see me no way. Will, what we getting into tonight, bro?"

"I got to go get Shaunna, my girl, and go see a movie tonight, but we'll hang out tomorrow."

"Bet! Ma, looks like you and Pops are cool."

"Yeah, we make it. But we're about to move out of here, though. It's dangerous around here."

Oh, yeah, we'll see about that shit.

"I can't even go the store without them young boys trying to sell me something or looking like they want to rob me, Jay. I tell you what, though, they ain't taking *shit* from me, Jay. You can believe that."

"Ma, you still crazy."

"Jay, now you know where we get if from," says Will.

"Shut up, boy!" Mom exclaims, "You act white, "Shit"."

"Ha, ha, ha, Ma. Very funny."

"Tell Jay where you live at," she says, trying to drive home her point.

"Uptown."

"Where is that at, Will?"

"Let me tell you," Mom says. "It's where all of the white folks live at."

"No, it ain't, Ma. There is a few blacks live in the building, too. I just don't want to have to be looking over my shoulder when I leave my apartment building."

"Damn, bro, you changed a whole lot."

"Nah, it ain't like that, Jay. I don't need that crap no more. I've grown up out of them kind of things, you know."

"Crap. Damn, when you speak like that, bro, yeah, you an Oreo nigga for sho."

"Well, I'm going to lay down, boys," Mom says. "Jay, here's a key for you when you leave."

"Thanks, Ma." I give her a nice hug and a kiss on the cheek and she walks down the hall to her room, then closes the door.

"Now back to you, bro. You lost your hood cred, huh? You have some type of want to be white boy now, huh? That shit is crazy, Joe."

"Who you calling Joe, Jay? That ain't my name, Jay."

"Damn, it's slang, bro. For homie, friend. You know."

"No, I don't know. So call me Will, Jay."

"Ok, give me some doe so I can get me a cunt and a few more things I need, son."

"Here, take this two thousand dollars and don't use it the wrong way either, boy. Buy clothes with it."

"Yeah. I know. Thanks, man. You straight with me"

"Drink a beer with me, bro."

"Yeah, I need one."

"Let me go to the ice box to get them for us."

"MGD tastes the best, Will."

"No, I like Heineken myself. But these will do."

Knock, knock, knock.

"Who dis?"

"Ghost."

"It's open, Joe. What's up, boy?"

"Jay, let's dip. I got Shaunna outside waiting. What it do, Will?"

"Nothing, Ghost. How are you?"

"Cool! We out."

Will goes out the door. "Holla at you tomorrow, Will," I say, then turn to Ghost. "C'mon so I can lock the door, son."

"Now you should have told me you was on your way, lil nigga," Ghost says. "Then I could have had you a bust down, you know. Man, fuck a bitch! I got to get paid, bro."

"I feel you on that one, boy."

"Now when we get into the whip, be cool, Jay. Shaunna's cool, but I need to drop her ass off so we can do us son."

We step into the new 745 BMW. All black, twenty-two-inch Lexani wheels, Perrelli tires, jet-black windows, two seventeen-inch TV monitors, two head rest TV monitors, four fifteen-inch SL audio subs pounding in the trunk, all Prada interior. This shit is laid the fuck out.

"Damn, that's clean, bro."

"Yeah, I know. She bought it for a player. Do your thing."

Ghost reached into the CD case and put in Top Authority: "I Had to Pop Him". I was feeling the music so much I almost forgot to speak to Shaunna when I got into the car. We ride on the freeway for a while, then make an exit. I lean forward.

"Hey, Shorty! How you doing?"

"Fine. And you?"

"I'm cool, lil mama. My name is Jay. What's yours?"

"Shaunna."

"Cool. We fam since you're with my big brother, huh?"

"Yeah. Ghost, where we going, baby?"

"We! You're going home so I can kick it with fam here. It's been years so I need to catch up on shit, Ma."

"I guess," she pouts.

"You know what, bitch? You better watch your mouth when you speak to me, hoe."

"I'm sorry, baby. Do you."

"That's better."

"Ghost, stop by a liquor store for me, Joe."

"Alright. There's one close by. What you want to drink, son?"

"A 12-pack of MGD and a pint of Hennessy."

We pull into the lot and it's full of people trying to get into the store before ten p.m. Ghost leaves the car, then Shaunna asks me how old I am.

"Sixteen."

"You're cute, Jay."

"Thank you." She don't know I'll bust her old ass down.

"Where you staying at?"

"My mom's right now."

"Well, if you need anything, call us, okay?"

"Yeah, I will."

Ghost comes out of the store, walking towards the car, looking funny. "What you talking about now, girl?"

"Nothing. Just talking about the city with Jay."

"Now don't tell me you jealous of me, nigga, talking to your boo, Joe."

"Nah, you just too slick for your own good, Jay. But fuck that. I got a case of beer and a liter of Hennessy for us, lil homie."

We slide out the packed lot with all eyes on the whip. Son, even 5.0 looking and shit.

I pop me a beer and sit back and try to remember Stacy and Tasha's phone number in Little Rock. Stacy is my bitch and Tasha is her sister. We did everything together. I miss them, too. I'm back in my own world when the car stops at the crib.

"Ghost, when you comin' back?"

"Later girl, so don't be blowing up my fucking phone."

"Shit. I'll be over my sister's house."

"Cool."

Shaunna gets out and I get in the front seat now. *Now where we at? Thirty-eighth and Fourth Street. The Bloods' hood. Ain't nothing changed about me, bro. I'm hood for sho, nigga.*

"Damn, Ghost, Will is on some new kids on the block shit, huh?"

"Well that's peanut for you, Jay. Not me, though."

"Shit, I need some dro."

"You can't smoke in the whip, though. I got a place to go to for that shit."

"Damn. Look, kill that damn shit right now, 'G'."

"I'm just fucking with you, Jay. Stop tripping, Joe."

"Let's be out now."

"I had to make sure she left safely, Jay. These streets are vicious, homie. We got the only new Range Rover around here, so I have to make sure when she drives, she's okay. Know what I mean? This ninety-shot Mac-10 will do just that."

"Damn, that's hot there, boy."

"I got you Jay, don't trip. Now that's what I'm talking about."

"Where we going? 'Cause it's too late for me to go shopping and I can't fit your shit, Joe."

"First, we going to see my man Lil D to get right, my nigga. Then we off to the strip club. My man Lil D got that purple shit. Man, his shit is so frosty that water would freeze dripping down it, Jay."

"Ooh, shit. I'm feeling this beer, Joe. Damn, look at them hoes looking at us in that 500 Benz."

"Watch this, Jay."

Ghost pulls up to the red light ahead and turns up the volume on the bass. Them hoes go buck. The one driving is a light-skinned redbone, long black hair down past her shoulders, deep red lipstick.

Chinky eyes. She is bad just looking through the window. We make eye contact for a few seconds, then she motions for us to pull over. I turn down the music, grab the Mac-10, and say, "Pull over, fam. I got you if they ain't straight, bro."

They pull into a McDonald's parking lot on Lake Street and we pull up beside them. The driver gets out first. *Damn, she is finer than a super model.*

Ghost gets out and walks to the passenger side of the Benz to holler at her friend. The driver walks up to my side of the car as I cock the Mac and put it under my hoodie to look after fam. I step out slowly like I'm not sweating her fine ass like that. "Hey, shorty, what's good?"

"You. What's your name?"

"Kendra," she says, her head held high like a queen.

"Kendra, I'm Jay. Nice to meet you, Ma."

"Likewise. Nice car you guys riding in."

"Thanks. It's my brother's."

"You riding fly, too, shorty? Is that your man's whip?"

"Nah, baby. I'm independent. I don't need no nigga to take care of me, boo boo. See my tags?"

Says Queenie, "Enough of that already. Where are you two going?"

"I don't know, Shorty. I'm from Little Rock and I don't know nothing about Minneapolis."

"Ooh, that explains your accent, then. Want to blow some smoke, Jay?"

"Yeah, if it's cush only. Not swally."

"Let's get into my Benz."

"Cool. 'Cause he don't blow in the BMW."

When she turns to walk to her car, that ass is just jumping in every direction known to man. Them apple bottom jeans do magic on my eyes. I give her a smirk when she looks to see if I am looking, like the true player I am. "Shit. Looks like they started without us, huh?" As we approach the car, I smell nugs burning and they smell fine, too. We open the doors and dro flows out in clouds of smoke in our faces. We quickly sit down in the back seats to join in on the smoke feast. "Looks like you're cool, bro."

"Yeah, cud, this here is Mercedes. She cool people, too, Ghost says. "Mercedes, this my lil brother Jay. He's fresh from down South."

"Nice to meet you, Jay."

"Likewise, Shorty. Now that that's out of the way, let's do the funk."

"Damn. Mercedes, bitch, I told you to wait for us. Shit. Quit crying, hoe. We got plenty to smoke. So don't act like that. You two look like two Chinks smoking."

Ghost passes the nug over the seat to me. The first hit tastes so sweet, like blueberry. Now I feel like I'm about to be right. I take a deep pull and my head instantly starts to sweat. So I hold the smoke for a few seconds, then release it, only to start choking. I got a head rush so fast and my heart starts to racing like crazy.

Kendra starts patting my back, saying, "Are you okay?"

"Yeah. That's some bomb shit right there."

"I know, Jay. Only the best for me."

"I can dig that, shorty."

Kendra puts the blunt up to her full lips and takes a deep pull herself. She doesn't choke, sweat, or look like she couldn't handle it. I'm impressed now.

Ghost is looking to our left at the BMW, kind of strange. So I look past Kendra to see what he's looking at. Shit. It's two niggas in blue bandanas posted on the hood of the car looking around, mugging, and shit. These hoes better not be on some setup shit or they through for sho.

Ghost looks back at me like "It's on you." I nod my head to let him know I got the Mac-10. These hoes don't know what's about to go down. I slide out the back seat without them two niggas even seeing me do it. I'm posted at the back of the Benz, listening to the two dudes talk.

"Yeah, cuz. Where that nigga Ghost? I got this .45 Magnum for they ass tonight, cuz. Fuck them slob-ass niggas, cuz."

That's all I need to hear about my brother. I slide my hoodie on over my head and creep to the back of the BMW to get good aim and the two dead men. I creep up to the front of the car and put the mack to the head of the one holding his strap under his pants. He freezes, shocked. His homie looks at Ghost, now in the front seat of the Benz, unaware that I got his crab-ass homeboy on point. He hollers out, "Shotgun Crip. Slob-ass nigga."

Pop, pop, pop, pop, pop, pop spits the Mac at point-blank range to his homie's skull, blowing his brains on the side of his boy's face. Before his ass hits the ground, I'm on his dome. Bap to the back of the head with the Mac. Ghost jumps out of the Benz. "Hold up, Jay. Let me see that."

The whole time the two women just look like it's nothing new to them. "Damn, that's Coogie and Trap. The two Crip niggas who have been riding through the Four Block looking for me, cud. Now buck that nigga and let's bounce, fam."

Ghost walks up to the crab nigga and buck, buck buck, buck, buck, to the face. People are running, hollering and ducking. Kendra says, "Let's go over to my crib. It's on Thirty-seventh and Pleasant."

Cool. 'Cause I can hear police sirens coming now. We pull out of the lot just in time to miss being caught. "Good looking, Jay. I owe you, Joe."

"Nah, you my bro. I got your back, son. Damn, I ain't been here twenty-four hours yet and you got me in some murder one shit."

"Let me call Lil D and tell him to meet me over there. Pass me a brew, dog."

"Here, Ghost."

Beep, beep. Ghost speed dials Lil D. "What's hood, my dog?" Lil D asks.

"Meet me on the corner of Thirty-seventh and Pleasant ASAP, homie."

"No doubt," replies Lil D.

"Bring me some purp, too, dog, 'cause I need it right now," Ghost says tiredly.

"I'm on my way, dog. One."

Ghost looks at me. "I see you still the same."

"Always hood to death. The streets is my pussy, just waiting to be fucked, dog."

"Jay, you a fool."

"Ghost, now them hoes are down."

"Yeah, I know. We could use bitches like them for real."

"Now we have to keep an eye on them and get to know them more or we kill them right now."

"I know, Jay. No witness, no case. We here now, so grab the brew and the Henny so we can see where their minds is, dog."

We get out of the car and look for something that isn't right. "All of the lights look like they're on to me, Ghost," I say.

"I'm going to grab my Mac." He walks back to the car to get the burner. "Now I feel better, Jay, with my heartless hoe on my hip. Let's go up to the door. I hope Shaunna don't ride by and see my fucking car, bro. Push open the door, Jay."

"This crib is straight, Joe."

Chirp, chirp. "Nigga, I'm up the block," says Lil D.

"Damn," says Ghost. "My car is outside. Pull up and park. Kendra, my guy is up the street with my purple, so I'm going to wait outside 'til he pull up."

"Okay. You and Jay come in when he gets here, baby."

"Can he come in, too?" Ghost asks.

"I don't usually let people come over to my home, but I will make an exception this time."

"Thank you. There he go, my dog."

"Shit, that's a fly-ass whip, too, Ghost," I say. "What is it?"

"A '69 Cutlass drop top."

Lil D parks across the street from the BMW and jumps out. He's in murder mode, burner in hand and flamed up from head to toe. He slowly walks toward us as he spots us on the steps.

Ghost says, "My nigga."

"What's hood?" Lil D asks.

"Damn. Static with them crab niggas tonight, Coogie and Trap," Ghost replies. "Look they wet, son."

"Man, let's get in the house to talk," I urge my brother.

"Yeah, you right, Jay. Lil D, this my little brother, Jay."

"What up," says Lil D.

"Nah, not me, 'G'. It's all good."

We walk through the front door and Kendra and Mercedes are in panties and bras, rolling nugs to smoke. "Hey, I thought you guys left us."

"Not a chance, Shorty. I need to finish what I started in the car."

"That's what I'm talking about, Jay," says Ghost. "Ladies, this is my man, Lil D."

"'Sup, ladies?" Lil D says politely.

"Hey!" Ghost says. "Let's see this purple you got, Lil D."

"No problem, ma."

Now, my mind is on what to do about these hoes. Mercedes has a flawless body like none I've ever seen before. No stretch marks. No fat except on her ass and breasts. Shit, her toes are so well taken care of, you want to suck them. She has a short Halle Berry haircut that looks just right on her. Creamy skin that's so smooth-looking.

I get so into looking at Mercedes that I almost forget about Kendra. I snap out of my daze when Lil D asks Ghost what happened tonight.

"Damn, me and Jay meet these hoes at a stop light on Lake Street and pull over at McDonald's to spit game. Then I look over at my whip to see them two bitch-ass crab niggas, Coogie and Trap, sitting on my fucking hood, dog, like it's all good and shit. I look at Jay like, 'It's on' and he took it from there, dog. Before I knew it, he was out the car with the Mac spitting."

"Man, where was these hoes, dog?" Lil D asks.

"Right next to us smoking like nothing was going on. Damn, what's up with that shit?"

Lil D replies, "Damn, I don't know, but I will, you know?"

Kendra interrupts. "Can't you guys talk later, Jay?"

"Yeah, Ma. We straight now."

"Why don't you and them come over here so we can entertain each one of you?"

"Yeah, it's enough pussy and mouth to go around, guys."

"Let's pop the Henny, dog," I say.

"Cool. Let's bust these hoes down, Jay," says Ghost. "Now that's what I'm talking about."

"Kendra, come here, baby. Let daddy help you out that thong, Shorty."

I hear Keith Sweat playing "Make It Last Forever" on the system. Mercedes is on the table, dancing for Ghost and Lil D now like a born stripper. Shit, the way her ass is jumping has my attention. Then I feel a hand pull down my zipper. I look down, and it's Kendra on her knees with her sexy lips ready to please a pimp. I loosen my belt, unbutton my pants, then let them fall to the floor. Before they get to my ankles, she has my boxers down and her nice warm, wet mouth and lips wrapped around my shaft.

Wet lips, softly deep throating my shit, rubbing my balls. With each stroke, her smooth tongue moves up and down the bottom of my dick. My knees get so weak I have to lie down.

I look across the room to see Ghost and Lil D with Mercedes moaning loud over the music. Ghost is behind her, pounding her wet, swollen pussy from the back. Sweat drips from his face on to her back as he grunts with every stroke from the tight pussy he's getting. Lil

D has his dick deep down her throat, holding the back of her head to keep a steady motion. This was a fuck fest for sure.

"Shit, baby. This is the shit, Ma." I bust ice cream all down Kendra's throat, then lay back on the couch to relax for a second. I hear, "Whose pussy is this, shorty?"

"Yours!"

"Yours, who?"

"Ghost's pussy! Oohhhh... yeah..."

"Whose mouth is this?"

"Yours!"

"Whose, Shorty?"

"Lil D's mouth!"

Then the house gets quiet, except for the CD playing Kelly Price with Ron Isley. Kendra speaks up. "That was fun, Jay. Can I fuck you now?"

"Hold on, Ma. We got to talk right quick."

"About what?"

"You know what, Kendra."

"You straight, Jay. We see murder all the time."

That catches my attention. What kind of woman is this tough? There can only be two kinds in my book, police or set-up bitch. Either way, I can't trust that note. She gots to go.

"Baby, forget that now and let's go upstairs," she entreats.

"Okay, but hold on. Let's see what they going to do, shorty."

"My room is the first on the left when you get to the top of the stairs." She glides from the couch, up the stairs and disappears.

Ghost looks at me. "Dog, what's up with you?" he asks.

"Man, you talk to that hoe, Ghost?"

"Yeah, she's funny. I asked her why they was so calm and she said her brother is M.C. and they killed people in the Chi all the time. Nah, that shit don't sit cool with me."

"We need to flat-line these hoes and dip, fam."

"I'm with that, dog. Lil D, you heated dog."

"Yessum, my nigga."

"Clean up our shit so it looks like no one was here with them, dog."

"Ghost, I'm going upstairs to do me," I say.

"Take care of your shit now, Joe," Lil D says.

"Lil D, I don't know you, but don't play, son."

"Listen, lil dude. I been putting in work since you've been in Pampers. So handle yours. I got this. Damn. Bounty hunters for life! C'mon, it's late."

I walk halfway up the stairs without looking up. I hear a metallic cocking sound. Damn, this bitch has a burner pointed at me. "Hurry up, nigga. Get your punk ass up here now," she demands.

"Okay, shorty. Slow down. What's with this, ma?"

"You know damn well what it is. Your whip, your stash, or your life, nigga."

Damn, I knew those hoes was up to something! I walk into her bedroom with a 50-caliber pressed to the back of my head. As soon as I get past the door, I get hit on the side of my head by a dude wearing a blue bandana.

Downstairs, Mercedes calls. "Ghost, come here, baby."

"Where are you?" Ghost asks.

"My room is through the kitchen."

"I'm getting us a drink, shorty. You clean up, Lil D?"

"Yeah, dog."

"Follow me," Ghost whispers. "I think that bitch Mercedes is some hoe I've seen sometime before, dog. Oh, yeah. I just can't put my hand on it yet."

Down in the kitchen, the lights are off. Be cool and on point. "Hey, it's dark in here, baby. Where's the light switch?"

Lil D is in the basement, waiting. He taps Ghost. "Look at your shirt, Ghost."

Pop, pop, pop. Lil D shoots in the direction of the light beam with his silenced .45 Glock. They hear a body drop not too far away. We're on point now. Ghost enters the basement first with a drink in one hand and the Mac in the other. "Bitch, come here."

Mercedes walks over about two feet in from of Ghost when Lil D shoots four times. Two to the face busts her brains out the back of her skull; two more to the chest blow out her heart through her back. It lands on the bed, still beating with life.

"Damn, dog, you could have hit me," Ghost says.

"Nah, I'm a professional," Lil D replies. "This is what I do, remember, Ghost? Man, now where is Jay?"

I wake up with my arms tied together and feet, too, and a dirty pair of panties taped in my mouth. I mumble, "You're dead, Joe." I get slapped with a twelve-gauge shot gun. "Cuz, you the only nigger in here tonight that's going to die. And, oh, yeah, by now, your brother's just like you. 'Crip for life'! Give me the keys to the BMW outside, cuz."

"It's not my car, Joe."

Bap, bap. Blood starts to run down my chin, falling into my lap. Death is in my eyes now.

"You answer me right now, cuz, or I'll blow your fucking knee off, nigga. I want the stash house address and don't lie, cuz."

"You slob-ass niggas will never learn, cuz."

"These are Shotgun Crip streets, cuz."

Downstairs, Ghost lays a hand on Lil D's arm. "Dog, let's creep upstairs in case there's more of them around. Stay close behind me, dog." They walk up the stairs, looking in every direction for surprises. They get closer to the door. "Dog, you hear that voice? It sounds like Fat Cuz don't it, Lil D?"

"Yeah, dog. Ain't he from Cali?"

"Yeah. He jacks for a living."

Upstairs, Kendra says, "Pop him, baby. He'll talk then." The dude turns on her. "Shut up, bitch! I got this here. Get your ass up and go make sure cuz is cool."

Lil D whispers, "Move to the side so this bitch can't see us outside the door and we can snatch her ass, Ghost."

The door opens as soon as they move out of the way. Kendra yells, "Fuck you, Chuck!" The door closes and Kendra takes three steps. Slap, slap, slap with the Mac to the back of the head. Lil D catches her ass before she hits the floor. "Cuz, this will put a hole the size of your pussy in your face," he tells her. "Homie, I'll be gone before the fuzz even find your corpse."

Slap, slap, slap. "Wake up, bitch. Cover her mouth. You scream, you die. How many more crabs are here besides the dead one in the kitchen?"

"Just Chuck in the room. Don't kill me, please! He made me do it."

"Shut up, bitch," Ghost says. "My brother better be cool. You're gonna walk in the room and we gonna come right behind you, so don't try shit. Got it?"

"Yeah."

"Clean your face, bitch and quit crying."

Ghost and Lil D creep to the door. Kendra opens it and walks through it like nothing's wrong. The dude asks, "Baby loc, good down there, Kendra?"

"Nah, crab-ass nigga. He dead, just like you," says Ghost. Tat, tat, tat, tat, tat, the Mac spits. Bullets hit Fat Cuz in the chest and stomach, but he's still standing.

"Ah, shit, you bitch-ass," the dude yells. Pop, pop, from Lil D's .45 Glock. The 12-gauge drops from the dude's hands in front of me.

"You hurt?" asks Ghost.

"Nah," I say. "Untie me, fam."

"Oh, yeah, my bad, Jay."

"Man, what the fuck took you so fucking long, Ghost? Damn, I almost thought the worst, my nigga," I say.

"I'm the truth, dog. Never that," says Kendra.

"Bitch, I knew you was on some shit from jump!" I say.

"Nah," she begs, "listen!"

I pick up the box cutter. "Is this what you two was going to cut me with?" Slice, slice, slice across her throat. Blood squirts in my face from the open wounds. "Damn, this box cutter is sharp, Joe," I say to Ghost.

"We done," Ghost says. "Let's dip."

"You two go ahead and dip," Lil D volunteers. "I'll chirp you one. Now, let me have a look around this bitch before I dispose of the bodies. I'll start down stairs and work my way upstairs. Damn, this bitch is bleeding like a motherfucker."

I look around and see what looks like a two-way mirror over on the wall. I need something to throw through it to see. Good, there's an iron. Swoossh…crack…breaks the glass. I was right. A camcorder is running. Shit. I remove the shattered glass so I can crawl through the small space. This room is hooked up like a police interrogation room. I need to get the fuck out of here! I grab the video camera and the extra tapes for later viewing.

Lil D goes outside to grab the acid and gas that he keeps in the trunk. As he walks back toward the house, he sees a car cruise by slowly, looking at the house. Now he know it's time to swoop out of there. By the time he gets to the yard, the blue S.O. Mustang has pulled over to the side of the street. Then it pulls up right in front of him and doesn't move. The windows stay up and he freezes for a second to contemplate his next move.

The window rolls down and he pulls out his 9 mm Millennium. The driver says, "Hold up. It's me, dog. Big Chief. Blood, you play too much, nigga. Riding around with all this fly shit on your whip, dog."

"I didn't know who the fuck you were," Lil D says.

Big Chief replies, "Ghost sent me to look out for you, dog."

"Well," says Lil D, "get your ass the fuck out and let's finish this shit, dog."

"Lead the way, cud."

They walk through the door and the smell of death is strong. "Downstairs first, son," says Lil D. "Put this acid over the bitch in the basement and pour some of this gas over the bed she's laying on. I'll be in the kitchen doing the same with the dead crab nigga. Move quick, 'cause time is of the essence, dog. It will be daylight soon and people will be going to work."

"Yeah, I got you," says Big Chief.

"Then meet me upstairs to finish up, dog."

"Cool."

Big Chief walks down to the basement. He can smell blood in the air so thick his stomach starts to turn flips. He looks around and sees the prettiest bitch he's ever seen sprawled out in a pool of blood on the bed. He pours the acid over her whole body. Instantly, her body starts to melt before his eyes. The bed starts to smoke. He quickly tosses gasoline all over the walls and floors.

He walks back upstairs to find Lil D and smells burning flesh all around. "Dog, where you at, son?" he yells.

"I'm coming down right now," Lil D replies. "Keep your voice down, nigga. Go to the fucking car, son, if you did what you was supposed to do."

Big Chief heads outside and Lil D lights the bottom of the stairs that Big Chief doused with gasoline. Foosh, it starts. Another job well done. Lil D shuts the door and he and Big Chief dip quietly and fast.

Ring, ring.

"Who dis?" Ghost says.

"What the fuck you mean, 'who dis'? You got some other bitch calling you, nigga?"

"Nah, baby, I'm fucking with you. I got caller ID, you know."

"Ghost, I ain't playing with you, boy. That's my dick, so don't play with me. Where are you? It's late."

"In traffic. I'll be home in about twenty minutes with Jay, so get the guest room ready."

"Okay. Lacy's, here, too."

"Good. She can keep him company."

"I've already told her how cute he is, so he good. She's been wait-ing for him to get here."

"That's why I love you so much, Shaunna."

"Whatever, nigga. You love this pussy more."

"Nah, you my boo. Roll us some dro."

"I thought you was meeting Lil D to get purple."

"I'll tell you when I get home. Love you!"

"I love you, too. Bye!"

"Now, Jay, that is the other half of my brain right there."

"Fuck that sentimental shit, cud. You got me already in some shit and I ain't been here twenty-four hours yet," I say.

"Cool, ain't it?" says Ghost. "I'll die for you, dog. You my fam, Joe."

We drive for about ten minutes, then we're home. "Jay, I got you something," Ghost says.

"Don't tell me. I don't want to know," I answer. We park in the garage.

"Now, don't say shit, Jay. Let me talk to my bitch."

"I could use a smoke before I lay down, cud."

"We cool. Jay, I'm a boss player, boy."

"I see!" The door opens before we get to open it, and there stands some broad I haven't met yet. She's cute, about five-foot-two, long braided hair to her shoulders. Green eyes with long eyelashes. The darkest skin that I've ever seen on a woman, but very smooth-looking. Breasts that stand up without a bra on that I can see. Short, thick legs that are begging for attention. When she reaches up to hug Ghost, the shirt goes up in the back, so I get a look at the two watermelons back there. I feel her. I really don't like dark women, but she's fine. My last look is at her toes and feet, and they're perfect. The pedicure she has doesn't compare to how pretty her feet are.

"What up, Lacy? I didn't know that you was over," Ghost greets her.

"I been with Shaunna all night," she says. "She come to get me when you left."

Ghost introduces us. "Shorty, this is my brother Jay."

"Hi, Jay!"

"What's good, lil mamma?"

"Nice to meet you, Jay."

"Nice to meet you, too, ma." We stand there looking into each other's eyes for what seems like hours.

"Girl, bring your fast ass in here and shut that door," yells Shaunna.

Ghost chimes in yeah J come on dog so we can chief some dro son.

I'm blown away by how big my brother is living. I walk in on mink carpet floors. Shit, there's flat screen TVs on three walls, and fifty-two-inch ones at that. The couches are imported, and they're stamped with the Gucci logo. My brother has a stereo system that looks like a mini studio. "Now this is laid the fuck out, fam. You doing your thing for real," I say.

"I'm good, fam."

Shaunna hands me some blunts. "Here, take these and go upstairs to the guest room. Lacy, show Jay where he's sleeping. I have to talk to Ghost right quick, then we'll come up to blow one with you two, okay?"

"Alright, girl," says Lacy. "Jay, you want something to drink?"

"Yeah, what you got?"

"Some Bombay. You drink that?"

"Not really, but it will do right now."

"Follow me, Jay."

I smile. "No problem there," I tell her.

"What you mean by that?"

"Nothing!"

The room is all the way to the back, she tells me. I tell her to lead the way. Every step she takes makes me harder and harder. With each bounce of her ass, I have to stop myself from grabbing it. *Man, fuck this shit. I don't sweat hoes.* I'm so focused on watching that ass that when she stops at the top of the stairs, I bump into the cushion. It's the softest piece of ass I've touched so far.

"If you're done, come on, playboy," she teases.

"You can tell, huh," I say.

"Nah, I'm just joking."

Downstairs, Shaunna lights into Ghost. "Ghost, where the fuck you been?"

"Girl, don't start that momma shit right now, 'cause I'm not in the fucking mood for your twenty questions right now," he says.

"Nigga, pull out your dick so I can smell it, then," she counters. He tries to placate her. "Why you so insecure, baby?"

"I'm not," she insists. "You been out hoeing and shit, Ghost. I told you I won't stand for that shit no more."

"Light that blunt up, baby, for daddy and chill out. My brother is upstairs, remember, Shaunna."

"Ghost, you're on thin ice, boy."

"Bitch, watch your mouth before I put my foot in your ass, you hear?"

"You'll need me!"

"Bitch, I need you right now. Go run me some bath water, baby."

"Sure, whatever you want, Ghost." She goes to draw the bath water. *You will get yours for treating me like this. If he only knew I been fucking Lil D on the low and he loves me, too. He'll kill his ass for me. I'll get the last laugh, though. Fuck... This is a bad time for his little brother to be here.*

"Baby, put some of that bubble shit into the water for me," Ghost hollers. "I got you," she replies. *Don't I always?*

"That's my girl."

I just hope Lacy's pussy and head game is on point. I need her to keep his head in the clouds until I do my thing with Ghost.

Upstairs, Lacy and I get to know each other. "How old are you, Jay?" she asks.

"Sixteen, ma."

"Where you from?"

"Little Rock, Arkansas. The country."

"Yeah! That's why you sound like Master P and them boys."

"Nah, I don't sound like that. They from a whole 'nother state, ma. What's up with you? You got a man?"

"Nope. I'm single, I'm seventeen and about to finish school. I want to be a doctor so I can save some of you fine thugs' lives."

"Oh, you on some save the world shit now, ma?"

"Nah, I want to get paid in full."

"Shorty, I'm faded. I need to hit the sack, ma."

"What? You don't like my company, playboy?"

If only you knew what kind of day the kid done had today.

"Cool. I'll holler at you in the morning, Jay."

"I'll be good then." *I bet you will, too.*

"Nice to meet you, Jay."

"Yeah, lil momma."

Lacy shuts the door and I fall on the bed in my clothes and instantly fall out.

Chapter 2

"Wake up, Jay! Let's go shopping, my nigga."

I moan. "I just fell asleep!"

"Pimp, it's about 5:00 p.m. Get yo ass the fuck up before Will gets over, 'cause I don't want to see him right now," my brother says.

"I know what you mean," I answer. "Ghost, did you watch the news today?"

"Yeah," he says, "the nine o'clock news. It said that four bodies were found about seven o'clock this morning in a burning house on Thirty-seventh and Pleasant South. No I.D. on the victims. No suspect yet. We good, fam. Lil D and Big Chief know what they're doing. Fam, this is *my* fucking city!"

Shaunna sticks her head in the door. "Ghost, I'll be back later, do you need me to do anything while I'm out?"

"No, I'm good," he says.

"Lacy will be here, though," she hesitates.

He shrugs. "Okay."

"Baby, be good now," she cautions. Ghost grins.

"Don't I always?"

"I don't know about that!"

"Whatever, nigga!"

"Bye, Jay."

"Bye, Shaunna." She leaves, and Ghost's phone starts to ring.

"Damn!" he exclaims. "Who's blowing up my phone? Hello, what up, baby?"

"I'm walking out the door right now," says a voice on the other end, obviously female.

"Where you goin'? I need to see you like yesterday," Ghost tells her.

"I need to go downtown to the V.I.P. to get my nails done first."

"I'll be down there outside, baby," he says.

"What are you driving? The Rover?"

"Yeah."

"That shit was not on point for your people. They got fucked up real bad, too. If you know, I had to show up."

"Yeah, I know, but we aren't done yet."

"I know. That shit is right. Damn."

"You're my boo, baby, and it's going to stay that way."

"I got to get word out about Fat Cuz getting wacked. Let me tell you this, his Cali people ain't going to like that shit. He's a O.G. Crip. There is going to be some real shit behind that one."

"Let me handle that. I got your back."

"Baby, I'll be downtown in about twenty minutes."

"Okay. Call me when you outside. Bye, baby."

Ghost jostles me. "Man, get your ass up out of that bed already so we can dip!"

""Ghost, I'm so fucking tired."

"Nah, nigga. You want to fuck Lacy, don't you?"

"Yeah, but that can wait, son."

"Fuck. Let's bounce, bro."

We walk down the stairs as Lacy is coming up. "See you later, Jay," she purrs. "I hope you slept good."

"I did," I say. "Tonight it will be better with you beside me, though."

She laughs. "I got this nigga whipped already!"

"We'll see," I say.

Ghost is impatient. "Jay, come on. I'm in the garage already, nigga."

"My bad," I tell him. "Here I come!" I turn once more to Lacy. "I'll catch up with your fine ass later, Shorty."

"Okay. Be careful," she warns.

"Fo sho." I skip stairs as I run to the garage door. I wonder why she said that last statement. As I enter the garage, I see Ghost sitting in a 600 Benz LS. Now we rolling big boy status.

"Get in," Ghost says tersely, "and don't talk me to death."

"Fuck you."

"Let me call Lil D and Big Chief to lay some charge on them," he says. "Pass me the Nextel out of the glove box." I hand it to him.

"Here, dog."

Chirp. Chirp.

"What it do, nigga?" Ghost says heartily. "You want that? Nah, I'll see you later, dog, for that shit. Lil D, I never got to get my purple."

Lil D responds, "You right. Where you at, dog?"

We pull out of the garage. "Leaving the crib," Ghost says. "I'm about to take Jay shopping."

"I'll be there by the time you get there," says Lil D. "I'm heading that way."

"Cool." Ghost hangs up.

"This nigga keeps fucking up my pussy shit."

"Ghost," I ask. "You trust Lil D?"

"Yeah, me and him have killed a lot of crabs together, Jay."

I stretch my arm across the back of the seat. "I'm here now, though. So he got to take a back seat ride, know what I mean, bro?"

"So real," agrees Ghost.

"Man," I say. "Will gave me two grand to spend."

Ghost slaps the steering wheel. "That cheap-ass nigga. He got that rich-ass bitch and that's all he slid you?" He pulls over to the curb.

"Who are we picking up now?" I ask.

"My nigga Big Bear. He the realest O.G. Blood in Minnesota. Period."

We roll down Fourth Street to Lake Street and make a right turn. We head straight for a second, then pull over in front of a place on Chicago by the liquor store we went to last night.

I look out the window at low brick building. "Is this a bar?"

Ghost nods. "Yeah, Sammy's. It's more of a spot than a bar. Them Family Cartel cats be up in this bitch, too, but they don't fuck with us, you know."

Chicago and Lake Street. I got to remember that for future info.

"Let me pull into the back to get his ass, Jay. It's niggas standing everywhere around here, dog. They got blows, crack, and weed over here. I got this on lock, too, dog. We can get him and bounce."

We park the car by the door, hop out and some lame-looking dude walks up to us as soon as he sees us. "What up, Ghost?"

"Nothing. Damn. How you living, cud?"

"Like a superstar, dog."

"J.R., where is Big Bear?"

The dude gestures inside. "At the pool table."

"Stay up, dog," Ghost says. We walk in and Big Bear is standing by the bar talking to a chicken head. Ghost yells to him, "Dog, let that bitch go so we can skeet, man!"

"Who the … aw, man, stop that shit, dog. You almost got it, fam," Big Bear says, replacing an annoyed look on his face with a more cordial one.

Ghost gestures toward the door. "Come on, we got shit to talk about."

Big Bear turns to the woman and says, "I'll holler, baby." She sighs and says, "Call me."

"I will, ma," he promises.

Damn, this dude is about six foot three in height and about two hundred and fifty pounds of pure prison muscle. He has long braids past his shoulders to his back, hands the size of basketballs and the look of a true killer. Very, very dark skin. I can tell he's not a ladies' man.

Ghost introduces us. "My nigga, this my little brother. He just got here last night. Jay, meet O.G. Big Bear." My hand disappears in one of his as Big Bear asks, "What up, fam?"

"Not too much, O.G. How long you up?"

"For good, son."

"Cool."

We walk back to the whip. I slip into the back so I can be on point. I don't know this homie. We pull out of the lot and sowallie rolls by slowly, look at us pull out of the alley onto Lake Street. Both Ghost and Big Bear say the same thing: "That's Red Beard's thirsty ass and keep it moving."

"Where we headed?" Big Bear asks.

"The mall," Ghost replies.

"You got heat?"

"You know this," Ghost says. "Jay pull on the bottom of the headrest in front of you."

I do, and the TV moves up and a chrome .45 moves out. "I got it," I tell him.

"Ghost, you know the mall got a lot of crabs in there," Big Bear mentions cautiously.

"We good," Ghost says. "My brother ain't no punk."

Chirp, chirp. Big Bear picks up the Nextel. "I'm about five minutes away, crab killer," he says.

"Who that?" Lil D replies.

"Me, dog," Big Bear grins.

"Me who?"

"O.G. Big Bear."

"Oh, shit, what up, my dog? In five, dog. I'm in front of the entrance by the car rental place."

We pull up alongside an all-red Dodge Magnum, twenty-four inch Lexanis, tinted windows, beats banging so fucking hard, with smoke leaking out the windows at random. Ghost jumps out of the Benz, followed by O.G. Lil D jumps out of the Magnum with purple in his hand, smoking. "Here, dog," he says. "Smoke this shit right here. Don't pull onto it too hard, though. Its dipped, homie."

I can smell the dip before I get out of the car. Ghost takes a very deep pull of the nolya. Instantly, his eyes turn red and watery. O.G. Big Bear reaches for the dipped blunt and we make our way to the entrance to the mall. He looks at me. "You want to hit this grown men shit, Jay?"

"Nah, O.G. I'm cool."

"What? You scared, blood?" he teases.

"Nah. I'm on point," I say.

Big Bear smiles. "I like him, Ghost. He a 'rida'."

"That shit runs in our blood, fam," Ghost says.

We walk through the mall door. O.G. drops the blunt roach on the pavement in front of the door. "The Footlocker first, fam," I say to Ghost. "I need me some Air Force Ones in every color that they have."

"It's packed like a motherfucker in this bitch," Ghost says.

"Yeah," says Big Bear. "That nigga, R. Kelly, is at the Target Center tonight, blood."

I look around the store. *Shit. It's hoes up in this store, too.* "I'll be over here, dog," I say to Ghost.

A girl in a striped referee shirt comes over. "Can I help you with something?"

"Yes, Shorty. I need every color of Air Force Ones you have in size ten and a half," I say. Her eyes open wide. "Every color?"

"Yes, ma."

O.G. taps me on the shoulder, then walks away saying something about some dude named Tank. I shrug my shoulders. The girl comes back juggling a stack of boxes. "Here's your shoes, sir. Would you like to try them on?"

"Nah, I'm cool, lil mama. Ring them up for me."

She hands me the cash register tape. "Your total is eight hundred and twenty-six dollars."

"Here's nine hundred. Keep the change." I turn to Lil D, who's been hanging with me the whole time. "Lil D, where them two niggas go, fam?"

He shrugs. "I don't know, Jay. Let's go see." We leave the store and start scouting the mall.

"Man, I heard O.G. say something about Tank. Who that be, Lil D?"

"A crab nigga, fam. You strapped?"

"You know this, man. Take two of these bags for me so I can adjust the mag."

"Look over there by the Legends store! Come on, Jay, it looks like we missed something, dog."

I rush over to my brother's side to feel the vibe.

"Nigga, you know what it is, crab-ass nigga? "

"Fuck. Shotgun Crip, damn."

"Come on cuz, don't even trip."

"Fuck you, slob-ass nig—"

Whap. O.G. slaps the nigga before he finishes his words. Bap, bap, bap. Lil D hits the nigga with a three-piece combo the face so quick, he wasn't ready for the blows. Tank's on his ass, trying to focus his eyes. O. G punches him so hard it sounds like a car wreck. Tank is out cold.

"Now, let's push out this bitch, blood." We walk right past security like nothing happened. Suddenly, a Good Samaritan says, "There. Right there. They're getting away! Hey, you guys stop right there!"

The security guard is on his walkie talkie, running toward us fast. I pull out the Magnum and blast four shots in the air to stop him in his tracks. People everywhere hit the floor screaming while we escape out the nearest exit door. Smooth.

"Damn, you niggas hot, fam!" exclaims O.G. "I see you damn niggas stay in some shit, Ghost."

"We make shit happen," says Ghost, "not ask what happened, bro. Lil D, let's go downtown to finish shopping for my lil brother. Blood, meet me there."

We jump into the Benz and pull out into traffic and we're gone. "Jay, you my nigga for life," says O.G., "even though you ain't a Blood yet, fam."

"That's cool to know, O.G.," I say, "but I'm a gangsta for life, fam. Cool like that. O.G., since I'm here, I got to put on for my city. That's why I didn't smoke dip with you guys earlier, to be sharp and on point. I still need to blow some smoke, cud."

"I got a blunt of some dro, Jay. I was going to smoke it with that bitch at Sammy's before the two of you came to get me, fam. But here, my dog, fire it up 'cause we'll be downtown in five minutes on the freeway, dog."

I been waiting on this nigga Lil D for about thirty minutes. Now I got to go. He ain't answering his celly for me, either. The thought angers Shaunna. *What's up with that shit? I know he wants some of this pussy. Fuck him, I'm fixing to dip and go to the bar for a quick drink. I wonder what's the deal with that shit? Let me leave him a message, though.* "This me, baby. Call me when you get this message, boo boo. Love you."

In California, Rich is on the phone with Lacy, talking about what happened last night with Fat Cuz. "Yeah," she says. "Them slob-ass niggas killed him."

"What you mean, bitch? Killed who?

"Your homie, Fat Cuz!"

"Shit. Tell Shaunna I'll be back tomorrow and to call Tank to pick me the fuck up. Bitch, you hear m?"

"Yeah." Click. *Now, it's on with you 30s niggas. These lame-ass niggas' life is over now. No more fucking playing the peace game. No more.*

"Cuz, what's up?"

"We got to make a flight back to Minneapolis, cuz, to war right now. So get the boys ready to dip, cuz, now. Let me call the spot in the hood right now."

Ring, ring, ring. "Thirty-two for life. Who this?"

"It's me, cuz, Pit Bull."

"Get them young ridas ready. We leave in the morning. I need they info so we can fly out. I'll call you back, cuz."

Shaunna will be pleased that I made the first move for her, Lacy thinks. *Now I need to get on Jay's good side to lead him to his death, too. I'm like a black widow spider in a way. I kill my mate after his use is up.*

"Let me call this bitch to see where she is at," says Ghost. "I need to dip up out of this place for a while."

"The Nextel phone you are trying to reach is not available right now," says a mechanical female voice.

"Damn. Who she talking to?" He sounds frustrated.

"Man, who the fuck was that dude you Roy Jones back there?" I ask. This crab-ass nigga Tank whose been a pain in my ass for awhile.

O.G. Blood when you bang, you pay the price not matter how old you are. Remember that, lil homie."

"I know that, son."

We pull into a parking garage, pay the ticket price and get out of the car. We start walking toward a building saying Civic Center. Ghost's phone hits. Chirp, chirp. "Where you dogs at?"

"Walking through the doors in the front of the Civic Center as we speak."

"Cool. I'm in Legends with a couple of my young guns, blood."

"Be right there. One. That was Lil D. He here now in the store."

We walk for a second in silence to the store. I look at the sign on the top and it says Twin Cities Town , just like at the other malls. They must like these stores, or this is where the ballers got to shop. I spot me some Guess jeans, matching shirts, a few polo sweaters. "They got some fly shit, fam," I tell Ghost. "I like that Scarface leather coat, too."

"Try it on, bro," he encourages.

It fits. I tell the clerk, "Hey, homie, put that on my tab, too. Yo, give me every color of New York fitted hats, too. Damn. Man, put every color of Enyce jeans and shirts on my tab, too." I turn to Ghost. "I'm good now, fam."

Twin, one of the owners, says, "Well, sir, your total comes to six thousand, six hundred and seventy dollars with tax."

Ghost reaches around me with a wad of bills. "I got you, fam, put your change back into your pocket. You cool now for a while, Jay."

I agree. "Yeah, we can dip now, man."

Lil D and two young dudes approach us. "Jay," he says, "meet Big Chief and Tre Duce."

"What's good?" I say.

"Money, fam."

"We on the same shit, Joe."

"These lil dogs will look out for you," Lil D says to me. I shake my head. "I'm good, Lil D. I can handle my own."

"Let me rephrase that," Lil D says. "They will show you around."

"Now that's cool!" I say.

"We out," says Lil D. "Come on, dogs!"

The Owner stops us before we walk out the door. "Ghost, the new clothes will come in on Monday," he says. "I'll call you."

"Okay, Twin," my brother says. "Be cool."

Twin stops Lil D now. "Hold up, Lil D, for a second! You got that purp, son?"

"Yeah. Hold on so my dog can go to the ghost whip to get it," he replies.

"Fam, I got some shit to do, dog," says O.G. "I got a hoe waiting on me to push up in."

"I'm going by the crib anyway so Jay can change and pop some tags, O.G.," Ghost says. "Lil D, I'll see you and the lil homies later, dog."

"C.K., my nigga," Lil D says.

"Crab Killer for life, dog," Ghost affirms.

I turn to my new friends. "Big Chief and Tre Duce, I'll get up with the two of you later, fam, to show me around the city."

"We got you, fam," Big Chief says.

We leave the store with about twelve bags of my shit, full to the rim. "Ghost, thanks, bro, for all of this shit," I say. Ghost shrugs.

"Nah, don't mention it. It's what big brothers do, Jay. Come on, let's dip so I can get wet, fam. I need to split, dog."

We walk out of the Civic Center to the Benz and spot Shaunna coming out of Applebee's. "Hey, baby, come here," Ghost calls to her. She gets a funny look on her face like she's thinking, "Oh, shit. It's Ghost." She strolls over to the Benz and we all look at her.

"Hey, baby, what's up?" Ghost asks.

"I didn't know you was down here, too," she says.

"Who the fuck you with, Shaunna?" he demands.

"Nobody. I was having a drink by myself after I got my nails done, boo. Hey, O.G."

He greets her. "What's good, Shaunna?"

"Some smoke," she answers. "Who got it and not that dipped shit, either."

"Not me," he says. "I'm going to get me some wet."

"You need to stop that shit, O.G.," she says.

Ghost interrupts. "Shaunna, go home. Matter of fact, Lil D is in Legends. Go and buy us an ounce of purp. I forgot that shit again. I'll call you when I get home, if I beat you there."

We get into the Benz and pull out of the parking lot. We see some of Fat Cuz's boys looking at us as we pass by. One of them points at us. "Cuz, there go that hoe-ass nigga's Benz right there! Let's bust a cap on they ass, cuz" says Dallas. "You know Rich said kill on sight, cuz. Shoot to kill."

"Shit, do they know?" Ghost asks us.

"Know what?" asks O.G.

"Damn," says Ghost. "I forgot to talk to you about it, fam."

I look in the passenger side mirror. "Fam, they busting a U-turn. Hit 94."

We head for the freeway and Ghost says, "We got to talk tonight, O.G., about some serious shit, fam. He looks in the rearview mirror and grins. "They stuck at a red light with the fuzz. We cool to hit the freeway. Man put on the new Bun B, bro."

Then I'm a G
These niggas don't know about me

comes blaring out of the system. I fall back and get into my own make of mind. I know I got to bust my gun fucking with these cats. I'm all for that shit, too. Now I got to do me. I need me some dope to push.

We pull up at Sammy's and O.G. slips out and walks to the drivers' side to do the Blood shake with Ghost before he dips. "I'll holler, fam. Be cool, Jay."

"One love, O.G," Ghost says.

We pull away from the curb and Ghost says, "Lacy should still be at the crib, Jay."

"I was hoping that shit," I answer. We get to the first red light and the police pull us over.

"Fuck this thirsty ass pig, Jay" Ghost mutters.

"Pull over" says a voice from the squad car. I look to Ghost for guidance.

"Be cool, Jay. I got this. He's on the take."

A chubby, short, red-faced and bearded cop wearing a baseball cap and plain clothes walks up to the driver's side window. Tap, tap, tap on the window. "Ghost, roll down your window. What's with the disrespect now?" says the cop

Ghost pushes the button and window slides down. "I got shit to do, Red!"

"Well, I thought you should know Fat Cuz is dead and there are no suspects yet. And, oh yeah, I need my cut tomorrow."

"You straight," Ghost says.

We pull out as quickly as we pulled over. Riding down Lake Street to Fourth Street, Ghost tells me to call Lacy and have her open the garage. I pick Ghost's cell phone off the seat and dial his crib number. "Hello," Lacy says, so sexy into the phone.

"Hey, Shorty," I say. "Ghost and me are up the street, so open the garage for him, okay?"

We approach the garage and the door opens as we pull into the driveway. "Damn, Lacy is looking good today, fam."

"I know, Jay."

"Do she always dress so appealing, dog?"

"Nah, not at all, Jay. I guess she likes you, bro."

"Cool."

We step out of the Benz in the garage and she's all over a player. "Looks like someone's been shopping, huh?" she states the obvious.

"Can you help me with my bags?"

"Sure. Where's mine at?" she teases.

"I got you next time, Shorty."

"I'm-a hold you to that," she says.

"She sure is. You can believe it. Come on," Ghost says. "Quit playing."

We make our way through the house up to the room where I'm lamping at. I push the door open to put my bags down beside my bed. Then Lacy pushes me down on the bed, pulling at my pants and saying, "Are you tired now, playboy?"

"Nah, close the door!"

"I got that for you," Ghost says. "Be nice to him, Lacy."

"Oh, I will for sure," she promises.

As soon as Ghost puts my bags down and shut the door, it's on. Lacy takes my boxers down with my pants. My dick is at full attention. I close my eyes for what awaits me next. I fall back onto my bed with

Lacy's hand slowly stroking my pole up and down. I feel her tongue slowly going around the head of me, gently rubbing my balls in the process. In a flash I am all the way deep down her throat. "Ummmm ... shit, ma, that feels so good."

Lacy's tongue and lips get to working on me at the same time. Every pull back up, her lips squeeze softly, making me even harder in her mouth. When it gets back up to the head, her tongue licks on the pre-cum coming out like a dripping ice cream cone. "Ohhhh ... Ahhhhhh..."

The motion of her head has me gone now. I have to look. *Damn, she looks so fucking sexy with a dick in her mouth.* My hand goes to the back of her head to fuck her mouth. My legs get stiff, so she knows that I'm about the blow a warm juice down her throat. I can't hold out. Not a second longer. I feel her grab my ass and push me further into her warm mouth. Then it blows. And I tell you it's a hard and long bust. "Shitttt ... Lacyaaaaa ... goddammit ... maaaa..."

I fall back onto the bed. I feel like I just fought a heavyweight fight, man. My whole body sweats like I just came in out of the rain. Lacy slides off of me. "Jay, you can put on your clothes now, but I need to get fucked real good with 'my' dick, baby. Tonight!"

"I'm all yours," I tell her. "I need to shower and make some moves, ma."

"I'll see you downstairs, Jay."

When she walks away, I feel a strange feeling that has never come over me until now. *Need.* I feel like I need her and I don't even know her. Shit. It must be the bomb-ass head she got.

I finish undressing and walk over to the shower. Damn, it's like a hot tub in here. I clean up, find me a pair of Enyce jeans, shirt, blue Air Force Ones and a N.Y. fitted cap. I'm good now to stroll the city.

Chapter 3

"Let me call this sister of yours, Lacy," Ghost says. "Hello, baby, where the fuck are you at?"

"Down the street, Ghost, why?"

"Shit, it's almost twenty-five minutes since I left you!" he exclaims.

"I know, baby! I had to get gas and blunts."

"You got my purp?"

"Yes sir, Mr. Is the alarm on, boo?" she asks.

"Nah, Shaunna."

"I'm pulling into the driveway now," she responds.

Ghost sits back on the couch, satisfied. "Cool."

Shaunna walks in the front door, putting her cell into her purse. "Hey, girl," she says to Lacy. Lacy gives her a "don't 'hey girl' me, bitch" look. "Ghost, here's your purp." She drops it on the coffee table in front of them and keeps moving to the kitchen. "I need to charge my phone right now, and I need a snack," she says to herself. "Let me make a tuna sandwich real quick before I smoke. Are you guys hungry?"

"Yeah!" Ghost and Lacy say together.

I stroll down the stairs. "Fam, I thought Lacy put your ass to sleep, dog," Ghost teases.

"Quit fronting, Ghost," I tell him. "You're the only pussy whip nigga here."

Ghost grins. "Nah, lil bro. That's where you're wrong. I whip the pussy, son. I got dick by the bulk, dog."

"Fuck that, son. Let's blow some of that purple shit you been talking about for the last couple of days. Hey, Lacy, turn up the news."

She turns up the volume on the television and the news announcer says, "The police have I.D.s on the two murders that happened two days ago on Lake Street. Donte Wilson and Demarcus James were found shot to death in a McDonald's parking lot. Police say it looks to be gang-related." Pictures of Coogie and Trap appear on the screen, then the camera switches to a cop. "If anyone has any information about this call, should be case, call Minneapolis Homicide. You can remain anonymous. We have no suspects at this time, so we urge the public to help solve these brutal murders." The news anchor comes back on. "Now, to the weather."

"Turn it back down now," Ghost says. Lacy grabs the remote off of the coffee table and lowers the volume. "I've rolled a couple of blunts to smoke," she says.

"Light up," I say.

"Hand me a lighter, Jay?"

"I don't have one, Lacy."

"Pass me my purse off the table, Ghost."

"Nah, I don't work for you nor am I fucking you, girl," he says, folding his arms.

Shaunna comes in from the kitchen with a plate of sandwiches. "Here's our sandwiches, baby."

"Shaunna, throw me my purse. Ghost's being an asshole," Lacy complains. Shaunna complies, and Lacy says, "Now I can light this nice piece of work I rolled."

She lights the tip of the blunt and the scent goes straight to my nose. She pulls strong on the purp, only to choke instantly, expelling air from her lungs violently, with slobber coming from her mouth. Not a pretty sight to see from a pretty girl like her.

"Pass that shit, shorty," I say. "Let a true player hit that shit. It's evident that you can't handle that grown man shit, ma."

"You're exaggerating, Jay," she coughs.

Ghost's cell starts to vibrate in his pocket. He answers. "Who dis be, dog?"

The voice on the other end says, "Me, Curren$y, dog!"

"What's the deal, fam," Ghost asks.

"C.K. Nigga, you know! But on the real, I'm in town. Are you ready for me, dog, or what?"

"Yeah," Ghost says. "Where we be at?"

"Damn. I'll hit you in twenty, fam."

"One." Ghost ends the call.

I take a second pull of the purple and hold it for the full effect. I release, then gasp for air as I begin to choke, too. Disgusted, Ghost grabs the purple from me and pulls so strong that the blunt burns halfway up. He starts issuing orders.

"Jay, I need you to roll with me to do something, fam. Shaunna, go to my safe and take out two hundred and seventy thousand for me and two duffle bags, baby. That will cover for the twenty-seven bricks of raw cocaine I'm about to get," he says.

"Okay, Ghost," Shaunna says. "Let me hit that blunt, too."

"Here, baby, take it with you."

As she leaves the room, Ghost explains, "I need you to ride shotgun, Jay."

"Cool, my nigga. I got you."

"That's what the fuck I'm talking about, fam," he nods. "Now I can make some moves. Stack me some paper for this extravagant lifestyle. I go to the extreme, dog."

"I feel you, Ghost," I answer. "Go hard."

"Jay, I'm a fanatic when it comes to the almighty dollar."

As he rises from the couch, Shaunna walks in with a big bag of money and throws it on the coffee table with two duffle bags. "Here you go, boo," she says sweetly. "Do you need me to do anything else?"

"Nah, you straight, ma," he says, then has a second thought. "Hold up, Shaunna. I do need you to go by the spot on Thirty-first and Bloomington and tell Pit Bull to give you that and to call me later on."

"Okay, baby, I got you," she says.

Ghost grabs the stack of one hundred-dollar bills wrapped in plastic and the duffle bags. We make our way to the Rover. Ghost puts the money in the back of the truck and we head out. We pull into traffic with extra caution now that we're Lil D. I look into the glove box for the straps and they're there, a .40 Glock and a 9 mm Taurus.

"I like to be prepared for the worst, Jay," Ghost says.

"I know, big bro," I nod. "We dominate everything we do, fam."

"But remember," Ghost cautions, "the U.S. monetary can be a man's in the game downfall." He pulls out his cell to call his boy and his connect, Curren$y.

"What it do?"

"Elevate, my nigga. The Embassy Suites, downtown Minneapolis, room 602."

"I'll be there soon, dog." Ghost puts an emphasis on *soon*.

Chapter 4

Tank is up in his apartment building, playing 2Pac's rap. "Thug nig-gas 'til we die" is coming out of his Sony speakers loud enough to hear outside the building. *Damn them slob niggas! Wait 'til I catch up with Rich*, he says to himself as he slowly pulls on a wet stick. He becomes more agitated by the second. His cell phone vibrates in his pocket. "Who dis? Shotgun cuz! Tres-deuce, fam."

"What's really good, Tank?"

"Ah, shit, my main man, Biggie."

"Yeah, cuz. I heard what happened at the mall with O.G. Slob Big Bear, fam."

"I slept, cuz. I wasn't heated, you know."

"Fuck that shit. I'm outside, cuz. So come on, let's go get some burner bruises."

"Since that shit happened, I've been contemplating what kind of consequences to do to all of them lames, cuz."

"Come on!"

"I'm out the door, fam. Oh, shit, let me grab my Tech 9."

Tank gets to the bottom of the steps and up to the car door when the wet stick kicks in full-fold. *I got to make it to the car with this strap. But I'm walking so fucking slow.* Biggie gets out of the car to help him. "Damn, fam, give me that heater," he says, "and come on before we get locked up, cuz."

They get into Biggie's Cutlass and pull out. "Fam, you look like the devil, cuz. Where is the shit at, fam, that you're on? Cuz, don't you hear me talking to you?"

"Damn, Biggie. My bad, cuz. Where we headed?" Tank mumbles.

"Nah, fam," Biggie says. "Answer me first. What you say? Who got that piss you been smoking?"

Glassy-eyed, Tank says, "Jug. Let's hit him up now so I can get right."

Biggie glances at him as he drives. "Tank, where is your cell at, cuz?"

"I left it at the crib. Man, just pull up at Lowry and Humboldt to see if his Cadi is parked outside."

Biggie busts a U-turn in traffic and almost hits a Ford Bronco. The driver of the truck flips him off as they pass him by in the opposite direction. "Fuck him, cuz," Tank says slowly. "I got my burner, cuz, so we tight."

They pull up on the corner of Lowry and Humboldt. Ten cars are sitting there, filled with homies waiting for the same thing they want. "Look cuz, there go Angel with her fine ass. Right there, cuz," says Biggie.

"Pull up behind her truck, cuz," Tank says. Biggie jumps out, wearing a crisp blue Sean Jean jumpsuit with a platinum chain. A cross full of diamonds is suspended from the chain, swinging from side to side as he strolls over to Angel's truck. He stops when he spots Angel sitting across the street but regains his composure quickly. *Cuz got the tech so I'm cool*, he thinks.

He taps on the driver's side window of Angel's 4Runner. She's having a conversation with Dwight, a true wet head. She motions for him to hold up one second. While he waits for her to finish up her deal, he ponders robbing her ass for stepping on Cuz's toes. Then again, he can also imagine himself plummeting his hard dick down her throat.

"Hey, cuz," shouts Jug. Biggie walks over the '62 Impala parked four cars behind his. "What you doing talking to Brickhead's bitch, cuz? Was you copping from her?"

"Homie, I just saw her parked there and I was fixing to shoot my game at her so I could fuck that plump ass," Biggie jokes. "Jug, I need some of that piss that Tank got, 'cause he lost in space right now. Just look at him over there, cuz."

"He needs to slow down before he needs some psychotherapy, homie," says Jug.

"Cuz, let me get one of those fifty-dollar vals from you," Biggie says.

"Smoke this shit slow, cuz, 'cause it's in its rawness, you know," Jug cautions.

"I'm a grown man, cuz," Biggie says.

Jug passes the little val bottle through the window to Biggie, who pulls out a fifty-dollar bill and slides it to him. "Cuz, you hot with all of this traffic, homie," Biggie observes.

"Mind your biz, cuz," Jug replies.

"You getting reckless, fam," Biggie says. "I'm out, cuz."

They shake hands and Biggie heads back to his whip. Tank is knocked out with the strap on his lap. Biggie slams the door hard to wake him up. He reacts by putting the mag on Biggie. "Be cool, cuz. It's me. Stop playing, cuz. We out."

They pull off from the curb and merge with traffic. They head to the liquor store on Penn and Lowry. "I need to smooth out my high, cuz," Tank says.

"I know, Tank," says Biggie. You fucked up, fam," he chuckles.

Biggie walks into the liquor store. Cookie is standing in line with her old-ass sugar daddy, Big O. "What's good, C?" Biggie asks.

"Nothing, Biggie."

He walks to the cooler to grab a twelve-pack of Old English, then to the counter to get a liter of sin juice. While he pays for his items, he notices the old man looking at him funny, like he's tough. Biggie and Tank bounce from the liquor store to head for the South Side. He drives onto 94 and points the car toward the spot they like to chill at.

They pull up at Twenty-sixth and Bryant Avenue South. All of the homies' cars are lined up out front. They get out and are greeted by T.C., who's on his way out the door. "Cuz, Rich is in there, and he's smoking mad at you, Tank, for not coming to pick him up at the airport, cuz."

"I didn't know he need me to, cuz," Tank slurs.

"Well, it's on you, cuz," T.C. says. "I'll be back in about twenty minutes. I got to go get my kids from their mom."

"Be cool, cuz," says Biggie.

"One, homie," T.C. replies.

Biggie gets to the door and hears a lot of commotion going on inside, as if there's a meeting they didn't know about. Tank puts his hand on Biggie's arm. "Biggie, I rather die than let shit slide, homie. I'm what these niggas suppose to be."

They enter the door without knocking. They're greeted by sad faces. Rich has the look of death in his eyes. "Where the fuck you been, cuz? Don't even answer, 'cause it's not important anymore." He turns to the group. "Cuz, look. That nigga Ghost and Lil D gots to go on sight, cuz. Oh, yeah, his bitch-ass little brother, too, homie. Them slobs killed four of the homies, as you all should know by now. Cuz, they killed O.G. Fat. Our grind is our life. We got to hit O.G. Bear first, homies. I want his fucking head first!

"Now, you are the only ones I want to know about what gots to be done. Fuck them two hoes; they're replaceable. Tank, didn't Lacy or Shaunna call you to come get me from the airport, cuz?"

"Nah, cuz. I haven't talked to not one of them yet."

Rich snorts. "That's 'cause you stay fucked up on them lovelies, cuz. I've heard about our run-in with them slobs, too, cuz."

Tank hangs his head. "I slept, cuz, but never again."

"That coulda been your deathbed, cuz," says Killer Boy. Killer Boy is a born killer from Gardenia, California, six-foot-seven in height, long dreds, about two hundred pounds of straight prison muscle. His eyes are so red that they could light a fire when he's mad. Killer Boy has about forty slobs killed under his belt. No one ever fucks with him, including the O.G.s when he's here.

Everybody in the room is about business for real. Killer Boy walks out of the room, saying, "We're going to turn this city into a ghost town." Then he's out the door.

"This meeting is over, cuz," says Rich. Everybody bounces, walking to their cars.

Rich calls Biggie over to rap for a quick second. "What's up, O.G.?" Biggie asks.

"I got twenty bricks coming tomorrow, and I need you to pass out and pick up what cuz and them owe me. Feel me?"

"Yeah, homie."

"Here's the address you need to be, homie. Keep twenty for yourself to knock off, cuz."

"I got you, fam, and I got the two hundred thousand that I owe you for the last shit, fam."

"Good. I'm out, cuz."

"Yeah, O.G."

"Do your business all by your lonely."

"For sho, homie."

Biggie walks to the car where Tank is waiting for him, dipping a wet stick. "Cuz, what do he want," Tank asks him.

"Nothing, cuz. Just hollering at me."

"Let's go find Lacy and Shaunna's asses," Tank says angrily. "Them bitches put me in the fucking hot seat with Cuz."

"I know," says Biggie sympathetically, "and in front of Killer, too, fam."

"I got to go check that bitch," Tank says determinedly.

They pull off after Tank lights the cheroot to go hit some of the spots.

I got slob Bear," says Killer Boy in a way that makes Rich nervous. *Killer Boy can be a vicious motherfucker if you're on the receiving end of his punishment.* Rich looks over at his long-time friend.

"Tank is falling off, cuz," Killer says as he drives toward the west side of the city.

"I know, Killer," Rich sighs. "Where we headed?"

"To see an old friend, cuz. To do what I do, cuz, you need to have friends on both sides. Money that's spread around makes things happen."

They pull up to a house on Thomas and Golden Valley Road. "Wait here, cuz, I'll be right back," Killer says.

Who this nigga know over here? This is my backyard and I don't know.

Killer walks to the door and it opens up as he approaches. It shuts as quickly as it opens. Rich narrows his eyes and watches closely.

"Hey, Squeek baby, what up with you, Shorty?" he says to the woman inside.

"Money. And you better have a lot of it, Boy," she says.

Girl come over here and give your guy a kiss." he entreats.

"You got the wrong bitch!"

They walk over to an old refrigerator in the kitchen. She stops in front of it. "You got my ten grand, Boy?

"Yeah, we good, ma. Show me my shit."

"What up, loc?" says a voice that startles Killer Boy. "Bam, where you come from, fam?" he asks.

"I'm back, cuz, to watch over Mom's back. So don't mind me, loc. We need to hook up sometime," Bam says.

Squeek puts her hands on her hips. "If the two of you is finished having a family reunion," she says, "can we do business now?"

Killer grins. "My bad, ma."

The refrigerator door opens to reveal every kind of murder weapon known to man. "Those at the bottom is what you wanted, C. Now where's my cash, loc?"

Killer reaches into both of his front pockets and pulls out two rubber bands of one hundred-dollar bills and hands them to Squeek. "Here, Shorty." He turns to Bam. "We'll catch up before I leave town," he promises.

"I can do that," Bam replies.

Squeek says to her son, "Bam, go get me that Army duffle bag over there, please."

He comes back with it and Killer Boy loads up the arsenal and brings it out to the car. "Cuz, pop the lock to the trunk," he says to Rich.

Rich takes in the huge, bulging duffle bag. "Damn, Boy, you got a body in there, cuz?"

"No, loc. This is my exclusive shit, homie." Killer Boy looks over at Rich with a "don't ask" face. "All I can say, loc, is I'm about to exterminate."

They exchange conspiring glances, then focus on the surrounding traffic.

"Loc, let's go pick up Spook," says Tank. "You know he will get an obsession with killing slobs."

"First, call them bitches to see what's up with not letting you know the business," says Biggie.

"Biggie, let me have your cell. Mine's at the crib." Biggie hands over his phone, the new Blackberry. "This cool, cuz," Tank says. He flips up the caller and dials Lacy's cell number. She answers, "Hello?"

"Bitch, you almost got my ass chewed the fuck out, hoc," he accuses.

"Nigga, you better check yo fucking mouth before you it get stomped out, Tank," she yells back. "You high, ain't you, boy?"

"So what if I am!" he says belligerently.

"Is Rich here, nigga?" she asks.

"Yeah. Why?"

"Look, I tried to call your cell but it went straight through to voice mail."

"No, the fuck you didn't. Where you at anyway, girl?"

"On the set," she answers.

"Tell her I say what's up, loc?" Biggie says.

"Biggie says what's up, Lacy," Tank reports.

"Oh, let me speak to him, Tank," Lacy says.

They arrive at Spook's crib. "Go in and get him, Tank," Biggie says. The car door shuts and Tank creeps up the sidewalk like he's on a mission. Biggie shakes his head, then turns to the phone.

"Hey, baby. You miss daddy?"

"I sure do," Lacy replies. "I need some of that ten inches, baby, like yesterday. Why haven't you called me, Biggie? You got so many hoes now that I don't count?"

"Never, Lacy. I got some shit to do right now, baby. As soon as I finish up, I'm-a hit you on the hip, ma."

"Cool. And tell that motherfucker Tank to watch his mouth."

"I got you. One."

As soon as Biggie pushes "end" on the cell phone, Tank arrives with Spook in tow. "B-Dog," Spook says as he nears the whip. "What it do, cuz?"

"Death," Biggie says.

"Now you're talking my shit, cuz!" Spook exclaims.

Tank still looks lost as he slides into the passenger seat. "Biggie, it's on. Let's strike slobs right now, loc," he says. They pull off to hit the Blood hood in a drive-by. They head to the freeway to cruise the South Side.

"Damn," says Spook. "You niggas is higher than a motherfucker! I can smell the dip and see the look in y'all's eyes. And by the way Tank's acting, I know it's some fire, Biggie. So dip me one, cuz."

"Dig, cuz. Dip your own poison, loc."

They turn left on Lake Street and ride to Popeye's for a bit to eat. "Get me a jumbo, cuz," says Spook. "I got to get right real quick."

"I know," says Tank. "I got you, fam."

"That nigga crazy, loc," says Biggie.

Spook says, "I know, fam. Let's go." He grabs Biggie by the arm.

"Fam, look at the light."

"Oh, shit," says Biggie. "Spook."

"Yeah, cuz. Sleep is the cousin of death, you know," says Tank.

"Revenge is better served cold," Biggie replies. "Come on, before we lose him in traffic." They push open the restaurant's glass doors so hard they crack. They run to the car.

"Where's my jumbo, loc?" complains Spook.

"No time for that shit, cuz. Hand me the Tech 9 in the back seat, Spook."

Biggie starts the G-ride and pulls about six cars behind O.G. Big Bear. Tank rumbles through the CD case to find MC Eiht's "We Come Strapped" album. "Now my mind is right, loc," he says. "This is some strong shit, cuz."

"Shotgun Crip for life," they all say together at the same time.

"Don't lose the slob, loc," says Spook. "He made a right, cuz. Move it!"

"I got the driving," says Biggie. "Spook, pass me the mag."

"Nah, pull up on the side of the dude and I'm going to Swiss cheese his ass, cuz," Spook replies eagerly.

"Spook, he stole on my ass at the mall and knocked me the fuck out, loc. Now pass me my shit," says Tank, animated now he's off the wet stick.

"Here, cuz. Do you fam."

O.G. stops at the liquor store across the street from the grocery store on the corner. "Fuck, he's got a bitch with him! Do the both of them, Tank," says Spook, "or let me hold you down, cuz."

"Nah, I got this," Tank says. "Biggie, pull right in front of the L.Q. so I can get them coming out, cuz."

Biggie busts a U-turn and stops in front of the liquor store. As soon as the car stops, O.G. and the woman come out, hugged up like newlyweds. Tank jumps out, wearing a hoodie and ski mask. He runs up on Bear and his broad so fast that it spooks her. She drops the bag she has in her arms. Bottles splash to the concrete as she looks at him with the look of death in her face. Before they can take one step, Tank lets off about forty shots, blowing them both through the double glass door and filling them with bullets before they even hit the ground.

Tank stands there for about five seconds, then walks over the top of both of them and fires until the clip is empty. "Fuck you, slob. Steal on that, bitch-ass nigga. That's for Fat Cuz and me."

"Come on, cuz," says Biggie. "Let's bounce, nigga."

Tank walks back to the whip, pointing the burner at anyone who looks at him. He sits down in the passenger seat and Biggie makes the tires screech, leaving smoke. "Pass me the dip, cuz," says Tank.

"You official," Spook says admiringly. "Let's bring backwards to these slobs, cuz. Let's ride to T.T.'s house. They got dro, fam."

"We headed to Foolish's house on Penn, fam," says Biggie.

"Yeah," Tank says. "We can chill there until nighttime, cuz."

"Let's call him first, 'cause you know how his bitch can be, fam," Spook says.

"Be cool," says Biggie, looking in the rearview mirror. "Po po is coming up behind us fast, cuz, in an unmarked car, so chill."

"If they put the lights on, we goin' pop they ass," Spook says enthusiastically. The car pulls away. Biggie sighs. "Shit, that was close."

"Fam, jump on the e-way," says Spook. "Tank, pass me the cell. Hello? What up, cuz?"

"Who dis?"

"Spook, Foolish. We on the e-way to your spot to blow."

"Come on, I need to smoke anyway, fam. Tank with you?"

"Yeah."

"Let me holler at him."

Spook hands the phone back to Tank, who takes it and says, "Speak, fool."

"I got that for you, Tank."

"Good. I'll call B.B. to come see you before the night is over,

Foolish,"Tank says. "I'm in the backyard."

"So pull back there."

"One."Tank hangs up. "Cuz, did you see them two motherfuckers do the Harlem shake while they was getting pumped with lead?"

"Yeah, cuz.They looked like P. Diddy and Mase out there today," says Biggie. "I'm proud of you, cuz. Don't tell Foolish what's up, Spook."

"Who you talkin' to, amateur?" Spook says.

"I'm just sayin', cuz," replies Biggie.

They spy a tricked-out car in the driveway. "Damn, whose old-school is that in Foolish's backyard, cuz?" asks Spook. "That's hot. It looks like it got juice, too, cuz."

Biggie leans over and whispers to Tank. "Give Foolish the Tech to sell for you, Tank."

"Good idea, Biggie."

Chapter 5

I hate coming over here, thinks Shaunna. *Shit.* Ding dong. Ding dong. "What it do?" says a voice on the other side of the door.

"Open up this door, Pit Bull. It's me, Shaunna."

"Okay, shorty." Buzz. The door unlocks for entry. *Damn, it smells like shit and piss in here.*

"What do you need, baby?" drawls a dope fiend in the hallway.

Pit Bull appears to escort her to his apartment. "Nigga, step the fuck off before I have to drop your ass, blood," Pit Bull says. The doper smiles foolishly and says, "My bad, Pit Bull."

"It's hot as hell today for some reason, ma," he says. "Ain't Nothin' Like a Little Bump and Grind" comes out of the sound system in the living room. He shuts the door. "How you doing these days, lil mama?"

"Good, Pit Bull. Let me get that doe so I can bounce."

"Chill for a second and blow a blunt with your guy..," he suggests.

"I got to do a few things, Pit Bull. Quit wasting my fucking time, nigga. I don't fuck the help." Suddenly, she says, "Oh, fuck it. I'll blow with you right quick, homie, but keep your eyes and hands to yourself, boy."

Pit Bull sits down next to her with lust in his eyes. "Here, light this up while I go get the doe," he says. One flick of the lighter and she pulls.

Knock, knock, knock. "Pit Bull, your door," Shaunna yells.

"I got it. Speak," he says to the door.

"Open up. I need a re-up. I'm out," says a female voice.

"That's Scooter's girl," he tells Shaunna. "Hold up, blood, for a minute. I'm busy," he says to the woman behind the door.

"Ah, hurry up!"

"Here's the sixty thousand," he says to Shaunna. You want to count it?"

"Nah, I'm cool. This some fine shit, Pit Bull."

"I know." He looks like he's going to ask her to stay with him for a while. "I got to dip, Pit Bull. You flipping that doe over here as I can see."

Shaunna walks out of the building to find a cop sitting on the hood of her Yukon. "Hey, sexy," he says. "Where's your man at?"

She frowns at him. "Red Beard, what the fuck you doing sitting on my fucking truck?"

"My bad, ma," he apologizes as he slides off the hood and walks toward her. "I need to see him like ASAP."

"Call his cell phone," she suggests.

"He ain't answering my calls."

"He must be busy."

"Shaunna, you cool down there?" asks Pit Bull, who's leaning out the window.

She looks up at him and says, "Yeah, we straight." She looks back at Red Beard.

"We need to settle up today," he says.

"I'll tell him I saw you," she answers.

"Okay, make sure you do that, Shaunna." The walkie talkie on his shoulder squawks. She hears something about "all available come to the scene to assist." "I have to go, but I'll see him later," Red Beard says. He gets into his squad and roars off, siren screaming. Shaunna gets thoughtfully into the Yukon and pulls off.

"Jay, grab the mags and leave the doe in the trunk," says my brother. "When we get to the room follow my lead, but don't do shit 'til you see me pull out, homie."

"We on a jack, Ghost?"

"Yeah. I think some funny shit is going on with Curren$y, dog. I just can't put my finger on it yet, you know?"

"I got you, bro."

We pull into the Embassy Suites parking lot. "We're here." A valet approaches the car. "How are you doing today, sir?"

"Fine," Ghost says. "Take care of my whip, son." He passes the valet a C-note. The kid smiles, gives Ghost a claim stub and leaves with the car, a happy young blood.

We walk past the front desk unnoticed by the clerk. The elevator is empty. On the way up, I'm prepared for the worst. The elevator door opens in the sixth floor. A maid drags her cleaning cart from room to room.

Tap, tap. The door to room 602 opens and a tall yellow pretty boy dressed in an all-red jumpsuit answers the door. "Man, what took you so long to get here, blood? And who is shorty, dog?" he asks.

"My little brother, "J", from the South," Ghost answers. I shut the door with a bad vibe.

"Sit down, shorty. Have a drink or light up a blunt to chill," offers Curren$y.

"Nah, my man. I'm cool," I say.

Ghost gets down to business. "We straight, blood, with the new shit, dog?" he asks.

"You know this, man," Curren$y says steadily. "And it's one hundred percent pure. Test this shit right here, b-dog."

Ghost dumps some of the kilo on the table in some white solution and it instantly turns blue. A smile comes over his face. "The car is downstairs in valet parking with twenty-seven bricks of raw in the trunk, Ghost," Curren$y volunteers.

"My car is down there, too," Ghost says.

A woman walks out of the door to the adjoining room and I up two burners. "Stop, bitch!" I yell. "What's this?" I say.

Curren$y says, "Chill, shorty."

"Nah," says Ghost. "You chill, nigga. Dog, pass me the valet ticket. And bitch, get your ass over there on the chair next to your man and shut the fuck up. Who else is over next door, dog?"

"No one," swears Curren$y. "This my girl from Cali, dog. I told you about her."

Pop, pop from the silenced .40 Glock and her head burst like a glass hit the floor.

"Shorty, why you shoot my bitch, dog?" Curren$y asks incredulously. I say nothing in response.

"Look, dog, I know you on some funny shit, so don't play games with me, blood," Ghost says crossly.

"Ghost, I don't kn…"

Bap, bap with the butt of the 9 mm to Curren$y's head before he can finish his sentence. "I can't see out my right eye, blood," he complains.

"Jay, take the valet ticket from him."

Curren$y reaches into his pocket and says, "Here, dog. Don't kill me now."

Ghost presses him. "Talk, dog."

"About what?"

"Let me know the deal," Ghost insists. The pretty yellow boy sighs and takes a deep breath.

"Rich knows that y'all killed Fat Cuz, and he gave me twenty-seven kilos to set you up, dog. I know that's fucked up, fam, but twenty-seven bricks is some dough, fam. He's my cousin, dog. Rich."

Pop, pop, pop. Three to the chest from my Glock and he's dead. "Baby boy, let's wipe this place down real good and bounce," Ghost says. "Jay, shit is about to get real raw real soon, fam. We good, though. We got twenty-seven bricks for free."

"I'm on," I say. "Wipe me down."

"Come on," Ghost says. "Let's go get the cars."

The valet is surprised to see us. "Leaving so soon, sir?" he asks.

"We need both cars," Ghost says commandingly.

"I'll be right back, sir."

The cars pull up to the hotel entrance and we each take one. I follow Ghost to some house on Penn and Twenty-ninth in North Minneapolis. We park in the back yard.

"Jay, grab that duffle bag out of the trunk for me real quick," instructs my brother.

"There's two of them, bro."

"Pass me one of them," he says.

"Here. Whose spot is this?"

"My bitch, Nina. She cool. I've been using her spot for years. Lil D don't even know about it."

Ghost doesn't know that Killer Boy has been hot on his ass, following his every move. *Damn, this nigga is a cold-blooded killer like me, but he's slipping fo sho. And it's me who's going to catch him when he falls. But who is Shorty with him?* he asks himself while he dips a blunt. *Let me get a closer look at him real quick.* Killer Boy pulls into the alleyway, driving slowly to check Jay out.

"Ghost, you see that blue Impala riding slow right there?" I ask.

"Yeah, let's put this money and shit up and dip and see if we can catch up with that car, dog." Ghost's cell rings to the Hot Boys song, "Bling Bling". "Hello. Dog, where you at?"

"On my way to get into traffic, dog."

"Notify me when you're in the street, dog," Lil D says, and they hang up.

"Go downstairs and put the doe into the dryer for me, Jay, then come on so we can see who that was, bro. Oh yeah, put these burners in there, too." *Where are the keys to the Malibu at? Oh, shit, I got them on my key chain.*

We lock the house door and enter the garage. "Now let's go see who that dude is, Jay." We turn left onto Penn Avenue North and the car is right in front of us. The driver doesn't know we're behind him now.

Killer Boy bumps C-Bo's "'Til My Casket Drops" and he feels the stick he just lit a while ago. He clutches the calico in his lap. *Fuck them slobs. I'm-a kill Lil D, Ghost and Shorty and bounce with they doe, too.*

"Don't pull up on the side of him, Ghost," I say uneasily.

"He can't see into this car with this dark tint, Jay. I'm going to take a photo of him to show the fellas to see if anybody knows him."

"That's what's up, big bro, then you can show that pig, too, huh?"

Click, click, click. "That's right, nigga. Smile for the camera. I'm good now. Let's go to the hood to chill out, Jay."

It's still evening when we pull up at Thirty-second and Fourth. A couple of homies watch us get out of the car. "Man, who that parked on the corner over there, blood?" Big Chief says.

"Let's see, dog," says Tre Duce. "Put your hoodie on, Big Chief. That's the big homie and Jay, fool. Yo, Big Dog, what up, homie?"

"Come here, little dogs," says Ghost.

"What it do, Jay?"

"Shit, fam," I reply.

Ghost hands me two stacks to spend. "Here, Jay, you go kick it with Big Chief and Tre Duce until later, dog."

"Cool." We get into the Malibu and I put on the Hot Boys' "Let Them Burn." We're out.

"Jay, you know we at war, huh?" asks Big Chief.

I nod. "Yeah, I'm with ya to the end," I say.

"I got a lick on the North side," he says.

I'm not sure how to get there. "Where at, Big Chief?"

"Let me drive," says Big Chief. "It'll be easier."

I pull over at the Taco Bell and we switch places. "Now we good," I say. "You got heat?"

"Yeah," says Big Chief.

"Pass it here, fam."

We pull up to North Commons Park. It's packed with people smoking weed, dipping blunts, hoes choosing players. "I'm looking for that nigga Johnny," says Big Chief as he scans the area.

"Damn, fam, he ain't paid you yet for them two zowies, blood?"

"Nah, but today I'm-a get it in his blood, dog. There he is, over by the basketball court, dog! Split up and I'll come at him to see if he got my doe."

"Look, if he don't," I say, "let me know by taking off your hat by him, then I got it from there, fam."

Big Chief starts walking toward Johnny. "Yo, Johnny, come here for one second," he beckons.

"Big Chief, I need one more day, homie. What you doing on my stomping ground anyway?" Johnny asks nervously.

"Looking for you, homie. It's been over a week now. Johnny, you trying to play me, nigga?" Big Chief throws down the challenge.

"Who the fuck you talking to, slob-ass nigga?" Johnny retorts. "You forget that you're alone and this my hood, fool."

People start watching the confrontation between the two. "Well, we straight, homie, keep the money," Big Chief says.

"You damn right, slob!"

Big Chief takes his hat off apologetically. "I didn't know it was like that, fam. "I'm out, blood."

I'm standing right behind the two of them, talking to Tre Duce. "Go get the car, Duce. Tell Big Chief to pull at the end of the park over there by the trees, fam. And keep the engine running." Duce splits to catch Big Chief.

Johnny sticks his chest out. "Man, fuck that nigga!" he yells. "Who the fuck he think he is to come to the Northside and try to check me?"

"Johnny. Yo, Johnny," I call out. The crowd splits, giving me a clear view of my victim. He turns toward me and narrows his eyes.

"Who you, nigga?"

Pop. He's hit in the shoulder. "Shit, man!" he exclaims. Everybody runs. Pop. Pop. The .50 caliber blows two holes into his legs and Johnny drops backwards on the concrete. "Help me, somebody," he calls, but he's all alone now. "Take my money."

"Nah, I don't want it, son." I put the .50 caliber to his mouth and pull the trigger three times. "Now you can't disrespect none of the homies no more," I say. I walk to the waiting car.

"What took you so long to hit him up, Jay?" asks Duce as I get in the back seat.

"I wanted him to suffer and know his mouth got him fucked up, fam." Suddenly, I'm tired. "I need to get high, fam. I need some dip, you know? I can't postpone my obsession any longer. I need to take a load off right now."

"Homie, I got you," Big Chief says. "It's official. You more down than a motherfucker, son."

"Big Chief," I say, "that nigga had a real mouthpiece on him, fam."

"I know, Jay. My baby lives around the block from here, down the street from the school. I'll run in and cop a vial for us to blow on me, scud. I'll be right out with some piss, dog."

"You know, Duce, sometimes I think that I'm living in a motion picture," I say wearily.

"Shit, Jay, that's crazy, dog," he replies.

"Here, dog, dip these Moore cigarettes," says Big Chief. "We out. Back to the hood, dog," he tells Duce. "Our business is done."

Chapter 6

"Hey, that looks like O.G. Bear laying there."

"Damn, it sure is, Officer Jones. Do you know what that means?"

"No, Red, what?"

"It means that we have to call the Gang Unit in on this, detective," the narc explains. "It seems that a Cali gang war is going on. The four guys that were killed a couple days ago were Shotgun Crips, and this man here is an O.G. Blood. The feds might come sniffing around, too. Call the Gang Unit. I gotta go back to the office." Red Beard walks to his unmarked car and pulls off.

Let me call this piece of shit and see if he answers now, he thinks. "B-dog, love!" he says into his cell.

"Who dis?"

"It's the po po, dog."

"What up?"

"Hey, Ghost, man, listen up. Twelve o'clock midnight. Dream Girls downtown, dog." Click. *That should get his fucking attention. I need to charge his fucking ass more money for the risk that I'm taking fucking with his ass. These are my motherfuckin' streets when it's all said and done!*

I should cruise through the hood to see if any of them Family Cartel cats are out. I'm going to have to check his pig ass for that shit, Ghost thinks. "Dog, have them hoes got over there yet?" he says to the man sitting next to him in the car.

"Nah, they ain't called me yet, Ghost," says Crooked. "Blood, you got two bricks soft for your man at a good price, homie?"

"Yeah," Ghost replies. "Fo sho, I got you, dog. You my main man. Let me call and see if Nina's around, dog." He pulls out his cell and hits speed dial for Nina's number.

"Hello, baby," he croons into the telephone. "What's up, shorty?"

"I miss you, Ghost."

"Yeah, I'm thinking about you, too, baby."

"I see you were here, however."

"Yeah, I took the Malibu."

"I know. What you want, nigga?

"Stop it, boo."

"But on the real, I need you to come by the hood with two Jolly Ranchers for me, baby."

"Okay, about twenty minutes."

"Pull up behind your whip, baby."

Crooked catches Ghost's attention. "Look, nigga, that looks like Shaunna pulling up the block, Ghost."

"Damn. What the fuck she want now?" Ghost sounds exasperated. Honk, honk.

"Come here, Ghost." He gets out of the car and walks to hers.

"Shaunna, why are you here?"

"I went to see Pit Bull, and Red Beard was sitting outside on the hood of my truck, saying he needs to get at you ASAP and shit. I don't fucking appreciate that shit, either," she pouts.

"I talked to him just a minute ago, so he tight now," Ghost says.

"When you coming home?" she asks.

"Later, baby. You know I just took care of some business, so I'll be late." He hands her a package. "Just put that away for me and keep five thousand for yourself to shop with, boo."

"I love you, Ghost. And be careful!"

"I love you, too, baby." They kiss through the window and Shaunna pulls off just in time to miss Nina pulling up from behind.

"Boy, your luck is good, dog," says Crooked when Ghost returns to the car.

Ghost grins, "Nah, I'm the fucking man."

"Shaunna sure kill your ass if she catch your ass, blood."

Ghost hasn't noticed the white van up the left side of the street. Two federal agents, Dan Lyons and Clayton Downs, listen to the conversation between Ghost and Crooked. "He's a very good C.I., Lyons," says Downs. "The wire in his belt is perfect. We got to get Ghost on federal charges now. The grand jury will love to get him on an indictment."

"I know, Downs. It's incredible to get him after all these years."

"But we got his ass now, partner. One move now and we will be able to break down their infrastructure."

"Hold on, Crooked, let me holler at my bitch," Ghost says as he gets out of the car.

Nina wastes no time. "Ghost, get in the car for a second." Ghost opens the passenger side door and sits down. Nina pulls off with a spooked look on her face.

"Why you look crazy, baby, like you seen Satan or something?" he asks.

"Look, Ghost. Right there to our left."

"Shit! The law. Turn right, then left."

"Did he see us, Lyons?"

"I don't know."

Ghost and Nina stop at a house a few blocks away. "Stop right here, baby," Ghost says. "Shorty, come here." Ten-year-old B-B walks up to the car, his round face solemn as an undertaker's.

"What that B like, homie?" B-B asks as he surveys Nina's Dodge Magnum.

Ghost shakes his head. "No time for that, lil homie. Take that package off of the back seat and go see Kiki for me, blood. Don't open it up."

"I got you, O.G."

"Here, take these five C-notes." B-B trots off. Ghost turns to Nina. "Now let's go back to screen Crooked."

Where did they go, man? Thinks Crooked. *I know I'm playing with death, fucking with Ghost, but I'm jammed the fuck up right now.* Sweat drips down his face onto his hoodie. *Damn, it getting dark now. Shit. I hope they got a good eye on my ass. Good. There they come now.*

"Baby, let me out by him and you keep it moving. But don't go right home," Ghost instructs Nina. "There might be a tail on you. So take this two thousand dollars and hit the mall or something and call me later. By the way, whose whip is this anyway?"

She smiles. "Don't worry about that."

"Cool. We'll talk later, shorty." They kiss and Nina bounces.

"This is Agent Lyons. Put a tail on her."

"Copy that," says one of the agents.

"Downs, we need to know who she is like yesterday, 'cause that wasn't Shaunna, partner."

"I know. Look over there." Downs points at a group of girls standing on the corner.

"Damn, these young girls grow up so fast," says Lyons, shaking his head.

"What's up, homie?" Ghost notices the sweat dripping off Crooked's chin, but says nothing.

"Trying to get paid, Ghost," answers Crooked.

"Crooked, get your doe out of my truck, blood, and I'll catch up with you later, dog. 'Cause she didn't bring shit, 'cause I don't do that shit, dog."

"I'll hit you up later, Ghost."

"Do that."

Crooked's heart pounds out his chest as he thinks about what Ghost just said. "Crooked, let's chill later tonight, bro." Crooked turns and nods his head.

This fool-ass nigga got the kid fucked up, Ghost thinks.

"He made us, Lyons. She must have seen us when she drove by."

"This is Special Agent in Charge Lyons. It's a no-go. I repeat, a no-go. Stand down. All agents meet me at the Federal Building to discuss today's events."

"Come ride with me real quick, fam," says Ghost to Smoke.

"Blood, let's dip, dog," replies Smoke. Ghost and Smoke take off in the Malibu.

"You got your cell, Smoke?"

"Yeah." He pulls out his Boost mobile and hands it to Ghost.

"I need to hit Pit Bull up real quick before we get there." Ghost flips the phone open. "You got Pit Bull's number on lock?"

"Yeah, scroll down, Ghost. You got that Jim Jones' 'Ballin'?"

"Put it in, fam. Pit Bull, I'm on my way. I need you to get Lil D and Big Chief over there ASAP, dog." Click.

Damn. It seems like it's on, Pit Bull says to himself.

Downtown at the Federal Building, Crooked is told what he must do. "Now, Kevin Larson, Sr., you know that your ass is in some very deep water, son. We can't help you if you don't help yourself now. Would you like a drink, son?"

"No, sir."

"Do you know who that woman was in that black Dodge Magnum?" Crooked shakes his head. "No."

"We have someone following her as we speak. Now, what went wrong out there today, Kevin?"

He shrugs. "I don't know. One second we was on, then we wasn't."

The conference room door opens and Agent Martinson says, "We have a guest, Agent Lyons." Lyons gives everyone in the room a confused look. "Why are you interrupting this meeting?" he asks the newcomer.

"Well, let me introduce myself. I'm Special Agent Adam Crown. The reason I'm here is because this is a matter that has international ties. I'm with the Federal Gang Task Force Unit in California. I've been sent here by my superior to investigate the wave of gang killings." Agent Lyons looks like he's going to interrupt, but Crown holds up his hand. "Let me interpret that last statement. We've been looking at the Park City Bloods for a while now, and we have inside information that ties them to the Mexican mafia."

Lyons says, "I'm Agent Lyons, and I'm in charge of this investigation. Whatever assistance we can be to each other will benefit the Bureau. But to let you know, I'm in charge, and what you learn comes through me first before you make any moves, agent."

"Clear," says Crown.

"Have a seat and we can continue with our meeting."

"Thank you."

꧁❖꧂

Pit Bull texts Lil D to meet him at his spot ASAP and texts Big Chief to join. *Shit, let me get these hoes the fuck up out of here before they get here.* Candy is already working him over.

"Shit, that feels so motherfuckin' gooood, Candy. But dammmmmmm … ahhhh … baby, your head is the bomb." Candy pulls Pit Bull's dick out of her mouth quickly, spits on the head and then rubs it around with her thumb.

"You like that, baby?" she breathes.

"Hell, yeahhhh."

Candy deep throats Pit Bull's whole eight-and-a-half inches and jacks off into her mouth. "I'm about to nut, baby! Ohhhhaaaa …. Uhhhhhh." Candy sucks every drop out of Pit Bull. Pit Bull lays his head back against the headrest on the chair to catch his breath. "Candy, you're so headstrong with your jaw," he pants. "Baby, there's some extras on the TV for you, but y'all got to bounce 'til later. Tell them bitches in the back what's up."

Candy looks at Pit Bull with a frustrated look on her face. "Mandy and Ayesha, come on, we got to leave," she screeches.

Knock, knock. Pit Bull fumbles out of the chair, trying to pull his pants up in a hurry. "Who that?" he addresses the door.

"Me, nigga," Ghost says.

Pit Bull turns to Candy. "Come on, y'all. My guy is here, ma."

Mandy and Ayesha walk out of the back room looking exotic. From the expression on both of their faces, Pit Bull just missed out on an explosive session with both of them. The door opens as Candy reaches for the door knob. "See you later, Pit Bull," she says.

"Okay, ladies."

"Damn, what do we have here now, Pit Bull?" Ghost asks as he eyes the women. "Look like you've been getting very explicit here."

"Nah, them my home girls, dog."

Shit, the one in front is finer than a motherfucker, Ghost thinks to himself. "Pit Bull, who that in the front of the pack, B?" he asks while still standing in the doorway looking at their asses.

"Candy, dog."

"You know, I would love to explore some of that, homie, but we got a problem that we need to fix right now."

"Close the door, Ghost," Pit Bull says. *Damn. This nigga thinks he can fuck anybody's bitch.*

Ghost and Smoke sit down in chairs near the windows so they can watch the street. "Where the fuck is the boys at, Pit Bull?" Ghost asks impatiently.

"I texted Lil D to come ASAP," Pit Bull replies.

"Never mind, they're outside now."

Smoke looks at Pit Bull and seems amused. "Damn, you look fatigued, blood. Them hoes must have some fire, dog."

"I've been up all night making moves," says Pit Bull. "You get that popper, Ghost?"

"Yeah, we straight, fam."

"Let me go open the door so they can come straight in, fam," says Pit Bull.

"Do that, fam," Ghost says.

Big Chief and Lil D come through the front door wearing all-black hoodies and black Sean Jean jeans with heat tucked.

"Blood, who's dying tonight, fam? Pull up a chair and sit down, you two, and check this out, blood," Ghost says. "Blood, we have to fortify our circle, fam. Look, today I was just on the block with Crooked, and he was trying to get two bricks from me. When Nina came with the shit, the police was up the street in a white van watching us. I would-a have slept if she would-a have come from another direction, you know?"

"Damn, Ghost, Crooked's flagrant," says Lil D. "I got that nigga, dog. Don't worry, fam."

"I will have more knowledge about the situation later tonight when I go meet with Red Beard, fam," Ghost tells them.

"Who got some dip, baby?" asks Smoke.

"I don't want none of y'all to blow that shit tonight, blood," Ghost says sternly. "I need all of y'all on point with this shit later, 'cause we got to be smooth."

A smirk creeps across Big Chief's face, then he laughs. "What's so funny, dog?" Ghost asks.

"Nothing, dog. Just tripping off the legacy we're going to leave behind us for the lil homies to battle over, dog."

"I'll hit you on that later on tonight."

Lil D says, "Ghost, that nigga is a fucking liability to us, dog. The way he's going to die is lethal."

"For real, dog," says Pit Bull.

Ghost and Smoke head out the door.

Chapter 7

"Cuz, let's bounce to Karma tonight. I got the hookup on V.I.P.," says Rich. "Biggie, did you take care of that business?"

"Yeah, cuz, we good. I kept twenty of them things like you said to."

"Where Tank at, cuz?"

"I left him and Spook over North at Foolish's house, smoking dip, cuz. That reminds me, Rich, I need to let you know what happened earlier today, fam. We held court in the street today for Fat Cuz, homie. I'm proud of the lil homies for laying down that nigga, O.G. Slob Big Bear earlier at the L.Q., and his bitch, too."

"What the fuck, fam? My lil nigga did that shit?" Rich is amazed. "I gotta bonus for fam when I catch up to his ass! I got to call that faggot-ass cop, Red Beard, to see what's the deal with that shit, too. But right now, I need to party. Yo. Damn, I need to call Cali, too, cuz. I got too much shit to do and not enough time to do it all, cuz.

"Look, homie, I copped this chain from Jacob. It's one hundred carats of flawless diamonds in this cross, and the chain is platinum with diamond cuts in it." Rich looks into the mirror to check himself out for the night. "Biggie, hit cuz and them up so they can meet us at the club. I'll call Killer Boy, Jamal, and Do-Right, they will spread the word, too, cuz."

"What car you want to floss in tonight, Biggie?"

"Let's pull out the H2, cuz, with the twenty-sixes on it. The hoes go crazy over that whip."

"It's 10:30 p.m., cuz. Let's bounce."

"Hold up, Biggie, I'm not ready yet, cuz. Grab an ounce of that dro in the dresser over there, homie, and start rolling up. We hood rich, cuz. Money won't change us. Money over bitches, all day hustling, cuz," says Rich.

"I know, baby. We neighborhood super stars, 'cause we never fold under pressure." Biggie rolls up, then they smash out to the club in downtown Minneapolis.

"Damn, cuz, look at the line at the door, Rich. I know it's some hoes up in there tonight, too. Look, there goes cuz in the parking lot across the street." Biggie rolls down the passenger side window and throws up Shotgun Crip to Jamal.

"What up, cuz?" says Jamal.

Rich turns up the four eighteen-inch J.L. Audio subs in the back to attract all the honeys as he pulls in the lot. Before the truck stops, however, Biggie jumps out with a blunt in his mouth, crab-walking to Bun B's "I'm a Gangsta Niggas Don't Know About Me." Rich parks the truck next to the fellas and gets out with a blunt in his mouth, too, as he walks to the booth to pay for parking.

"Cuz, we are at war," says Biggie, "so stay on point tonight." He gives Dread the Crip shake.

"Cuz, I always knew that Rich had true potential to hold it down," says Do-Right.

"We produce killers. Fuck them slobs," says C-loc.

"Let's hurry up and smoke so we can fade up in the club deep, cuz," says Rich.

They all arrive at the V.I.P. section. "How many is with you to-night, Rich?" asks the bouncer.

"Let me see, about fifteen tonight, homie. Look, I don't want to walk through no metal detector, fam. Take this two grand, yo, plus the door fee. Whatever it is for us to walk straight to the Velvet Room."

"Cool. Follow me. Let them pass, Mike. I'll escort you, fellas."

They proceed through the crowd while the D.J. bums "Stunning Like My Daddy" by Bird Man and Lil Wayne. The crowd gets hyped now. Rich and the rest of the crew are seated in the V.I.P. section of the club. The waitress comes over. "Gentlemen, what may I bring you to drink tonight?"

"A whole lot of you," says Do-Right.

"Man, quit playing with your no-game having ass, cuz," says B-loc.

"Baby, bring us fifteen bottles of Ace champagne and fifteen double shots of Louis XIII," says Rich.

"I'll be right back, sir."

Damn, she going home with me tonight and she don't even know it yet, thinks Rich.

Ghost, Big Chief, Lil D, and Tre Duce walk through the doors at Dream Girls. He's early, waiting for Red Beard to show up. "Hold up. Can I see some I.D. from you two?" the door man says to him and Big Chief.

"Let me talk to him, fellas," says Ghost, coming up from behind them. "Look these are my two nephews and they're eighteen years old. I want to show them a good time tonight. Feel me."

"Nah, not yet," says the doorman.

"Here's one thousand dollars to you, if you feelin' me now," Ghost says.

The doorman stands aside. "Don't start no shit," he warns.

"We cool," Ghost replies. "And we'll spend more than that tonight on the girls, too."

The atmosphere in the strip joint is live. Attendance is beyond astonishing. As the crew nears the stage, they see why. Buffy the Body is up on stage making her cheeks clap. Big Chief asks the attendant if he can get closer to the stage to get a better view. Ghost passes the attendant three C-notes and he springs into action: "I'm sorry, fellas, this table is reserved. The hostess forgot to put the sign on the table. I'm sorry for the mix-up, fellas, but guest who reserved the table is here now."

The four men at the table look at the attendant like they're going to assassinate him on the spot for moving them from the best table in the joint. They move sullenly to a less desirable table.

"I want you guys to sit there," Ghost says. "I'll be all over the joint, blood, getting lap dances 'til he shows."

"Cool, dog. We straight, fam," Lil D replies. "I want to authenticate this bitch anyway, 'cause the word is, she'll let you fuck for the price, dog."

"Come in. I have audio-visual on your suspects. Copy?"

"I'm down the street at Karma with my eyes on the Crip crew," says Downs.

"Good. We can kill two birds with one Crown tonight. Call up Burgess and see what he came up with on the mystery girl."

Downs leaves the dance floor to make a quick call to Agent Burgess and knocks a woman's drink off the bar as he goes by. "What, lady? Oh, I'm sorry, I didn't see your drink sitting there. I'll replace it when I get off the phone. Okay, nigga. These women nowadays. Excuse me one second."

"Agent Burgess? Where are you?" Downs speaks into the phone. "Copy."

"I'm at the Bureau," Burgess says. "I lost her at the mall hours ago, but I got the plate number to that Dodge Magnum she was driving."

"Good work. That's a start."

"Where are you, Agent Downs?" Burgess asks.

"Karma. Following Rich."

"I'm on my way. I don't want to miss all of the fun. Copy."

Red Beard parks across the street from Dream Girls in the pay parking lot. *I wonder who he has with him tonight.* He walks into the strip joint.

"How are you doing tonight, sir?" asks the attendant.

"Fine. And you?"

"Cool."

Red Beard pays the twenty-dollar fee to enter the club. As he walks through the crowd, he surveys the people around him. His swagger changes as he spots Ghost in the V.I.P. section getting a lap dance. Red Beard attempts to make eye contact with Ghost, but can't from the view he has right now.

"Attention, blood, look over your shoulder," says Big Chief. "There's that cop we here to meet." Everyone's attitude changes from fun to business.

"If Ghost hits his chirp button, blaze his ass. Now I want all of you to be where you can blind-side him if you have to, homie," says Lil D.

They move into different parts of the club. Red Beard walks up to the table where Ghost is enjoying himself immensely. "Is this seat taken?" he asks.

"Nah," Ghost says. "Shorty, come over and take care of my comrade." He calls the bouncer over to tell him that he wants privacy and passes him four C-notes. The curtain comes down over the door.

"Now you can quit procrastinating with my money, son," growls Red Beard.

"Yeah, I know, dog. I have your proceeds with me, so let's keep this professional." Ghost reaches into his front pockets and pulls out two knots of one hundred-dollar bills. "Here's your fee, plus some, because I need to know who this man is right here." He pulls out his cell phone to show the photo he took of the person driving through the alley. "I want a profile on him, so fucking probe, yo. I know you're very proficient at what you do, Red Beard, so enjoy the night on me. And, oh yeah, you can take this phone with you. It's a pre-pay."

"I have some very bad news to tell you, Ghost," Red Beard says apologetically.

Ghost's cool, but suspicious. "What you got to tell me now?"

"O.G. Big Bear and a broad he was with was killed earlier today."

Ghost throws the fat-ass woman off of him and onto the floor and walks out before she or Red Beard can say a word.

Damn, there he goes, Agent Lyons says to himself. *I thought I lost him. Where the fuck has he been? I can't lose him now, he looks upset.*

Lil D sees Ghost moving fast toward the exit, so he motions for the rest of them to follow him out. As soon as they reach the cars, Ghost says to them, "They got O.G. Big Bear today, and we have to recruit some killers from the jungle in Cali to help out with this one here, blood."

"Fuck them niggas! We got this, blood," says Tre Duce. The rage of death is in his voice.

"Hold on now, lil homie! O.G.'s rank is beyond any of ours, so we have to go to the top of the chain on this one, dog. Cali calls the shots," Ghost explains.

"Damn," says Lil D. "But we regulate this chapter of the set, dog."

"I know, dog. It reflects on us, though, how we handle this situation." Ghost continues, "With that said, I'm reluctant on bringing in anyone else on this hit besides the people the O.G.s send down to blaze shit up. I will hold every one of you responsible if you open your motherfucking mouth, understood?"

"Yeah," they all say.

"Now our reputation is on the line, so let me make some calls so we can resolve this shit, yo." Ghost says.

"So you want us to chill, homie?" Lil D asks.

"Yeah, but stay strapped, 'cause it's on!"

They jump into their whips and dip off on their separate ways.

Now that didn't look right, thinks Agent Lyons. *I'll bet my salary on that shit.* He stands in front of Dream Girls scribbling down the license plates of cars parked near the club. *It's late. I'm going to call it a night.* He pulls out his cell and calls Agent Downs.

"Do you have anything incriminating, Downs?"

"No, not yet. They've all been drinking all night long with different people that are of interest to us. They have been making it rain all night, tonight. People have been trampling each other to get the money they're throwing on the dance floor. I've given them a close scrutinizing with the small camera I have."

"That sounds great, Downs. Let's call it a night, pardner, and go home. We'll talk to the U.S. Attorney in the morning about getting more agents on the case."

"My sentiments exactly," says Downs.

Chapter 8

The next morning Killer Boy calls Scab to come meet him at Amos and Amos on Broadway Avenue North. *I know this A-1 dope-sucking motherfucker got some news that I can use*, Killer thinks as he mugs himself in the rearview mirror of the black Grand National.

Scab pulls up in a red Ford Taurus. *Just look at this sunken-face nigga here. One day he's going to succumb to his pleasures of coke.* Scab approaches Killer's car. He has a mopey look on his face. "What up, Killer?" he asks, making hand motions to unlock the passenger-side door.

Killer rolls down the window. "Get in, homie."

"Man, when did you get in town?" Scab asks as he gets in the car.

"Don't worry yourself about shit you don't need to know. Now, I need your fucking mouthpiece so I can send me some slobs to the fucking morgue." Scab pulls out his cell phone.

"You know I got you," he says, sympathetically. "I heard about Fat Cuz, too, homie, and all of you got my condolences."

"Now listen to me, lil homie – oh, shit! Hold up for one second. That looks like one of them Southside 30s niggas."

Killer pulls off before Scab can try to get out of the car. "Look," he says. "Shut the fuck up and grab that Colt .45 out of the bag on the back seat. We're going to confront these hoe-ass b-dogs right now, fam."

Scab gives Killer a confused look. The Grand National moves in and out of traffic, lane after lane, until Killer spots the enemy up ahead at Penn Avenue North and Broadway. They're four cars behind the white Yukon. Killer glares at Scab. "Look, get your fuckin' confidence in order and hand me the AK-47 on the floor behind me, cuz." He gives Scab a look of death. Scab knows the situation he's in and knows there's no turning back now.

"This shit is fire, big homie," he says.

"I know."

Damn, I don't want to be no casualty today. I haven't even had no morning hit shit.

The Grand National pulls up to the side of the Yukon. "Man, that's Crooked and some white man," says Killer. "Both of them is about to cease to exist." With that, he raises the AK toward the passenger-side window and exhibits exquisite shots at the stop light. He puts the car into park and gets out to empty the whole clip while Scab lights up the driver's side window as he walks slowly up to the truck. . Killer and Scab move on the truck with expert experience, like marksmen at war.

All of the windows shatter. The driver of the truck slumps over on the steering wheel. The truck runs into the fire hydrant on the corner. Both occupants are hit in the face and neck. The gangstas turn to leave the crime scene when the back window of the truck explodes. They turn around at the same time and fire shots at the young soldier who's firing at them. TThey hit him execution style in the dome, making the back of his head explode out the front windshield.

"Come on, Scab, let's bounce!" They jump into the Grand National and pull off toward Golden Valley Road.

"Pull over in the back of that house over there, Killer." Scab points to a blue house about three doors from the corner.

"Who stay there?" Killer asks.

"Foolish," explains Scab.

"Oh, shit. That's on time," Killer says appreciatively.

Killer makes a left turn, pulls right up to the steps and jumps out with Scab in tow. Foolish opens the door. He's about to leave when he sees them running up the walk. Foolish ups a .357 Magnum into

Killer's face at point-blank range.

"Ma, it's me, nigga. Put that shit away before you make me bust this AK, fool."

"My bad, homie," Foolish apologizes. "What's the deal?"

"We need to chill for a second."

"That's cool. Tank's in there, sleeping."

"Fuck him. Call Rich," says Scab. "That's who I owe my fidelity to."

"Go ahead and go in. And be quiet. My kids are here."

"Man, how long my brother been here, Foolish?" asks Killer Boy.

"Since yesterday. Biggie was over, too, but dipped out."

Scab fumbles with his thoughts about the killing of O.G. Big Bear.

"It's hard out here for a Crip," says Killer.

"I'm going to wake up Tank and you call Rich," says Scab. He walks into a bedroom and gets Tank out of bed.

Killer thinks, *Like I need you to tell me anything, genius.* "Where the phone at, gladiator of the crackheads?"

"Over by the TV." Scab gives Killer a glance that says, "Stop with that shit." *This nigga has no gratitude for no one. I just put my fucking life on the line for this crab. No more, though, for me. I set up niggas, not kill them.*

Cookie comes out of the bedroom wearing a thong and nothing else. "I didn't know we had company," she says sleepily.

"Don't mind me, baby. I guarantee you are in good hands," says Killer. She gives him a seductive look.

"Look, homie, I'll be over later at Candy's," says Scab. "So meet me at that bitch's house, homie."

Killer walks over to Cookie and runs his fingers around her breast. "Damn, baby. You feel like marshmallows, so soft."

"Shit. You look so masculine and strong. Where is my man at?"

"Foolish left," Killer tells her.

"So we have time to fuck," says Cookie. They disappear into the bedroom.

Scab and Tank look on from the bottom of the stairway. "How in the fuck did he manage that shit so fuckin' quick?" asks Tank in amazement.

Tank shakes his head. "I don't know, bro, but I do know she has some magnificent head on her, fam. This nigga better get his nut off before my man gets back, though, Scab." They steal up the steps to watch.

Cookie pushes Killer back toward the mattress and maneuvers herself in between his legs before his back hits the mattress. Killer unbuttons his pants and throws them to the far right of the bedroom.

"It's very easy for Cookie to manipulate a man into sex," whispers Tank to Scab. They watch through the cracked door. Killer reaches into his Tommy Hilfiger boxers and pulls out his massive ten-and-a-half-inches of hard dick and puts it in Cookie' face.

Cookie lets out a soft moan as she slides the head into her mouth to savor for a second while she masturbates him slowly. "Baby, now this is a woman's treat for sure. Now, let mama take good care of you."

"I'm in your hands, shorty." Killer is at maximum length. Slowly, Cookie swallows every inch of Killer's dick, making him shake lightly. *This will be some memorable shit here.* "Shit, baby. Ooooohhhh ... man ..." Killer grabs the back of Cookie' head to try to push more dick into her throat, but to his surprise, this is what she wanted him to do. Now he's mesmerized by her skills. Killer Boy can no longer take the back of her throat massaging his dick and he bursts in her throat like an erupting volcano, sweat dripping from his head like he just ran a hundred-yard dash.

Cookie hands are on his waist, pulling him closer so she can suck every drop out of him, slowly. "Baby, I have never cummed so fuckin' hard before in my life. Look, I feel so damn vulnerable right now, shorty."

"Fuck that shit you're talking," she says. "Nigga, you owe some dick!"

"Shorty, what is your name?"

"Cookie."

"Nah, shorty. Your name is Voluptuous, and I can vouch for that shit."

Cookie gets up from between his legs and begins visualizing them fucking. She Gauges out of her daze when the phone rings. Before she leaves to answer the phone, she pulls her thong to the side and sticks her finger into moist pussy jaws and pulls her wet finger out and sucks it clean for all of them to see. She knew Scab and Tank were watching! Then she turns and walks toward Killer while he's putting on his pants and licks his ear. She grabs his dick one more time and whispers, "Daddy, it's vital that you get at me soon. I'm your bitch, Boy."

Killer looks at Cookie with a whining face and she knows she's got him. She walks away to answer the phone. As soon as she picks up the receiver, Killer drops to his knees to get a whiff of that sweet pussy before walking out the door. Tank and Scab are standing out in the hallway with big grins on their faces.

"Cuz, I feel like a kid with a new toy," says Killer with a satisfied look on his face.

"I might have to whack that little dude, fam. It's weird that I feel that way, loc."

"Nah, loc, he's my nigga," says Tank. "Shit, you already violated him, homie. That bitch head she gave you is virulent to your health. That was visible if you only lasted five minutes or so."

"Rich says Dallas is on the way to swoop y'all up," screams Cookie.

"Word," Scab says to Tank. "Cuz, be on the vigilant when we leave for the law, son."

"Why?" asks Tank.

"My bad bro, we just smoked some slobs up the street."

"You a killer now, bro?"

"Yeah, you can say so."

"Them 30s niggas is some vindictive chumps, so you know if they find out it was you, there is no way you can vindicate yourself, fam. They will smoke you, bro, so don't sleep," Tank cautions. "It's on sight, cuz, with them fools."

Killer looks out the front window. He has a funny look on his face. *There's something he's not telling us about,* thinks Tank. "Big homie, what's the deal out there, loc?"

"Po po is everywhere out there, son. I hope cuz makes it soon."

The first officer on the scene looks into the Yukon and almost vomits at the human waste he sees. Then a voice tells him to move out of the way and put up yellow tape to keep citizens away from the crime scene. "This may be a very sensitive matter," he tells the cop.

"Who are you?" the officer asks.

"I'm Special Agent Adam Crown, FBI."

"Let me see your badge, please, sir," the cop says. Crown reaches into his coat and pulls out his wallet to show his I.D. "That says California," the cop says. "You don't have jurisdiction here. I'll have to call my sergeant to make the call."

"I'll settle for that until we get things straight," Crown replies. He walks over to the Yukon and peers inside. He shoots the officer a significant look and races to the passenger side. "Cop down!" he shouts.

All of the officers run to assist him at getting Agent Downs out of the Yukon. "He's been slaughtered, and he's one of us," Crown says. "There's no pulse and his heart isn't beating."

"Who is the other one slumped over the steering wheel?" asks another officer. "Lay him back so we can get a good look at him."

"Oh my God, his whole face is blown off, sir."

A homicide detective arrives on the scene, just behind an ambulance. "Block off this whole area for four miles," says the detective. "I'm Sergeant Jenkins and I want all of you out of my crime scene." The cops begin to clear the area as he issues more instructions. "I want every officer here to go by every shop on this block to see if anyone saw anything."

"This man is FBI," says Crown, pointing to Downs. "I met him and his partner a few days ago, but I don't know why he's riding around with this unknown man. I have to call the Bureau to get in contact with Agent Lyons. Here's my card, detective. Call me if you need me."

"Thank you for your cooperation," Jenkins says as he takes the card.

"Detective Jenkins! We've found a recorder on the floor in the Yukon," shouts an officer.

"Good. Tag it as evidence."

That will let me know what he was up to, but I have to talk to the U.S. Attorney to get that tape in my possession. This gang war just went out of control, Crown thinks. *This contingency has contributed to the downfall of some of the Bloods and Crips.*

Agent Crown walks to his unmarked car, opens the door, and flips his phone open when he sits down. He dials Agent Lyons's cell number.

"Hello, this is Agent Lyons. How may I help you?"

"I have bad news for you this morning," Crown begins.

"Who's speaking?"

"Agent Crown. This morning Agent Downs and an unknown black male were shot to death in North Minneapolis while riding in a white Yukon."

"That can't be right," Lyons says. "I just left Agent Downs downstairs with Kevin, our C.I."

"I hate to be the one to inform you of the bad news, but there was a cassette tape found on the floor of the truck at the crime scene. "

"I'm with the U.S. Attorney right now. We have to get that tape right away. Who's in charge?"

"Detective Jenkins."

"I know him. That won't be a problem. I'm leaving now. Meet me at the homicide office."

"Roger that."

Chapter 9

"Wake up, Jay! I need you," says Ghost. "Damn, shorty thick, son," as I pull back the covers to show off the sexy body of Pookie.

"Let me put on my shit real quick, fam," I tell him.

"Where you going, baby?" asks Pookie.

"Chill with that shit, ma."

I pull out a black T-shirt, black Sean Jean jumpsuit, black L.A. Raiders coat, black and white L.A. Raiders hat, and black Air Force Ones to match. "Cud, let me take a quick shower."

Pookie gets up naked with her ass shaking and her long hair down to her butt cheeks. Walking to the dresser, she stops and bends over to give Ghost a clear view of her nicely shaved pussy from the back. Ghost gives a light chuckle at the sight of her, then clenches his teeth. "Next time, baby," he says. He walks to the kitchen and grabs a bottle of gin off of the TV. *This is for my man, O.G. Big Bear. I have to commemorate my fallen dog.*

Pookie walks up to Ghost and says, "This cocktail tastes much better. Tell Jay to call me later." She saunters out the door.

"My nigga. What's good, fam?" Ghost asks.

"You don't have to say shit, fam. I can tell by the look on your face that we're on some murder one shit, fo sho."

"Where is Mom and Dad at, Jay?"

"Sleeping."

"Well, let's bounce so I can tell you the deal, son."

"Come on, then. Let me lock up."

"That bitch you was with is real loose, Jay. She bounced."

"Cool. I'm not no better," I say as I lock the door. "Let's take my whip today."

"What whip, son?" Ghost has a confused look on his face.

"Right there. That's my '89 Ford Bronco. You like?"

"That shit's right, bro!" Ghost exclaims.

My whip is fine, with five Mickey Thompson tires on it and custom-made twenty-six inch Daytons; black and green bowling ball paint; and jet black tint. "Ghost, wait 'til you hear the sound system," I say. We get into the truck and I click off the Viper alarm.

"Look, baby bro, I'm a gangster, something more than a seven-letter word. I'm a Tyrell time hustler, so call me the block bleeder," says Ghost as he takes another swig of gin. I pull off to hit a few curves to show off my whip. I push the power button on the CD player and "Go DJ" by Lil Ghost pounds in our ears. Eight fifteen-inch woofers pump loud bass. Ghost jumps at the sudden boom! of the bass.

"Turn that down, dog," he says. "I got to rap with you on some combat shit. Hit the freeway so we can just ride, son." I turn onto the entrance ramp and we cruise to the left lane, heading east on 94.

"Look, Jay, I know you ain't been here long and shit, but things have got to where I need all of my people to collide together for the cause and commit fully to this complex problem. O.G. Big Bear has been killed and Crooked is a fuckin' snitch.

"Now, I have thought about this all night, and there are only two people who are compatible with the competition like you are. Big Chief and Lil D are going to complement you in the complicated task that needs to be taken care of. Them two are the only companions you need to lay all of the heads of the crabs down."

He interrupts himself to give me directions. "Stay on 94 'til you run into Snelling Avenue in St. Paul. I'm going to compensate all of you for every crab y'all drop."

I put up my hand. "Hold up, Ghost. Don't compare me to none of your boys."

"Look, lil bro, I'm the head of this committee, so don't question me! I don't fuck with no lames. This is my block and I got shit on L.O.C.K., son! Jay, you're the most conniving person I know, so stay consistent.

"Exit here on Snelling and make a left at the light, then turn right on University."

"Cud, I need to know who I'm consuming," I say. "Like they say, Ghost, cut the head off, the body will fall."

"Yeah, I know," Ghost says, "but I need heads to roll before the big homies get here from Cali, Jay. I had to call and let them know what the deal is with O.G. Big Bear. He's a made man and they can make shit hard out this way. Now you know why I need continuous merking going on. I don't care how y'all coordinate this shit, but make sure that crabs know that 30s Blood is contributing to their demise.

"Turn left here and make the first right and park," my brother instructs. "Jay, I have every Blood set cooperating with us on this co-op effort. But most of all, I'm counting on your down-South country intuition," he says as he exits the truck.

Damn, I feel my brother's pain. I'm subsequent to what happens to these crab niggas. No prisoners, no surrender, only death to anyone in my way. I take a dip of wet to smoke while I wait for Ghost to come out.

He approaches the back door of the house on the corner of Charles Street. The door opens and Red Beard appears in the doorway with a smile on his face. "Come in, so I can apprise you of a few things," he says.

The door shuts behind Ghost. "Have a seat, Mr. Blood," Red Beard says graciously.

"This is not the appropriate time, pig, for your shit," Ghost says testily. "No, motherfucker. What do you have for me, cop?"

"Well, for one, I don't have to put dope on Kevin to apprehend him. He's dead now, along with a fed. Here is the info you wanted on the person in the phone."

Ghost looks over the information and mumbles to himself. "The nigga is from Cali. I remember him now. Killer Boy is what they call him," he says. "Damn. He's a real nasty killer, too. What is this shit right here, Red Beard?"

"It's an open investigation on your ass," Red Beard explains. "Kevin opened up on you, but since he was found dead, they have no case on you. They have to change tactics now. I know the feds are sweltering about the dead agent, so chill out, Ghost."

"Fuck both of them motherfuckers! Son, they get no sympathy from me. Who spot is this, Red?"

"Don't ask me shit," Red says. "Pay me my dough. I must say, you're real tangible, son."

Ghost hands him some money. "Here's the ten thousand I promised you, plus five thousand more to get me all the information on all the head crabs that's here."

"Cool," Red nods.

"I'm out, Red," Ghost says as he walks to the door. "And oh yeah, you need to spend some of that money to change your attire." He laughs as he closes the door.

Fuck you, nigga. I hope all you punks kill each other soon so I can extort some new fish, bitch. But wait 'til you get jammed by the feds. I'm going to astonish you, slob.

I'm in the Bronco babbling to myself about authenticating Lil D and Big Chief when Ghost returns. "It smells like candy in here, lil bro," he says. "Let's dip, dog." I pull off and head toward the freeway.

"Man, I might have to kill me that bitch-ass cop, Jay. That arrogant motherfucker has the audaciousness to pop slick with me. When this punk motherfucker gets me that list —" Ghost pauses to hit the stick. "I want home invasions on all of these crab niggas, son."

My cell starts to vibrate in my pocket. "Let me get this call real quick, bro," I say. "Hello?"

"Hello. Where my boo at?" croons Lacy.

"Chilling. What's up?"

"You, baby," Lacy replies. "You know you owe me some dick, Jay, and I want to collect tonight."

"I got you, ma. I'll hit you up later so we can chill. And do dinner, too. Would you like that, baby?"

"Hit me up, Jay, when you're ready," she whispers.

"Cool. I got to handle something real quick. Peace."

My brother looks at me sharply. "Nigga, who got you with an intimate smile on your face?"

"Lacy, if you must know every fucking thing, yo," I shoot back at him.

"Boy, you didn't let me know you got a cell phone."

"Pass me the stick, Ghost, before you smoke it all yourself." He looks at me with an intimidating look on his face. I can tell he's irked by what he just heard.

"Take me by the crib, yo," he commands.

"Just tell me the way, big bro." *Damn. Money and these wet sticks have made this nigga feel invincible*, I think as I watch my brother get high.

"Jay, this shit is fire as hell, dog." He begins shouting, "30s Blood for life, dog. C.K. rider to the end! Shotgun Killer." He begins throwing up gang signs. I jostle him with my elbow to get him to chill out before we get on the freeway. I don't want to get stopped for some dumb shit. I don't even have a driver's license yet, and there's a hammer in the glove box that's not legal to carry.

"I'm kosher, dog. Quit with the elbows and shit, homie. Pull into the back, Jay."

"Man, whoever did the landscaping around your pad did their thing big, bro. Your shit is lavish."

"Come on," Ghost says. "I need to get my money from a few cats that's delinquent."

We walk through the back door and catch Lacy in the living room relaxing in a chair with Black Mike, one of the homies. The TV is on B.E.T., 106 and park are blasting on the surround sound system. Lacy doesn't hear us enter the house and walk through the kitchen. I look at her and see her as the freak that she is and decide, *no more.*

Lacy senses someone is watching her and turns around. She's greeted by an angry Ghost. He gives her a look that's detrimental to her health, and Black Mike's, too. "Bitch, what I tell you about having niggas in my fuckin' crib, huh?" Pow. Ghost backhands her off of Mike's lap to the floor.

"Look, big homie," Mike says. "She told me it was cool to stop by for a second. I woulda have never come if I knew, blood. I brought that one hundred thousand that I owe you, fam. It's in my trunk outside, fam."

Ghost steps over Lacy balled up on the floor and says to her, "Bitch, you need to be disciplined about your discrepancies with me, 'cause you keep disobeying me in my fuckin' house, doing shit that I disapprove of. Now get the fuck up out of my fuckin' house, you street whore!"

Lacy crawls away on her knees to the other side of the living room with an ugly, underhanded smirk on her swollen face. I step up to Black Mike as he reaches for something in his back pocket. "Hold up, homie. I'm just getting my Land Rover keys to get the doe, fam."

"Chill, blood," says Ghost. "You know that I know that you're one of my straight-up b-dogs. You know why I'm so private about my shit, fam."

"I know, O.G. It's so unfortunate that I fell for her shit, son. That is unusual for me, and so unexpected."

Ghost turns to Lacy once more. "Lacy, get your shit, you low-down vagrant, and bounce, bitch, before I put my foot on your neck."

"Ghost," says Black Mike, "I value our friendship and our business relationship. So let me go grab that money so we can move on."

Ghost nods. "Cool, dog. Do that."

I ease over to the window to watch Lacy leave. *Damn, she got the bomb head job, yo. The vibes I get from her is this shit ain't over by far.*

Shaunna pulls up into the driveway and sees Lacy crying. "What's the matter, Lacy?" Shaunna asks as she jumps from the Yukon. Lacy points to the house. "Ghost hit me."

"Why?"

"For having Black Mike in the house," she sobs.

"You know not to have anybody in the house when we're gone, girl. Anything coulda have happened." Shaunna shakes her head. "I know he burnt up with your ass now."

"Fuck him!" Lacy spits the words out and sees me looking out the window at her. Black Mike strolls by, speaks to Shaunna and keeps it moving like he doesn't see Lacy's ass now. "That nigga a hoe, too, Shaunna," Lacy puts. "Fuck Black Mike, too!"

"Girl, get your ass in the truck and wait for me," Shaunna says. "Shit! You act like a spoiled brat more than a woman that's about to go to college."

Lacy takes the keys from Shaunna and walks over to the Yukon. But before Shaunna walks into the house, Lacy hollers, "Check that nigga about putting his motherfuckin' hands on me, girl. I ain't his bitch. You are!"

Not for long, Shaunna thinks as she reaches for the door handle. She opens the door. Ghost, Rob and I are laughing, and it irritates her more. She slams the door to get Ghost's attention. Black Mike gets up from the chair, gives Ghost dap and nods to me. As he passes her, he says, "'Bye, Shaunna."

"Whatever, nigga," Shaunna remarks. As the door closes behind him, she explodes. "Now, why in the fuck would you put your fuckin' hands on my sister, nigga?"

Ghost's face turns sour. "Bitch, this ain't no hoe house!" he retorts. "I don't want niggas running through my fucking crib. Bitch, have you lost your mind, too, Shaunna?"

"Nah, nigga, but you have. I can smell that wet shit on your breath."

"So what, bitch? I'm a grown man. I do what the fuck I want to." Ghost moves closer to Shaunna.

"I can't take her to my parents with a swollen face, nigga! What will they think?" Shaunna asks. "Ghost, they know she is over here."

"Take that little whore to a motel on me, then, but she's not allowed in my crib no more. You hear me?" His hands are in Shaunna's face.

"I got that," she says.

"Where you been, anyway?" he asks.

"Getting the Yukon detailed, nigga, so we can go to the casino later, fool."

"I can do that, baby. We need some 'us' time," he admits.

"Yes, we do, nigga."

Ghost relents. "Well, take Lacy to the Hilton, then come back and grab me. Tell her I'm sorry for hitting her, okay, baby?"

Shaunna gives in a little. "I'm still mad at you for that shit, though." He kisses her lips softly and she bounces out the door.

"Damn, bro," I say. "You be on some Jekyll and Hyde shit, fam."

"Nah," Ghost says. "I got too much shit on my mind to deal with them two pains in the ass. I just got off the last of the bricks that I had over here to Rob for two hundred and twenty thousand dollars, but I still got them ones at Nina's spot, too. And Kiki got two bricks, too." He mulls over his options.

The phone on the wall rings. "Want me to get that, Ghost?"

"Yeah."

I pick up the phone. A pre-recorded message greets me. "This is a pre-pay phone call from a federal correctional institution to Ghost from Boss Man. Press five to accept. Press seven to deny." I hand the phone to Ghost, who accepts the call.

"What up, loco?" asks Boss Man.

"Everything good, vato," Ghost replies.

"Well, amigo, I need you. I'm getting out next week, so be in Little Rock then, loco. We got shit to talk about."

"I'm there," Ghost says. The phone clicks and I hear a dial tone. *I wonder what's the deal*, Ghost thinks.

Chapter 10

Agent Lyons arrives at the morgue to identify Agent Downs and see the body himself. *Downs was my partner at the Bureau for ten years. This can't be happening now.* He gets a hard, fiery look in his eyes. "Whoever is involved with this is going down hard, by any means necessary," he says to U.S. Attorney Larry Kline. Kline nods.

"Larry, I need to get that tape from Homicide now," he says desperately.

"This is a federal investigation now. The locals can back off, Lyons."

"One of ours is dead and that means the ball is in our court, Larry," Lyons replies.

Kline gestures to the other body. "Do you know the John Doe?"

Lyons nods. "Yes, that's one of our C.I.s. Kevin. He was working the Blood case we were working on with the 30s in South Minneapolis."

"The case we were just discussing?"

"The very one," Lyons says. "Let's go. I have work to do."

Agent Crown is on the phone with the director of the FBI in Washington, D.C., giving him an update on the situation while he waits for Lyons to arrive at the Homicide office downtown. "Sir, there seems to be an international gang war going on here between the L.A. Crips and the Bloods, but they both have big ties to Leemma, the Mexican mafia, and a Somalian syndicate."

The director is impatient. "I don't care who they're tied to! One of our agents is down and so are they. Got it, Agent Crown?"

"Yes, sir," Crown says immediately.

"Whatever you need, call me and you'll get it, hear?"

"Yes, sir."

"Keep me posted."

"I will, sir."

He gauges his phone shut as Sgt. Jenkins enters the room. "Hi. How are you today, Sgt. Jenkins?"

"Fine, just fine, agent," Jenkins returns as they stand next to the clerk's desk.

"Have you made any progress, Sergeant?"

Jenkins shakes his head. "No, I haven't. There are no witnesses. No suspects at this time, either. I got a call from the Big Chief this morning and was told that this is a federal investigation now, but to help out if I can. Your people should be on their way to get the files on this case and the evidence, too." He eyes Crown curiously. "Agent Crown, what part of the FBI do you operate out of?"

"The Federal Gang Task Force," Crown replies.

Jenkins scratches his head. "What would you be doing around a murder investigation?"

Crown says, "I can't discuss that."

The door opens and several FBI agents stroll through and walk past them to the lieutenant on duty. "Who's Lt. Fred Cummins?" one of them demands.

"I am," says a short bald man in his early forties. "Who wants to know?"

"Can we talk in your office, sir?" asks the agent.

"Right this way, uh —"

"Agent Randal Wright."

All of the agents go in behind Lt. Cummins and close the door. Jenkins says, "Let me go get everything ready to hand over, Agent Crown." They shake hands. Jenkins disappears down the hallway. Crown starts for the door. He runs into Agent Lyons and the U.S. Attorney. "Excuse me, Agent Lyons," he says. "I was just leaving. There are more agents in the lieutenant's office right now."

"Damn," says Lyons. "It must be Agent Downs's brother. We have to get in there now, Larry! I'll call you later, Crown."

"Sure thing."

Rich, Killer Boy, Tank, Scab, and Dallas are chilling at Applebee's, talking about what just went down with Crooked and an unknown white male earlier today. "Cuz, that was some Pit Bull shit this nigga got my brother in, big homie," says Tank.

"Look, loc. It's on, on sight. Do you know what that means, cuz?" says Killer Boy.

"Now, you two chill out and lower your voices a tune," Rich says. "What do you guys want to drink?"

"Whatever, homie," says Killer Boy.

"I want a triple shot of Hennessy," says Scab, still feeling a little unsteady about the whole episode.

"Me, too, cuz." Rich flags down the waitress and gives the orders. She bounces to the bar with a sexy strut.

"Cuz, that's two for the price of one," says Killer Boy. "The white boy don't count. I got that hoe-ass nigga in the back, too. That's three for the price of two, my nigga."

The waitress returns with the drinks and leaves. "Now I can continue," says Killer Boy. "I left my fuckin' Grand National over at Foolish's spot, and my heaters, too."

"They cool, son. Don't nobody want no murder weapon, yo," says Dallas.

"Look, maniac, loc will be here tomorrow with some more of the homies from Cali," says Rich. "I want to be hearing about death, cuz."

"Damn. Just what I need. More niggas in my way, cuz," says Killer Boy, slapping the table top.

"Let's bounce to get money, cuz," says Dallas.

"Cool."

Rich lays two C-notes on the table, then they dip out to leave. "Drop me off at Amos & Andy's. My car is still there," he says.

"I'll ride with Scab, since he's my brother," Tank says.

"Cool, loc."

Lacy calls Biggie as soon as Shaunna leaves. "Baby, where are you, Big?"

"I'm in the trap, baby. What's good?" he says.

"I'm in the Hilton, waiting on you to fly me some room service dick, boo," she twists the phone cord in her fingers.

"Listen as soon as I make this one move, ma, I'll be to see you," he responds.

"I'm in room 502. Bring some drink and some smoke," she instructs.

"I can do that," he says agreeably.

"Don't take all day, either, 'cause I got something to discuss with you when you get here, Big. It's about some paper."

"I'm with that shit," he replies. "So, about twenty minutes, Lacy." He hangs up.

Yeah, that punk-ass nigga goin' regret putting his motherfuckin' hands on me, for real. Fuck Shaunna's ass, too. Now, let me get myself into the shower. Shit, I don't have no other clothes to put on. Let me start a bubble bath then call Shaunna's freakish ass to bring me some clothes.

Lacy starts the water in the tub. It's a wide one, with whirlpool action. When the warm water starts to flow, she calls Shaunna.

"What," Shaunna says in an irritated tone.

"Bitch, please," Lacy says. "You left me here with no clothes."

"Lacy, you know you're a pain in the ass, don't you? I'll stop by the mall to grab you something, girl, so don't kill yourself, okay?"

"Sure, bitch." Lacy hangs up.

I don't know who she keeps calling bitch. I'm-a have to check her ass when

I get there, Shaunna thinks.

"Let me call my baby to see what's the deal for tonight." Pookie flips open her Boost mobile. "Hey, I miss you, Jay," she says sweetly.

"I'm thinking about you, too. Where you at, Shorty?"

"At home."

"I'll be over in a little while," I say. "So don't leave. I need you to drive."

"I'm here for you. One." She ends the call. I turn to my brother. "I need to dip if you cool, now, bro."

"I'm straight, Jay."

I leave to head over to the North Side to see Pookie. *It's going to be one of them days, I know it.* I pull off onto 94. Traffic is crazy. *I need to blow me one before I get to this bitch's house. Where did I put my lovely at? Ah, there it is on the back seat. Now, where is my Black'n'milds at?*

Honk, honk. The driver behind me wants me to move up. I've been holding up traffic looking for my cigars. I hit the pedal to make my pipes roar loudly, turn up my banging system, and let my windows down to pump "All Eyes On Me" by 2Pac onto the street.

Fuck it, I'll blow later. Traffic finally becomes normal and I exit on Broadway. *Shit, the law is every-fuckin-where, like the Pope is here or something. Be cool. The truck is in Will's name, so I'm good.*

I pull up at the light on Broadway and Washington Avenue and see a blue two-door Riviera with two red-bone honeys in it. They look at my truck like they want to fuck it on the spot. I play like I don't notice them scoping a player. The light turns green and I pull over to the liquor store on the corner. They jump lanes to follow me. I get out of the truck and walk to the door, but I'm cut off before I get there.

"Hey. Come here for a second," the driver says. I stroll around the car.

"What up? You trying to injure me, ma?"

"You're cute. What's your name?" she asks.

"Jay, shorty. And yours?"

"Nicki. And this is Shorty, my home girl."

"Jay, where you from? You don't sound like you're from around here at all," Nicki says.

"I'm not. I'm from Little Rocks, Arkansas. Home of the Razorbacksssss." I look over the ladies with caution. *Damn, the driver is finer than a flawless diamond.* "Where you from, Nicki?"

St. Paul. How long you been here, Jay?"

"Not that long. Why?"

"You got a lady, Jay?"

"Nah."

"That's good, 'cause you're cute, baby boy. I got to go to work in a few, so let me get your cell number so we can hook up later, Jay."

"Cool. You got a pen and paper?"

She hands me a scrap of paper and a pen from the glove box. "Here, Nicki. Call me." I walk back to the truck. She sticks her head out the window.

"Hey, weren't you going to the L.Q.?"

"Nah. I was going to you," I smirk and dip back into traffic.

"Confident, are we? And a little arrogant, too," Nicki muses.

"Girl, he's really sexy, Nicki," says Shorty.

"I know, girl." They continue to talk as they near Nicki's place of employment, the gas station on the corner of Twenty-sixth and Penn. "Shorty, did you see his smile?"

"Yeah. He has very clean teeth and he's not missing any, either," Shorty points out.

"Damn. I bet his lips will feel good on my pussy," says Nicki.

"Girl, you so nasty!" protests Shorty. "But it's true, girl. Shit, looks like he got money, too."

They pull into the gas station lot and Nicki gets out to go to work. Shorty moves into the driver's seat. "I get off at nine o'clock. Tell Mom that," Nicki says.

"Okay." *She better hope I don't see him*, Sherry says to herself.

I pull up to Pookie's house. *Sherry a "ten" fo sho. Nicki looks mature, too*, I think as I walk up to the door and tap on the window.

"Who is it?" A male voice hollers on the other side of the door.

"Jay."

The door opens and a big male dressed all in blue stands there, acting like he can intimidate me by giving me hard looks. "Who you lookin' for cuz?" he asks. *Damn, not already*, I think.

"Pookie," I answer. "Is she here?'

"What you want with my lil sister, cuz? You know she fucks with Cuz?"

"Nah, home boy, I didn't know that." *Shit, I need to get my heat out of the truck.*

"Blue, who you talkin' to, boy?" asks Pookie's sister, Munchie. *Damn, she looks just like Pookie!*

"Some dude lookin' for Pookie," he grumps.

"Come on in," Munchie says to me. "Don't mind Blue. He high. Sit down, Jay. Pookie told me you was on your way. I go get her."

I sit down on the couch and the big dude sits beside me, still animated. I can see the handle of a pistol on his hip. "Where you from, cuz?" I tell him Little Rock, and he says, "You sound country, cuz."

Just in time, Pookie walks into the middle of our conversation and leads me back to her room. "Blue being overprotective, I see," she says.

"Whatever you want to call it, ma," I say, looking around.

"Sit down on my bed, Jay, while I finish doing my hair, then we can leave," Pookie says.

"So what do you want to do today, sexy?"

"Let's ride around for a second so I can show you off, Jay."

"Cool, I'm with that, lil mama. Pookie, what did he mean when he said you fucks with Cuz?"

Pookie looks irritated. "That nigga got me fucked up. I don't fuck with none of they asses. Come on, let's get this shit straight right now." We stroll out of the bedroom, through the kitchen and into the living room.

"Blue, what you say to Jay about me?" Pookie questions him accusingly.

"Nothing, lil sis." Blue stares at me with a "what, nigga?" look.

"I don't fuck with Cuz or anybody else for that matter, do I?"

Munchie jumps in. "Pookie, you good. Blue, stop," she commands.

"Come on, Jay," says Pookie. "Let's go."

I give Blue the C.K. glare. "Here's the keys, ma." Then I slap Pookie on the ass so Blue can see it and we bounce out the door.

"Fuck that broke-ass nigga," says Pookie. "All he does is beat Munchies ass." We get into the Bronco. "Where's my CD, Jay?"

"In the CD player for you," I say smoothly. Pookie turns the ignition key and "12 Play" by R. Kelly comes out of the speakers. I lean back and grab the bottle of wet and dip a Moore cigarette. Pookie objects. "That shit stinks, Jay."

"I know, baby."

"I know one thing. Blue better check his self," I say as I pull on the stick. "What is a he a '90s Crip? C.K. baby, fo sho."

"Jay, be nice," she pleads.

"For you, I will," I say. "Now let's chill."

Tank pulls up to the Stardust just off Riverside in South Minneapolis to meet with Red Beard. *Good, It's empty.* He parks the two-door Lexus coupe and walks straight to the bar. "Let me get a shot of Seagram's gin and a MGD," he says to the bartender. "Will that be all, sir?" she asks in a flirty tone.

"Yes."

Tank walks over to the last table and sits and waits. After about five minutes, Red Beard emerges from the bathroom. Tank waves him over with drink in hand. "How's my favorite cop today?" he asks genially.

"I'm good, but don't ever ask me to meet you here again," Red Beard says.

Tank smiles. "Cool. Now what you got for me, cop?"

Red Beard holds up his hands and starts counting on his fingers. "For starters, the FBI is going to be on everybody's ass until they find out who killed that federal agent yesterday. Some knucklehead killed Crooked and an unknown person at this time, and a federal agent. I hope you're not anywhere connected to that shit, Tank."

"Nah, not me."

"Second, this little war you got with the Bloods is out of control. Bodies are dropping all over the city, you know, and that's bad for your business."

"I know. But what do you know?"

"Well, Fat Cuz was killed by Ghost, Lil D, and Ghost's little brother. I don't have a name on him yet. There is an FBI agent here from Cali named Adam Crown. You heard of him?"

"Yeah. He's been a pain in my ass in Cali for years. What the fuck he doing here now?"

"To shut the Bloods and Crips down," Red Beard explains. "All of you big guys are under investigation as we speak. So I can't meet you like this no more."

"I got something for Crown. Leave him to me, cop", Tank says. *Damn, that white guy was a fed. Killer is in some deep shit now.*

"I'm working on rounding up some of the low-level Bloods so they can rat out some of the ones who are doing the killing," Red Beard continues. "Scare them with federal charges and they all talk."

"Yeah, you do that," Tank says. "Here's twenty thousand. Keep me posted." He shoves a stack of bills across the table and Red Beard pockets it quickly.

"I will," Red Beard promises. "But don't call me anymore. I'll get at you, 'cause your phone might be bugged. So be safe."

Tank gets up and leaves, a look of thoughtful concern on his face.

"I want a tail on every O.G. Crip and Blood that's in Minnesota, period," says Lyons to the gathered agents. "This is a priority case and is number one on our schedule. Now, this is Agent Adam Crown, and he will be working with us on this case. He knows all of the gang members from Cali, so don't hesitate to ask for identification for any member you don't know.

"To my left is senior ranking Agent Randall Wright. He's Downs' brother and he will be helping with the case as well. Let's put these low-lives behind bars quickly. Now, men, let's go do our jobs."

As the meeting adjourns, Wright comes up to Lyons. "Thank you for letting me join in the hunt for my brother's killers, Lyons," he says earnestly.

"Sure thing, pal," Lyons says. "I have to go listen to the tape recording that was found at the scene to see what we have so far. The U.S. Attorney is waiting for me in my office, so will you excuse me, Agent Wright?" Wright stands aside and Lyons walks swiftly to his office and shuts the door.

"Dan, how did the briefing go?" asks the attorney.

"Well, Larry, all of the agents are eager about the case. They want some closure to it. Now, it's time to see what Downs was up to."

Lyons turns on the tape recorder. Downs' voice fills the room. "Mr. Kevin, how do you know Ghost Jones, aka 'Money'?"

Crooked answers him. "We're Bloods from the same set. The 30s Bloods. Plus, we do a lot of business together."

"What kind of business?"

"We sell cocaine together. He gives me dope to sell when I buy it from him."

"So this is an organized thing?"

"Yes, we're a strong gang with ties to Leemma, the Mexican mafia."

Agent Lyons gestures to the attorney general. "Pause the tape for a second, Larry." Kline hits the pause button. "This is bigger than just L.A., Larry!" Lyons pushes "play" again.

"Where are we headed now, Mr. Kevin?"

"Ghost has a girlfriend named – "

Pop, pop, pop. Kevin is cut short by rapid gunfire. Lyons and Kline exchange a look of despair. "This didn't clear up a damn thing, Dan," says Kline. "We have nothing to go on here."

"I know, Larry," Lyons sounds mildly discouraged.

"Well, let me know of any new developments with the case. I'm going back to my office."

"I will, Larry."

The phone on Lyons's desk rings as the door shuts behind the U.S. Attorney. "FBI, Lyons speaking."

"Hi, Lyons," says a voice on the other end. "This is Agent Ron Burgess. I've been tailing the Shotgun 'Biggie' for some time now, and it seems to me that he's out dropping off cocaine to the Crips right now."

"Good job, Burgess. Where are you?"

"I'm on 94, headed toward Brooklyn Center."

"When he stops, stay with him," Lyons advises. "I'm on my way out there. Switch to line four."

Shaunna and Biggie pull into the Hilton Hotel parking lot one after another. Neither is aware that an FBI agent is watching Biggie. Shaunna grabs some shopping bags off of the back seat and walks toward the lobby entrance. She leaves the Yukon with the valet attendant.

Biggie parks at the far end of the lot, pancakes the '63 Impala, then exits the vehicle. Agent Burgess parks on the opposite far side of the lot and gets out to follow his suspect.

Shaunna stands in front of the elevator, waiting for it to come down. Biggie walks up with a smile on his face a mile long. "Hey, stranger!" he says. Shaunna turns on him with a "don't talk to me" face. When she sees it's Biggie, she smiles.

"'Sup, homie?" she asks.

"Getting paid, you know me," he answers.

"I can dig that, Big," she agrees.

"Shit, looks like you getting all the money, shorty." Biggie gestures toward the shopping bags in her hands. Their conversation is interrupted by the opening of the elevator doors.

"Come on," Shaunna says with a knowing smile. "I already know where you're going, boy."

"I'm caught," Biggie says with an answering grin.

As the elevator doors begin to close, Agent Burgess enters the car. "Could you push five for us please?" asks Shaunna.

"Sure, no problem."

"Thank you." She turns to Biggie. "Now if I knew she called your ballin' ass, I wouldn't-a have bought her shit."

"I got her. Whatever she needs is on me," Biggie says. "Matter of fact, take this four thousand to cover your pocket." Biggie pulls out a knot the size of an extra-large Subway sandwich.

"This is where we get off, Big." As they walk to the room, Agent Burgess holds the elevator door open to see where they go. *Yeah, room 502. I got you.* Burgess takes the elevator back down to the lobby, flips open his cell phone and chirps Agent Lyons on his Nextel.

"What's up, Agent Burgess?" asks Lyons.

"We're at the Hilton off of Shingle Creek. I'm parked on the south side of the parking lot, sir. Where are you?

"We're near the Shingle Creek exit. Agent Crown is with me."

"Things here are interesting, sir."

"Why do you say that, Burgess?"

"Ghost's girl, Shaunna, is here, too, and she knows Biggie, sir."

"Copy that. I'll be there in three minutes, Burgess. Ten-four."

Chapter 11

The music blasts in the spot where Jamal and Dallas count money with the money machine. "Cuz, you got the rest of the dope bagged up?" asks Jamal.

"Yeah, cuz. We straight. This fuckin' machine does all the hard work for us, Jamal."

Lil D, Big Chief and Tre Duce park a block away. "Blood, let's go in there and get the fuck out," says Lil D. "My peoples tell me this is one of their weight houses, so we should hit a good lick. Make sure you got an extra clip, son, and your silencers on, fam."

The three of them exit the black K-5 Chevy truck. Wearing all black, they slowly approach the spot. "Blood, it's good. Ain't too many people out this early, son," says Big Chief. They reach the back door. The house vibrates to the beat of the music.

"The music is so loud that they can't hear us, either, if we make noise," Tre Duce points out.

"Cuz, where you put the dro, fam?" Jamal asks.

"In the kitchen behind the triple beam, loc. By the drink. Roll us a couple, Jamal."

"Cool," Jamal says as he walks toward the kitchen.

Lil D reaches for the door knob to see if it's open. "Come on, blood, it's unlocked." The trio creeps through the back door. As it softly clicks shut, the music ends.

"Cuz," they hear. "Get the front door. It looks like Do-Right, fam."

"Shit Joe, you got me fucked up, cuz, with this ordering me around shit," Jamal protests.

"Just get the door and I'll get the weed," Dallas says. He crab-walks to the kitchen to get the pound of dro. Two 10mm pistols are put to each of his temples as soon as he reaches for it. Lil D shakes his finger to be quiet while Big Chief and Tre Duce put him on the floor on his stomach, the Mag to the back of his head.

"Cuz, ain't nobody at the fuckin' door," yells Jamal. "Them sticks be fuckin' with your brain, cuz. I'm fixing to change the track, fool. Yeah. I want to hear Compton's 'Most Wanted' anyway."

"Who else is here, crab?" Big Chief whispers.

Dallas shakes his head. "Nobody."

While Jamal has his back turned, Lil D moves quickly to put the Mag to the back of Jamal's head. Before he can put the CD into the player, Lil D says, "Get down, crab. There is no need for my soundtrack music."

Jamal gets down on his knees. "Don't shoot," he pleads.

"Fuck you, crab," Gauges Lil D. "Bring the other nigga in here, Big Chief. Well, well. Look who we caught sleeping, blood!"

"Motherfuckin' big-time Dallas and punk-ass Jamal the snitch," says Tre Duce. "Shit, it looks like they counted our doe for us, huh, Dallas?"

"Sit your pussy ass down beside your crab-ass homeboy. Big Chief, find something to put our cash in. Now, where the dope at, nigga?" asks Lil D.

"Man, it's --"

"Shut up, cuz!" Dallas orders.

"They gonna kill us anyway," protests Jamal.

Ten shots from the Mag spit into Dallas' knees.

"Ah, cuz. Look, it's in the closet over there by the front door," says Jamal. Blood soaks into the carpet so thickly that Jamal slides away from Dallas to stay dry.

"Don't move, crab," orders Lil D. "Duce, check that out, fam."

"It's here, Lil D."

"Snatch that shit up and let's bounce, blood. Jamal, your mouth is way too much for your body. Let me help you out, son. But before I do, tell me which one of you crabs shot O.G. Spook, and I'll let you live."

"Fuck you, slob," Dallas says defiantly. "Die slow, bitch." Big Chief stands over Dallas and unloads the whole clip into his face, sending brain fragments everywhere. "Fuck *you*."

Jamal panics. "Man, look, I heard it was Tank who pulled the trigger," Jamal says while he shits his pants, crying like a dope fiend.

"Now I know who did the big homie," Lil D says. "Thanks for the info and the cash and shit, but I gots to go, blood. Tre Duce, lay him to sleep."

Jamal puts his hands up as if they can somehow stop the bullets. Tre Duce puts down the bag, looks Jamal straight in the eyes. "Blood, you won't feel a thing, and you can have an open casket on me." He Put two bullets through Jamal's heart and half of his back flies out.

"Let's bounce," says Big Chief.

"Hold on, blood. Let's leave them to hear his crab-ass homeboy MC Eiht," says Tre Duce, picking up a CD.

"You a fool," Big Chief says.

They stroll out of the back door as though nothing is wrong. They reach the alley when an unknown man walks toward the house. "'Sup, cuz?" he says to Big Chief. "Jamal in there?"

"Yeah, he's sleeping, though," Big Chief replies.

"I can hear the beats pounding, cuz," the man says. They all frown, but keep their cool.

"Dallas in there getting his head blown back," Tre Duce explains. "We out."

"Shotgun!" the stranger shouts. They turn and walk toward the truck on the corner.

I've never seen them around here. Why do they have on black gloves at this time of the day? Did they have red shoe laces in their Chuck Tailors? By the time the unknown man comes out of his thoughts, the Blazer comes up the alley. The back window rolls down. All the man can do is grab his bullet-ridden body and fall to the ground.

"One for the road," says Lil D. "To the hood to count our lick, fam. Sticks on me, blood. That bitch Angel good with me, fam."

Ghost's cell phone rings. "Speak!" he says.

"Slob, you dead." Click. Ghost looks at his caller I.D. *Blocked call. Now, who knows this number? Damn, where in the fuck is this bitch? I got too much shit to do to be tripping off a phone call. I need to chill for today. That lovely have a nigga paranoid all fuckin' day.*

He watches "Paid in Full" on the plasma screen TV. *Killer Boy can pop that nigga for the bricks, fam. Only a sucker would tell a goon that dumb shit.* "Let me call this pig to see what's the deal," he says aloud. "But first, let me pour me a drink to level out my high some."

He walks over to the bar and pours a double shot of Belvedere vodka, stops on his way back to the couch and looks at himself in the mirror. *I feel something big is about to happen.* His cell phone plays a text message signal. He sits down and flips if open. It's a message from Shaunna: "I'm leaving the hotel now, so be ready, baby. Love, Shaunna." *It's about fuckin' time already.*

"Bitch, open up this door!"

"I'm coming! Hold on." *She fuckin' up my time with my nigga now. I just text his ass to let him know I'm on my way. Shit.*

The door flies open and a half-dressed Lacy stands back to let them enter. "You cool now, so I'm out," Shaunna says. "'Bye, Biggie."

"'Bye, Shaunna." Biggie slips through the door with bags of clothes in each hand.

"For me, baby?" Lacy says, wide-eyed.

"Yeah, I couldn't let Shaunna out-do me, you know."

The towel Lacy is wearing drops to the floor. "Let me shut the door, baby," says Biggie. "I don't want nobody to see all that body."

Lacy walks backward to the bed and lies down slowly. She opens her legs to show off her pussy's lips, sticks her finger deep into the wetness and tastes it. "Biggie, come taste," she breathes.

Everything in his hands hits the floor and his clothes come off in one slick motion. One second later, he's face-deep in Lacy's pussy.

That nigga thinks that I didn't see that bitch Nina leave the 'hood the other day. Shaunna pats her feet on the ground as she waits for the valet to bring up the truck. *I got his ass where I want him now.*

Agent Lyons and Agent Crown pull into the parking lot as Shaunna pays the attendant. "That woman right there is one of the O.G. Bloods' girlfriends. Here comes Burgess."

"It's about to be show time, sir," Burgess says as he gets into the back seat. "It's very odd, sir, how close she is with the Crip guy, Biggie. In the elevator they talked like they were old running buddies."

"She's not our first priority right now. What room is Biggie in?"

"Five-oh-two. I don't know who's in there with him right now. I can tell you this, though, sir. He has a lot of cash on him right now."

Agent Crown clears his throat. "His real name is Benny Thompson, Cali Shotgun Crip. He's one of the big dope pushers out there. Rich, a.k.a. Clayton Graham, is his big homey. I've been chasing them for a while. They are connected to some very powerful Jamaicans in Kingston. He has no drivers' license, so we can have a squad pull him over when he leaves. He's been connected to about seven homicides in Cali alone, but nothing ever sticks."

"Well, Agent Crown, if he has drugs in that car over there, we're going to change that today," nods Agent Lyons.

✂◈✄

"Lick this pussy, baby, ooh . . . ooh . . . right there. Don't stop don't stop, shi-i-i-i-t . . . Yeah, baby, I'm, I'm, I'm about to come!" Sweat rolls down Lacy's breast to her stomach. With her back arched upward, she grabs Biggie's head and pushes toward his face and climaxes as she never has before. Biggie pulls his tongue out of the Lacy, but licks off every drop of pussy juice before he pulls completely out.

"That pussy just tastes so good, baby." Lacy rubs her legs together, looking Biggie right in the eyes as she strokes his nine-and-a-half-inches.

"You want mama to suck that big dick, don't you?"

With a look of desperation, he answers, "Yes-s-s-s . . ."

"Baby, it feels so hard in my hand." Lacy scoots closer to Biggie so she can taste the pre-cum with her tongue, then puts the whole dick into her mouth, slowly, inch by inch, while holding Biggie's ass to push him forward. He moves back at the sensation of Lacy's warm mouth wrapped around him. Lacy pulls back to stroke his ego a little. "Why you make me wait so long, daddy? You know how hungry I can be, daddy."

"Never again, Lacy. Never again," Biggie swears as he puts his hand on her head to push forward. Lacy licks around the head, stroking slowly as head moves back and forward. Biggie's stomach muscles tighten at the work shes doing on him. Lacy looks up at Biggie. His eyes are fully closed; he's enjoying the blow job he's getting.

I get this nigga going, Lacy thinks. *Pussy and head is my poison on these niggas.*

Biggie grabs Lacy's head with two hands and starts to pump into her mouth. "Yeah, ma," he says.

"Please, big daddy," she answers.

"Suck daddy's two-by-four!"

Lacy pulls back so that only the head is in her mouth, and sucks and strokes until she feels a rush of cum shooting down her throat. She moans as she drinks every last drop. Biggie lets out a weird sound, like a bear caught in a trap. He drops face-first on the bed beside Lacy.

Looking over at Lacy, he says approvingly, "That's daddy's little girl." *Nah, that's mama's trick.*

Lacy snaps out of her daze when Biggie says, "You have the best fuckin' head I've ever had in my whole life, shit. Lacy, if you keep that up, I'm-a have to wife you, ma."

"I only want to please you, daddy." *Yeah, right, nigga.*

"Where you put the smoke, daddy?"

"In my pocket, on the floor. Roll up!"

"Brooklyn Center Police Department. How may I direct your call?"

"This is Agent Dan Lyons with the FBI. I need to speak with the sergeant on duty."

"Hold on, sir. Let me connect you to his office."

"Yes, this is Sgt. Fred Banks. How may I help you today?"

"I'm Agent Dan Lyons with the FBI, and I need a traffic stop done on a suspect we're following."

"Where are you?"

"At the Hilton."

"What kind of vehicle?"

"Sky-blue '63 Impala, gold rims, black tint, drop top, license plate LETS EAT."

"Should I be warned about any weapons?"

"Stop with caution."

"Okay. I'll come out to conduct the stop myself."

"Thank you for your cooperation."

"No problem."

"Oh, sergeant, I need a K-9 unit."

"Sure thing."

"Now that's taken care of, all we need to do is wait."

Biggie's cell phone vibrates on the floor. "Baby, hand me my phone, Lacy." *I wonder what cuz wants. I just left his ass. Cheaa!*

"Cuz, somebody smoked Jamal and Dallas at the spot and K-loc, too. Them niggas lost two hundred and fifty thousand dollars and fifteen bricks of dope, fam. And the big homie is pissed, too, son."

"I'm on my way."

"Do-Right."

"Enough said, loc." Biggie hangs up.

"Daddy, why you looking so cold?" Lacy is frightened by the sudden change in him.

"I got to bounce, cuz," he says, drawing on his clothes. "Here's three thousand to keep your room and anything else you need."

"Thank you." Biggie walks out the door without a backward glance. The door slams shut.

Fuck you, too, trick, and I didn't even have to fuck for a buck, Lacy thinks. I wonder what's up with that call? Shit, it don't involve me, so fuck it. I got dro.

"Here he comes, guys. I want everybody on Line 1, a clear channel, no mistakes," Lyons says.

Biggie jumps into the Impala, pulls out his .40 Glock from under the seat and slides a round in the chamber. He starts the car, unpancakes the switches and pulls off quickly. He's on a back street headed toward Shingle Creek Parkway and I-94. *Shit, a squad car on the freeway entrance and I don't got no D.L. Shit, he's pulling off now. I don't need this, then.* With a flick of his wrist, the Glock sails into the grass.

Crown sees the gun fly out of the car. "Stop, Agent Lyons, so we can retrieve that weapon. If we're lucky, it will have some bodies on it. I want to stick everything we can on him."

The squad car's red and blue lights flash on, signaling Biggie to pull over. *I'll just give them Cuz's info and the insurance card like before. Stay cool. Damn! A K-9 unit, and I got four bricks of hard in the trunk, too. I'm fucked.*

The cop steps out of the cruiser and walks slowly to the driver's side window. "Driver's license and registration, sir, and your insurance card," says Sgt. Banks. His hand rests on his revolver. "It's a nice day today, son."

Biggie opens up the glove box and a stack of money held together with a rubber band falls onto the floor. Sgt. Banks plays like he didn't see it.

"Here's my registration, and my insurance card, but I left my driver's license at home, sir."

"That's okay. What's your name, birthdate and address?"

"Tyrell Young, 4-20-74, 2207 Penn Avenue North."

Sgt. Banks writes down the phony information and smiles. "I'll be right back, Tyrell," he says. "Let me run this through my computer." He walks back to the squad. Biggie leans over and puts the money back into the glove box, thinking everything is cool.

Sgt. Banks gets out of the squad car and lets the K-9 out of the back door. Biggie starts to sweat as the dog walks toward the car. *Shit, more cops. Should I run or not? Shit, what am I going to do?*

"Well, Tyrell, your license is valid, but I have to make sure you're not carrying any drugs or guns. Do you mind if we let Kip sniff around the car?"

Biggie wills himself to stay calm. "I don't have a problem with that."

Sgt. Banks points under the driver side door. The K-9 sniffs it. Then Banks walks over to the gas cap and points at it. The dog sniffs it. Then he stands in back of the Impala and hits the trunk. The K-9 barks and scratches the trunk. Sgt. Banks gives Agent Burgess a nod and he pulls out his service pistol, a twenty-one-shot 9 mm Taurus.

"Put your hands up where I can see them and shut the engine off, sir."

Life in prison don't sound good to me. Fuck, let's hold court in the street. Biggie looks over at Agent Burgess for a brief second. Then, as Sgt. Banks walks up on the driver's side, he slams the car in gear and shoots gravel onto the squad car, Sgt. Banks and the dog.

"Agents Lyons and Crown in pursuit now," Crown radios the others. "Stay on him, Lyons. Don't let him get away!"

The Impala's .445 engine pulls Biggie away like a jet on wheels. Biggie shuffles to get hold of his cell phone and open it. He dials Low Down's number. "Cuz, get the lil homies out on the corner of Forty-ninth and Camden. The po po is on my ass and I need them to bust the heat at them and get them off my ass ASAP, loc."

Agent Lyons sighs as he sees Biggie reach the exit miles ahead of him. Biggie exits the freeway at seventy-five miles an hour with perfect skill, letting off on the gas just enough to skid into the right turn, then mashes the gas to barely skim by a parked car. Simultaneously, the lil homies post up on the corner to provide cover as he passes by. Biggie gives them a sinister look as he sinks down in the seat.

Agent Burgess is in the back seat of the squad car, sizzling at his slow reaction to events. "Come on, Lyons, move it!" yells Crown. "He's out of sight!" Crown is becoming very skeptical about Lyons's driving skills. They exit at 49th street and are hit with a slab of bullets. Agent Lyons tries to make a right turn at ninety miles an hour and hits the brakes to slide into a parked car.

Boom, smack. Sgt. Banks and Agent Burgess smash into the back of the agents' car. Smoke rises from all of the police cars. "Get down, people!" Crown yells. The agents and Sgt. Fred return fire.

Biggie pulls into the back of the house while C-loc opens up the garage so he can park inside. He jumps out before the garage door closes. "C-loc, you saved my ass today, cuz. I got a slew of cocaine in the trunk, son. You know I'm not Jamal, cuz. Get you one of them bricks out of the back for yourself, yo."

One by one, the baby locs get picked off by the expert sniper shooting by the officers on the scene. "Code Four, fellas." The walk over to check out the sophisticated weapons strewn across the ground. "This was one spectacle," says Sgt. Banks.

"I speculate that this was a very spontaneous act by our suspect who split," says Burgess. "Poof, he's gone and we're left to kill some young kids."

Chapter 12

Rich leans against the staircase, sputtering and trying to catch his breath after hitting the blunt. He staggers down the stairs and stops at the bottom to take up a stallion's stance.

"The stakes just went up. The stain in my pocket stabbed me deep today. To those who don't know these other cats I have here today, well, all you need to know is that they're the Family Cartel from the South Side."

"Why you go —" Rich squelches Do-Right quickly before he can finish.

"They have the same interests we do with them slobs, so we gone aid and assist one another on this,"

Rich explains.

"Them slop, slob niggas' credibility is very spurious, fam," says Spook. "The ones we cripple will be the ones that didn't die from their bullet wounds."

"Not if you bust their craniums, cuz," says Dread crankily.

"Damn, cuz, your wrist looks like frozen spring water," says Jug to break the tension. "Shit, all that wet you splurging, loc, you should be Donald Trump by now."

"Locs, chill out, drink, and smoke on me. This is the spot to come to and get A.A. with what you need, fam, from the coalition we've put together today," says Rich.

"The streets are talking now, son," says Spook, who's holding a blunt. "That shit don't mean shit, cuz. I'm Murder Mac. I'm addicted to the sound of the twelve-gauge, like a hype with a rock, fam, 'Ya understand me.' When I get ahold of Ghost, I'm-a duct tape his ass and bring him to the hood. I'm showing no love to these cowards. I don't give a fuck."

"Nigga, Family Cartel is a supply and demand of killers who swarm slobs with heat to suppress them to the end," says Ike.

"Murder, let me holler at you one second, fam," says Rich. "Roll with me real quick."

"Cool, loc," says Murder.

"Dread, is the low ride in the back?" asks Rich.

"Yeah, loc."

"Good. Follow me in the Cutlass real quick, loc."

"I'm game."

They walk to the rides in the backyard. "Rich," says Murder, "what's the deal?"

"Murder, you're a rare breed, or shall I say, species? See you, loc, specialize in your line of work." They get into the old Regal Sport to put down a quick move. "See, me and you together is synthesis. Your talent and your tactics are very valuable," Rich continues. "Look under your seat. It should be very tenuous in the palm of your hand. It's time for me to come out and put in work now. I have the tendency to fuck with the best when I terminate."

"I feel you, cuz," says Murder. "Where we going?"

"South side," says Rich.

"You sure you're straight, Rich?"

"Fo sho, cuz."

If Rich was a thermostat, he'll blow at that question.

The three thoroughbreds head to the South Side. They make a left turn and then make another left. "We're going to lay down our trade, man," says Rich.

"When we leave the slobs we hit, a tourniquet won't be able to save them, cuz," says Murder.

"I'm leaving the Shotgun totem with them today," Rich replies. He pulls out two AP9s with two extra-long clips in them. Murder clicks the mini AR-13 to chamber a shell.

"Look, cuz. The park is full of slobs today. Pull over in the middle. Here, Murder, put this ski mask on. Now let's show these slobs who's the most treacherous."

Rich directs Dread to park at the north end of the park as their escape driver.

"This is my tribunal for Cuz," shouts Rich as they exit the Regal. They both shout, "'Sup, Cuz!" as they let their trigger fingers loose.

One Blood close to Rich is hit in the neck with two shots; he falls two feet from the two shooters. Rich runs by the fallen man and puts two into his stomach. Murder covers his back and sprays the AR-13 into the crowd with the intent of killing everyone.

On instinct, Rich turns to his blind side to see two males in sight, creeping toward them with revolvers. They're no match for Rich, who quickly spits ten rounds into their bodies. They fly backwards to the ground. Two more sweeps of the AR-13 drops fifteen to twenty members of the Blood gang. Dread jumps out of the Cutlass. "Come on, cuz, the fuzz is on the way!"

As Rich and Murder flee the park to the awaiting car, Murder stops for a moment. There's an insane look on his face. *This is one of the many installments you bitches are going to get, cuz*, he thinks. Four carloads of Bloods exit their cars, looking inquisitively at the situation. Murder and Rich let off the rest of the clips in their direction and shout, "Shotgun Crips, nigga!" Murder chimes in with "Family Cartel, cuz!"

"Get in the car," Dread urges. "Here they come!" He pulls off into traffic and is out of sight in seconds.

"Roll down the window, cuz," says Murder in the back seat. "I need to toss this hammer and ."

They toss the heaters out the window. "Man," says Dread, you two are a fuckin' mess, loc. I'm glad it was getting dark so we could bounce easily, Rich. All I could see was bodies falling in groups. That shit looked like a paint ball fight down there."

"Them slobs couldn't even scramble. The scenery is our scenario, cuz," says Rich. "Back to the spot to kick it, fam."

"There's a science to the art of war. Sleep is the cousin of death. That is the price you pay," Murder says.

Do-Right pulls into the alley to so Killer Boy can pick up his Grand National. "Foolish in there, fam?" asks Do-Right.

"I don't know, cuz. I didn't call over here," says Killer Boy.

"But you smoothly slithered your way to Cookie," Do-Right says pointedly.

Killer doesn't even look back at that comment. He shuts the door of the 745 BMW.

"Be careful, loc," Do-Right says. "You know we lost a few soldiers earlier today."

Killer gives him an impatient look. "I know, nigga. What you gone give me, a sermon now? I'm the fuckin' Grim Reaper himself, Do-Right. My body is a sepulcher for lost souls."

"Get your whip and dip, fam."

"One."

"Damn, in the dark it's hard to see you, baby," Killer Boy talks to his car as he inspects it. "Let me see who's home now." But he changes his mind. His recidivism kicks in and he jumps into the Grand National. He pulls out backwards, then drives down the alley to rumble and go on a rampage on Nina.

I'm going to ransack that bitch's whole house until I get what I come for. He drinks from a bottle of Absolut vodka left from days ago. *This nigga gots to pay reparation for me and there is no one to remonstrate me tonight, either.*

Killer parks on the side street of Twenty-ninth Avenue North on the side of the building where Nina stays. He cuts the engine to chill until she shows or leaves the house. *While I'm waiting I might as well reminisce on the good days kicking it with Fat Cuz. He was the only O.G. who wouldn't relinquish me to the other O.G.s 'cause I'm a renegade and a free agent. Fat Cuz, this dip is for you, fam, up there in O.G. heaven.*

He eases the seat back to relax and release some tension. *This is the remedy I've been craving. It looks like someone is walking through the house.* He pulls on the stick with revenge on his mind. He's brought out of his thoughts when two squad cars come slowly from the next block over, shining the spotlight on parked cars. *Shit, the law.* As they move closer to where he's parked, Killer ducks down to avoid being seen.

Shit. I could be a fugitive right now. I got to smoke Scab to be one hundred percent safe.

Nina walks out the back door to the garage. Killer sees the garage door open and he's furious at the cops' slow pace. His face is a mask of total frustration. One squad car pulls over next to the Grand National. One of the cops gets out to confront a young-looking boy. "Come here." The boy takes off, running through the gangways to avoid the cops. A gargantuan woman cop comes running behind the rather small cop in the pursuit of their suspect.

Killer sees the back of the Malibu leave the alley, going straight past the squad cars. They're blocking his way. He can't follow her. *You live one more night, Shorty.*

Killer takes a deep breath to calm himself. He glares around the ghetto. The coast is clear. He decides to bounce while he has the chance. He starts the Grand National, glares at the house on the corner for a second, then disappears into the night.

Chapter 13

I wake up in a strange bed beside a strange woman. "Baby, you leaving?" asks Pookie.

"Nah, not yet, but I've been over here for several days now. I do need to grind, ma."

"I know, baby, but I like to grind with you, too. Can I come with you?"

"Haven't you cum enough?"

"Well, no, daddy."

"Pookie, have you seen my cell phone?"

"It's in the truck, sitting in the cup holder."

"I need to check to see if my brother called me." I get up, butt-ass naked, and put on my silk boxers and Sean Jean jeans. I slide on my Air Force Ones and walk shirtless through the kitchen to the front door. Munchie and Blue are sitting in the living room, watching TV. Munchie looks at me with lust in her eyes as she takes in my muscles.

"Hey, Jay, leaving?"

"Nah, just getting my phone out of my truck. How you doing, Munchie?"

"Fine. You got some smoke?"

"Yeah, some fire dro. You got blunts?"

"I do, cuz," says Blue. "We straight now, 'cause Pookie don't smoke."

"I know. Let me grab my phone out of the Bronco real quick."

Blue watches Munchie closely. The front door closes and I hit the remote to deactivate the Viper alarm. The lock pops up and I reach for the door handle as an all-white Bronco pulls up behind me. A tall, skinny, dark dude jumps out, eyeing me suspiciously. He moves swiftly toward the house with his hoodie up and hands concealed.

Shit, where I put the dro? Ah, in my hoodie on the back seat. I might as well put it on and grab my 10mm out of the glove box. I almost shut the door, then remember my cell. I grab it, shut the truck door and activate the alarm.

Damn, shorty been blowing up my shit. I've been thinking about your sexy ass, I say in my head to Nicki. I walk back to the house, and Pookie opens it as I get there. She's wearing my shirt and nothing else. "Baby, I thought you left me," she pouts.

"Nah, I had to put on my hoodie." She closes the door and all eyes are upon us.

"Girl, go to the back. We about to smoke," says Blue.

"Check yourself, Blue," Pookie retorts.

"Go on, Pookie," says Munchie.

"Don't be long, Jay," Pookie says to me.

"I won't."

I sit down by the new dude. "What up, cuz? That's a nice Bronco out there," I say to him.

"Chilling, playboy, he says, "and thanks, I'm "G".

Not at all "G" says. "The more the better the high." He asks the usual question, "Where you from?"

"Little Rock, Arkansas."

"I watched a documentary about banging down there," he says conversationally.

"That shit's overrated to me, homie," I say.

"You being?" he asks.

"I'm folks, fam."

"That's cool. I'm a 90 Crip homie, me and Blue. He's my cousin in real life, too. Roll up, Blue. Here's the dro, do you."

The door flies open and Pookie's mom rushes into the house. G-man, let me holler at you real quick," Rose says. "Hi, everybody."

She and G-man walk to the back room.

"Munchie, your mom be fana," says Blue as he licks the blunt closed.

"Don't start your shit today, Blue. Leave Mom alone."

"I'm just saying, it's way too early for that shit, ma."

Rose comes out of the back room and leaves as quickly as she came. G-man walks back into the living room. "Light up, cuz. We got to bounce shorty, cuz."

"You got a light, Jay?" asks Blue.

"Nah. Here, cuz." G-man hands him a lighter. "90s, cuz, for life."

Damn. My luck to knock a bitch who got crab homeboys. It can't get no worser than that. I'm already tired of hearing this crab shit. I don't know how much more I can take of it before I blow. Chill, Jay, for Pookie's sake.

Blue pulls on the white willow strong enough to push Munchie from his lap as he convulses from the hit he took. Coughing and spit flying out of his mouth, he passes the blunt to me and runs for the kitchen sink, where he spits and catches his breath. We all laugh at him. "Greedy ass," laughs Munchie. "Always trying to look tough in front of people. That's what he gets. That shit smells fire as hell, too, cuz."

I take a few light pulls and pass the blunt to G-man. It tastes like blueberries. "Here, Munchie, hit this shit while I chief the shit that sent Blue flying."

Pookie rolls over on her back, letting her imagination run wild. She knows that Jay is in the next room, and that re-ignites the flame between her legs. She has the illusion that Jay is touching her pussy as soon as her fingers touch her clit. She spreads her legs wider to put more fingers in her now-wet pussy. She pulls her fingers out again and licks them with gratitude written all over her face. She lies back and closes her eyes and pulls her breast up to her tongue so she can lick them slowly and rub her thumb around the tip. It swells up hard and marks her hornier.

I get a text message and look down to see "Call me." I pass the blunt to Munchie. "I need to get some air real quick, y'all," I say. I go outside to call Nicki back.

G-man gets up to use the restroom and finds Pookie back in her room with her door wide open, having sex with herself. She moans softly, her legs wide open. Fully naked, eyes closed, she pleasures herself with her long fingers moving in great haste. G-man stands there for a moment. Then the dro helps him make a quick decision to go heighten her pleasure.

G-man tiptoes to the bottom of the bed and quietly leans down to smell Pookie's pussy. He gets down on his knees and slides his tongue into Pookie. Pookie keeps her eyes closed, playing with her breast. She heaves her pussy into G-man's mouth, thinking it's Jay. Without touching Pookie for fear she'll open her eyes, G-man sticks his long tongue deep down into her body to cause havoc with her emotions. She moans louder to hearten him more. Pookie clamps her pussy muscles around G-man's tongue. He knows she's about to explode in his mouth. He starts to move his tongue like a hungry snake. She cums deep and long, then says, "Fuck me, Jay."

G-man gets up, and hesitates, then slips into the bathroom before she opens her eyes. Pookie looks around the room. G-man shuts the door silently, undetected.

I'm outside on the phone, making plans to meet up later with Nicki.

"I usually don't meet up with people I don't know, Jay," she tells me.

"Listen, ma. I have great Southern hospitality in ways you have never seen. I'm very modest, deeply respectful. And with the right person, very compassionate, too," I say persuasively.

"So you say," she remarks ironically.

"I see you have a sense of humor. I can sense a smile on your face, Nicki," I tease.

"Don't flatter yourself just yet," she says. "Do you have a woman?"

"Nah, but I have a good candidate, though."

She's doubtful. "Oh yeah? Is that so? What took you so long to get back at me then, huh?"

"Shorty, I've been on a few things, you know, trying to fit in where I can get in at. I like to coordinate my moves, if you feel me. But I've been thinking about you, Nicki. You've been on my mind."

"Now, what did I do to contribute to those thoughts?"

"My first thought about you is how you looked sitting in your car, so sexy. I bet you're a very congenial person," I egg her on.

"Meaning?"

"You're a very sociable woman. To be frank, I think you will be any man's perfect counterpart."

"You're kind of smart, Jay. I like your conversation. It's highly ir-regular that someone your age has the type of intelligence you have."

"I'll take that as a compliment, lil mama. You smoke, shorty?"

"Yeah. You got the good stuff?" she asks.

"Fo sho. Only the best."

"I'll call you later, Jay. I got to get ready for work right now. I get off at nine o'clock. If you want to pick me up when I get off, we can smoke later."

"Anyway we can bond, sexy," I say.

"I'm with it," she replies.

"So call me about 8:30, then I'll be on my way to your fine ass so I can appropriately appease you. Baby, I'll be waiting in anticipation of your call."

I can imagine Nicki blushing at the sweet compliments.

"Call you later, Jay. 'Bye."

"Holla," I say as she hangs up.

Damn, he's cuter than a motherfucker, and smart, and talks so sweet to me, too, Nicki thinks as she drops her robe and enters the shower.

Man, these bitches in Minneapolis is so fuckin' easy, it's crazy. My game is so ample, though. I never cease to amaze myself when it comes to hoes. I got to dip out on this hoe here, or she'll have a player pussy-whipped for sho. But I'll keep it amicable as possible with her.

I jump into the Bronco and head to Ghost's house.

G-man comes out of the bathroom and looks Pookie dead in the eyes. Satisfaction is on his face. He walks back to the living room

No, it couldn't have been him! Agony shoots through her body at the thought of that happening. Warning signals go off in her brain. *It could have been him. I didn't even open my eyes. Shit. Where are my clothes at? Shit, if it was him that ate this pussy with so much aggression . . . I'm afraid I liked it.*

A feeling of vulnerability comes over her. She puts on her clothes and walks into the living room. She decides to check his face to confirm her thoughts. G-man doesn't even look her way as she walks over and sits down on the couch beside him. It's obvious he's acting funny. *This nigga violated me. Payback is better served cold.* Pookie gets up and gives G-man a vindictive look before she disappears into her room. *It was him, because Jay's gone.*

Chapter 14

I've been up for days sucking crack and replaying that scene over and over in my head. It just won't stop, thinks Scab. He jumps into a potential sale's car.

"What you got?" asks the driver.

"It's over there, but I got to go in, 'cause you're white," Scab says.

"Is it good?"

"No soda ball, just butter," Scab assures him. "Turn left here and park. Here, puff this. I still got a potent hit left on my stem."

The white guy lights up the stem, takes a large pull of the smoke into his lungs and holds it for a second. He slowly pushes out the cloud of smoke while Scab gets his pipe back. Scab pushes it to take a pull himself, then asks, "How much you got?"

The white guy starts to drool. Spit runs down his chin. He fumbles through the car, looking for his money slowly, like he's in a zone.

These white guys are so fuckin' predictable when they hit that fire, thinks Scab.

"I got two hundred and fifty. Can I get one piece?"

"My man got whatever. Don't trip. You straight, son."

Scab grabs the money and steps out of the car with a smile on his face. *Shit, I can bounce now. I've been waiting on a lick like this for days. I can buy me an eight ball and slide out of here with one hundred and fifty left to chill with.*

Down the street, the Third Precinct crack team is waiting for a signal from the C.I. that the deal was made. One of the officers on foot walks by Scab to ID him as the target with the marked money. He talks into the microphone inside of his shirt to give the other officers a brief description of the suspect. "Roger that," the team leader replies. "This is Agent Dan Lyons. As soon as he comes out of the building, grab him and hit the whole building, every apartment. I don't want anybody to leave."

"Copy that, sir."

"We're going to hit every crack spot that they have," says Lyons to Red Beard.

"You have our full cooperation on this investigation, "says Red Beard.

"Man, what's taking him so long?" asks Agent Burgess.

Scab walks into the building.

"What up, blood?"

"Let me get an eight-ball, son."

"Hold on for a second. Give me the doe, fam."

Scab passes him the money and waits for the dealer to come back. The door behind him flies open and a young gangbanger comes through it, looking counterproductive. *Shit, I shouda put my money in my shoe.* "Sup, blood?" Scab nods at the young blood and pulls out his stem. He takes a puff.

"Take that shit back there, fool-ass crackhead," the young blood says.

Pit Bull's worker comes out of apartment 106 and signals for Scab to come to him. He eyes the young blood. "Blood, what you doing hanging in the halls, nigga? Shit, yo. You better not be fuckin' with my people, yo. If you are, I'll make sure you burgeon slow, son." He turns to Scab. "That nigga be on some rubbing shit too much," he explains, then tends to business.

"Here, blood, it's all these, plus some extras for running customers. You cool, fam?"

"Yeah, I'm good. Thanks for the benediction, fam," says Scab. "I'm out." He walks out the back door and runs into a bum-looking white guy. Scab gauges into awareness, but it's too late. The man throws him to the ground and tells him to shut the fuck up. He searches Scab's pockets and finds the marked bills. He puts handcuffs on him, then rolls him over and finds the crack lying under his body. "I have the suspect," he radios in. "Move in now!"

All the teams move in like an army. Pit Bull steps to the window to look outside and sees police cars all over the front lawn. Before he can leave the window, his apartment door flies off its hinges and lands across the room, followed by a huge puff of smoke. "Police. Get down. Search warrants. Police. Get down. Search warrants," comes a voice though a police bullhorn.

Officers wearing smoke masks come through the door and automatic weapons pointed at everyone in the building. They snatch people's arms and throw them face down on the floor with a knee in their backs.

As they sweep the rest of the building, they find Pit Bull on the floor with his hands behind his head. Mandy and Kim walk into the room to show Pit Bull their police badges and to cuff him. Pit Bull gets up with a smirk on his face. "Let us have a word with him," says Kim. The other officer leaves them alone to talk. Red Beard stays in the hallway to listen.

"You two bitches are the po po!" Pit Bull exclaims.

"Yeah, we're the law and you're federally fucked if you don't help yourself, Pit Bull," says Kim, whose badge reveals her to be Officer Patty Jensen.

Pit Bull is thoughtful. "That's why I never saw you smoke no cake, huh? But I do know you two bitches suck a good dick."

"You'll be sucking dick soon enough," says Officer Tracy Hays, otherwise known as Mandy.

Red Beard sticks his head in the door. "Take him in the front with the rest of the garbage," he says.

Pit Bull becomes more comfortable with the situation when he sees Red Beard. Tracy walks him to the living room and pushes him down in the corner.

"Tear this place up, people," orders Agent Lyons as he walks through the front door with Agent Burgess. "I want everybody charged federally, not state." He walks over to where Pit Bull lies and gives me the stare of one who's just won, then walks out of the room.

Pit Bull's head is facing the floor. "You two bitches won't see next year, fuckin' with me," he proclaims.

Officer Tracy walks over and flips him over to face her and spits in his face. "You're a statistic when we find your stash, dope boy." She's startled when Red Beard takes her by the arm and whispers into her ear. She leaves the apartment.

While other officers tear up every inch of the apartment, Red Beard takes Pit Bull downstairs to his cruiser and puts him in the back seat. As Red Beard settles into the driver's seat, Pit Bull starts in. "What the fuck, cop? You on some bullshit now, son, and we pay your ass for this kind of shit."

Red sighs and explains, "The stipend I receive from you guys doesn't include the FEDS. This is way out of my hands now. With all the killing going on, and the killing of that federal agent, stings like this will happen at random. As long as nothing comes out of that apartment you were caught in, you're good. You'll be downtown for thirty-six hours P.C. time, that's all. To be straightforward with you, shut down for a while. Change your strategy."

"I want both of them hoes' heads for playing me for a fool, Red, and I mean that, son," Pit Bull says angrily. "Whatever it takes."

"There goes the paddy wagon," says Red. "I'll take you downtown myself. Let me go clear it with Agent Lyons real quick."

He walks back to the building with long, vigorous strides. He meets Lyons at the door. Lyons smiles. "What a good blow to their structure today! We've got lots of drugs, guns and money in several apartments in this building, plus people willing to talk. We're going to be busy with interviews today. But there wasn't anything in the apartment Pit Bull was found in. So I guess he can go with the other people who were in the apartment with him. That way, we can watch him closely now."

"I'll take care of that, sir," volunteers Red Beard.

Chapter 15

Foolish and T.C. puff on a blunt, waiting on Foolish's front porch for Mario to show up and buy the AK-47 and the Colt .45 pistol.

"Man, Foolish, what you want for them heaters, G?"

"Fam," replies Foolish, "fifteen hundred to you, but I need two thousand from Scab. That nigga be on some bullshit when I fuck with him, T.C."

"I know he a dirty little fucker," T.C. agrees. "Foolish, this sure some fire shit. My loc homie got the bomb. Why you fuck with them so damn much?"

"Look, G," Foolish pauses as he pulls deep on the blunt and exhales purple smoke. "Man, I eat with them cats real good, 'you understand me.' But I fucks with them to an extent, too." He gets up to look down the block to get a better view of the fiends coming down the street toward them. "Never exclusively, though. I keep my options open for my G niggas. Here, T.C., take this while I handle this." He hands him the blunt.

A young blood approaches the porch steps. "I got one hundred dollars. Can I get a ball?" he asks.

"Hold up one second, Clyde," answers Foolish. "I got you. Sit down." He walks into the house and comes back with a plastic bag filled with work. He passes Clyde two grams of crack. Clyde hands over the money without delay and walks back to the corner where another smoker waits for him.

"Fam," says T.C., "you doing your thing, Foolish."

"Nah. I run a shop that sells cooked or unprepared work to cater.

Whatever they want. This my block, fam. Everybody knows I run this over here, son."

"I'm going to have to come fuck with you more, G," says T.C.

"Do that," Foolish says agreeably. "Man, where this nigga Mario at, T.C.?"

T.C. points at a black Buick Regal. "There he come, down the block now."

Foolish calls to Cookie. "Cookie, bring that and put it by the door, baby."

"Okay. You hungry, baby?" she asks.

"I'm good," he replies as Mario pulls up. The Regal is a real trap car for the 'hood. Mario walks over to them with a pimp gangsta stroll.

"'Sup, 26 nigga?" he asks.

"Twenty-six, fam," T.C. says back with the 26 handshake.

"'Sup, gangsta, you up, nigga?" asks Mario as he reaches his hand toward Foolish to throw up the rakes.

"My dough, skud. You got it?" says Foolish.

"Yeah." Mario throws some money in Foolish's lap and sits down on the steps beside him. "They clean guns?"

"Yeah, fam," says Foolish.

"I got to bounce. Where my shit at?"

"In the doorway," Foolish gestures behind him.

"Cool." Mario goes to the door and grabs the bag. He peers inside it to inspect the mags. "Now this is what the fuck I'm talkin' about," he says. "This will make niggas lay the fuck down." He walks toward the Regal, then stops. "T.C., you rolling or what?"

"Here I come, fam. I'll get with you, Foolish," he says. "Be safe."

It's about time he left so I can do my shit. Foolish walks back into the house to post up and dump work.

T.C. shuts the car door and Mario pulls off toward Broadway and Twenty-sixth Avenue North. "Skud, you know them crabs and slobs are waiting for real," he says.

"Shit, from what I hear, fam, them crabs are demolishing they ass. They're lacking the skills to put the murder game down, and have failed to do what is required," says Mario.

"What's that, Mario?"

"Pay us to make them crab niggas cease to exist. Open up that bag on the back seat, T.C."

"I know what's in that bag," T.C. says. "So what's your point, Mario?"

"Nothin', cuz." Mario pulls into the station on Twenty-sixth and Penn Avenue North, then drives out the other side of the lot to avoid a squad car that's pulling in. "That was close, skud. Let me drop these off at the trap first, fam, then we can move around. It's too fuckin hot to roll."

"I feel you on that note," T.C. agrees.

Mario parks in front of 2608 Bryant Avenue North, grabs the black bag and dips into the spot. Tyrell walks out the door to get into the car with T.C. They wait for Mario to come out so they can go get their minds right. "Fam, what it do, T.C.?" he asks.

"Shit, dog, I need me one in me, fam," says T.C.

"Me too, skud. Mario needs to come on," Tyrell says.

"Here he come. Who got that piss Tyrell?"

"Jug or B.J.," replies Tyrell.

"Now, what the fuck you niggas want to do," asks Mario as he shuts the door.

"Blow."

"Hit B.J. up."

"Tyrell, I owe Jug a C-note from yesterday," says Mario.

They pull off into traffic. A fiend stops the car at the corner. "Hey, hey, hold up," he says. "I got two

hundred and fifty. What up, Mario?

"I got a teen on me," T.C. breaks in.

"And I got the rest," says Mario. They serve the dope fiend and push on.

"Now I got some play money, Mario. Sticks on me, skud."

"I already got a pack of Moore squares," says Tyrell.

"Who in the spot, Mario, while we gone?" asks T.C.

"Lonny, fam."

"It's only about forty-two ones left. We need some more work."

"Mario, let's go get my K-5 to move around in, so we can bump while we chase hoes, skud," suggests

T.C.

"B.J. said meet him up at the 200 in ten minutes," says Tyrell from the back seat, "and I got triple stacks

on me, too."

"We good then fam?" says Mario.

Twenty-four inches off the ground,
That's how you feel.
A young nigga selling forty by the pound,
That's how you feel.

Young Jeezy blares out of the stereo system as Ghost packs for his trip down South. "Shaunna, where is my Gucci shades at, baby?"

"I already packed all of our stunna shades, boo. Calm down, nigga," she yells up the stairs.

"That's why I love you," he answers. "Real talk."

"Come downstairs, Ghost. Jay's here," she shouts.

"Looks like y'all about to bounce on a trip, sis," I say.

"Ask your brother," she says.

"Tell him to come on up," Ghost yells down.

"I can hear you, scud," I say.

"Then get your sprung ass on up, lame."

I walk up the stairs slowly to annoy Ghost some more. "I'm in the guest room," he says. I jump into the doorway to find Ghost pointing a Tech-9 at me.

"Never second-guess your instincts, dog," he says.

"'Til I die, bounty hunter. Blood for life," I answer. "I can see some-one is already started early."

"Call it what you want, dog. I demand respect," my brother says.

"Whatever," I shrug.

He lowers the gun. "Shut the door, Jay. Sit down, dog. Look, I'm about to go see my connect. He just got out of prison. He's not out for another two days, but you might as well say he out now. I have to bounce back to Little Rock to hook up with him. So I need you to go see Nina, get what I have over there and make that happen. I've already sent her a text message to be looking out for you, son. It should be twenty-five bricks over there. Keep half for yourself.

"I don't know how long I'll be gone. So you can crash over here until I get back. Don't bring every bitch you want to fuck over here. This is my safe home, you understand me?"

"Fo sho, big bro. Now quit with the lecture and pass that dip, yo."

"I'm counting on you, lil bro, to handle your business, skud," Ghost says as he passes the stick.

Downstairs, Lacy walks through the front door. "Shaunna, I need for you to pay for my cab," she says.

"Bitch, where your money at?" Shaunna asks impatiently. "I know he hit you off real proper." She grabs a fifty-dollar bill out of her purse and hands it to Lacy. "Do it yourself," she says. "I'm busy. We have to talk, too," she says.

Lacy walks out the door to pay the cabbie and returns with shop-ping bags full of clothes. "Grab the other bags off of the porch for me, girl," she says to Shaunna.

"Shit, you a fuckin' hand full, Lacy," says her older sister.

"Bitch, quit playing like I didn't learn it from your ass." Lacy sits down on the couch, kicks her shoes off and falls back into the cushions. "Is Ghost cool now?"

"Yeah, he straight, but don't try to fuck up my shit no more, girl," Shaunna warns. "I love that man. He's all that I've ever had to really love me, Lacy. I need him. Do you understand that?" She sits down next to Lacy to touch her healed face.

"I would be dumb to not know that, girl. Ghost is my big brother I never had. I didn't mean to upset him or make him go off on me," Lacy says contritely. "You know, sometimes I act with the foolish boldness of our stubborn, persistent ways."

"Shit, he's the only other person who's got a high tolerance when it comes to you, Lacy, besides Mom and Dad," Shaunna points out.

"I know. I'll be more respectful towards him."

"Thank you, girl. Lacy, the game is over that we was playing with them," Shaunna says as she gets up to grab two champagne glasses from the bar and a bottle of Ace champagne. She hands Lacy a glass and sits down and pops the cork. Champagne spills out onto the coffee table. Shaunna jumps up to get a towel to clean the table.

"What you mean, Shaunna, by that?" Lacy asks.

Shaunna finishes wiping up the table and pours each of them a drink. "This shit is way the fuck out of hand now."

Lacy tilts her head and gives her a quizzical look.

"Them days you been up at the Hilton, them Crip niggas been putting in some major work on the 30s, girl."

Lacy plays with her tongue, thinking about Ghost about to fall.

"Girl, put that fleshy muscular organ back into your head before you burn me or something," Shaunna says.

"Fuck you, bitch. You jealous."

Shaunna continues, "So we need to quit while we're ahead. You feel me?"

"Okay, Shaunna. Whatever you say." Lacy lies back and puts her feet in Shaunna's lap and relaxes. "Men are easily controlled," she observes. "Such a tragedy to stop now when I was having fun."

"Listen, girl, we're leaving for Little Rock tonight, so be good here with Jay. I have to finish packing." Shaunna gets up to go to the bedroom. Lacy falls asleep on the couch.

"Ghost, why you listening to this crab-ass nigga?" I ask.

"'Cause he want to be a Blood, that's why. He's confused. And I like his music, dog," Ghost says.

"Man, them high street bitches I used to fuck with live up here, too," I tell my brother.

"Nah, quit playing," he says.

"No bullshit," I return. "Tasha stay over on Twenty-sixth and Bryant Avenue North."

Ghost leans forward. "That's the block I'm about to take over," he says. "It will be just like old times for me. I have to come by to get some of Dorothy's fine ass."

"She got a nigga, fam," I warn.

"So what? That don't stop no bitch from fucking, Jay," Ghost points out.

I nod. "You right about that shit, bro."

"We're a desired goal for any bitch, son."

Ghost gets up and pulls his sleeves up, revealing a fifty-carat brace-let on each writs, then pulls his fifty-carat diamond chain from under his shirt to lay flat on his chest. "One hundred and fifty carats. That means one hundred and fifty reasons a bitch know I'm a boss player in this game, Jay."

"Look, Ghost, we been in this room for hours, doing nothing."

We walk toward the door. Suddenly, Ghost turns around, looks me straight in the eye and says, "Scud, we play for big stakes. Never be spurious, fam." Then he staggers out the door.

I walk behind him to make sure he doesn't fall down the stairs. "I'm fixing to go holler at Nina right now, so I got to bounce, scud," I whisper to him. Ghost gives a nod of approval.

I don't notice Lacy asleep on the couch, but Ghost does. He squats beside her head and squeezes her cheek together, like you would do to an adorable child. Lacy wakes up and sees Ghost by her, speaking with involuntary pauses and repetitious apologies to her. Then he falls face first into the carpet. The weed and the sticks he and I just shared put him in a deep sleep.

Chapter 16

The Bronco comes to a stop at a house on Twenty-ninth and Penn Avenue North. I feel paranoid and look around the block to make sure no one is following me. I shake it off. *Fuck that shit. We doing it big, yo. The only bad true dreams I can have is living the night life 'til the pigs come and get me.*

I get out of the Bronco and walk to the back door, where Nina meets me. "It's about time you got here, sexy," she says. "Come on in."

I get an eyeful of her ass as she turns to walk into the house. The wet and the blunts are kicking in full force now, but I have to focus. This is business, not pleasure.

"Have a seat, Jay. I'll be right with you. Do you want something to drink?"

"Yeah, shorty," I answer.

""Make yourself at home and get what you want. This is your spot, too, so don't be shy." She gestures toward the refrigerator.

"Okay, thank you."

She disappears downstairs. *Shit, them jeans are full to the max.* I grab a MGD out of the icebox, twist the top off and gulp down the whole brew, all the while standing next to open icebox door.

"How long are you in town," asks Nina as she comes up the stairs.

"I'm young and restless, so I don't know yet," I say. "But I will tell you I like Minneapolis already, shorty."

"Here's fifteen bricks," Nina says, getting down to business. "I sold ten sticks to my people down in Duluth for a lick, so there's two hundred thousand in there, too. I got my forty thousand already, so you good, sexy."

"Damn, you a true hustler, ma," I say, somewhat surprised. *It's hard to suck up to somebody, when it comes from a bitch.* I study her closely, contemplating her making major moves like that.

"Money's my game. You smell me, playboy? It's a concrete jungle out here. Feel me."

"Yeah, I feel you," I say. I sit down at the table and look through the duffle bag to confirm what's in it.

"I trap to survive, Jay," Nina says.

"I can dig it," I answer. "It's true life out there, ma."

"Shorty, you ain't got to tell me about coming from nothing, because I know," she says. "We can do things together."

"I'm still new to these sticks," I point out. "I'm lost in these streets like a fiend on a glass pipe."

"Look, shit, Jay, this square is ours. This is where we eat, so don't trip you straight. I've been having bad vibes lately, ain't nothing sweet about it," Nina says.

"What you mean?" I ask.

"Just that my neighbor told me that a strange dude been parking on the side street lately. I got me a strap, but I'm only a woman."

"I got you, ma. I'll make it a personal favor from me to you to look out and check on you every day," I pledge.

"I would like that," she says simply.

"I got to bounce."

"Stay in touch."

I get up from the table and head for the door. Nina grabs my left hand and puts it on her ass and shakes it. "Come back so we can play," she entices. My other head says *Play now. Fuck later at the touch of her soft ass cheek. Keep your mind on your money, pimp. Fuck her later.*

"Call me," Nina says.

"I will."

I walk out of the house with the duffle bag on my shoulder and a hard dick in my pants. I jump into the truck, open up my cell and call Tasha. "What up, Tasha?"

"Shit, boy, where you at?" she responds.

"I'm on my way over there now, so be looking out for me in the back."

"Okay," she says. "One."

> *Bun-B,*
> *I'm a G*
> *You don't know about me*
> *But you ass gone learn*
> *And yo ass gone see*

bumps out of the system in the Bronco as I turn the corner to go down to Tasha's house not Nina's house. Everyone I pass feels the bass coming out of the truck. Windows shake on houses, other cars' rear-view mirrors vibrate on the side or in back of me. Hood rats throw up their heads and drop them like it's hot to see me. I cruise like the Don of the road and pay them no mind. I reach for the remote to add volume so the stereo blasts more as I approach Twenty-sixth and Bryant.

"Damn, T.C., you hear that bass?" asks Mario.

"Yeah, it feels like it's in this truck."

I hit the corner and all eyes are on me. T.C., Mario and Tyrell become briskly alive at the sight and sound of the strange Bronco coming down their hood block. "You strapped?" asks Tyrell.

"Nah, scud, I left them in the spot," replies Mario. "Let's get back to our customary activities."

"What's that?"

"Blowing."

"Now that's a fundamental element by itself! Come on, son. Look at Lonny in the window, fiending and shit."

They forget all about the strange Bronco and go into their spot.

Tasha observes me closely as I back up into the driveway. As I put the truck into park, I recognize the look on Tasha's face that says, "turn that shit down." I grab the remote, cut off the stereo system and wave for Tasha to come join me in the truck.

"Hey, boy. What I do?" I say.

"Shit," says Tasha as she climbs in to the passenger seat and shuts the door. "Jay, you so damn reckless. Do you ever consider what I go through when you clown?"

"Fuck that shit," I say. "Look into the bag on the back seat, and then talk shit."

Tasha reaches back and unzips the duffle bag and smiles.

"Look, Tasha, the Great Recessions is over. We good now. Just like old times, ya hear?"

"Who?" she asks.

"Don't ask questions, just listen. I need you to comprehend the situation completely. I've got a connect, so we can obtain bricks for a nice profit. I recognize from past experiences and acknowledge that you're the only person that I can trust," I say. "I love you, Tasha, like my sister. We've been through a lot together. Plus, you're the only other person I know is as extremely hungry as I am."

She interrupts. "You got some smoke, Jay?"

"Yeah, in the glove box. Roll up."

"Jay," Tasha says, you've always stood for ethical standards in my book. She breaks up the dro on a CD case. "Boy, just don't start living recklessly and extravagant on me."

I grab the duffle bag off the seat. We walk to the back door. I look around and say to Tasha as she licks the blunt closed, "I have to take possession of this block before another. Our squad will dominate this part of town, girl."

The door shuts and we walk down the stairs to her room. "Take one brick for yourself, and give A.D. one, too. I'm going to bounce in a minute, but I'll be back tomorrow to make some moves. Here, take this pocket change." I hand her three thousand dollars.

"Thanks, bro. You my heart."

"I need twenty thousand a brick," I tell her.

"Cool."

"Keep the blunt for yourself, Tasha. I got to be somewhere. Holla."

Damn, I'm ready to get off. "I'm going to step outside and suck a cigarette," Nicki says to her co-worker, Tom.

"Okay. I'll cover for you."

"Thank you." *Shit, I can finally blow me a premo and wind down.*

A customer on his way into the store and courteously holds the door for Nicki to exit. Nicki goes to stand by the air pump, pulls out her lighter, and puts fire to the premo. She takes a strong pull of smoke. *I need to call Mom and tell her I got a ride tonight. I'm kind of captivated with Jay's smile. And I'm fascinated with his swagger, too.* She takes another pull of the premo and drops the rest on the pavement and steps on it. *I hope he can hang with my rhythmic flow and movements in bed,* she thinks as she walks back to the store. She giggles at the thought of them fucking in her waterbed.

"Thank God you're back, Nicki. The phone has been off the hook and the line is getting long as hell," Tom says as she walks through the door.

"I got it, Tom," she says. "Is this all for you, sir?"

"Let me get two packs of Newport shorts and your phone number," the customer says.

"I have a man, but thank you for your attention," she replies sweetly. "Your total is $22.15, sir." He hands over twenty-five dollars and walks away. "Your change —" she yells after him.

"Keep it, shorty. You're too cute to be working here."

"Nicki, your mother is on line one," shouts Tom.

"Thank you. I got it," she shouts back. "Hey, Mom," she says into the phone.

"You sound busy," her mother says.

"I am, but I can talk to you. I was going to call you anyway to let you know I got a ride tonight."

"Who?"

"A friend, ma."

"Do I know him?"

"I don't think so. Hold on, Mom." She gives a customer his total. "It's $6.75. Will there be anything else? Mom, I have to go."

"Okay, baby. Call me."

"I will."

A group of guys come into the store, noisy and acting unrestrained and rowdy. Tom asks them to please lower their voices. The leader of the group gives Tom a cruel, murderous look and walks over to him and spits in his face.

The boldness of the action shocks Nicki. Tom wipes the spit off of his face and wishes he'd never made such a stupid mistake. He tries to return to his office, but the group blocks his path and denies him access. "I don't want any trouble, guys. I'm sorry for bothering you," he says.

I pull up to the gas pumps outside and start filling the tank. Nicki doesn't see me. I walk through the door and see Nicki with an agitated look on her face. "Hey, baby, you good," I say to try to break the mood she's in.

"Nah, look," she manages to croak out. I survey the situation.

"I got you," I tell her. "Yo, fam," I say to the group, "what's good?"

"Cuz, mind your business," says the leader.

"You my business now," I reply. I walk closer to the crowd. The younger kid in the crowd starts to blow violently, walking toward me. I lift my shirt to show him I'm packing and say, "Crab, I'm a biohazard to your health if you don't bounce. And watch your mouth, punk-ass nigga." I step between Tom and the gangbangers.

"Come on, cuz. Let's dip."

"I thought so, hoe-ass niggas," I say scornfully. They all look back at me to get a good look for future reference. Nicki comes from behind the counter to hug and thank me. "I didn't know you worked here, shorty," I say to her.

"You know him, Nicki?" asks Tom.

She nods. "Yeah."

"Thank you, umm . . ." He offers his hand.

"I'm Jay, and you're welcome."

"I'm off in ten minutes," Nicki tells me. "You might as well hang out."

"Okay. Let me get fifty dollars on Pump 1. I'll pump my gas, then pull up by the door." I walk out and find the gang of boys standing at the corner selling weed. As I pull the nozzle out of the tank to pump the gas, I notice one of the boys creeping up on me from the other side of the truck. I leave the gas pumping and pull out the Mag. I meet him with the strap pointed at his face.

"My bad, big homie," he apologizes. "I just wanted to know if you want to buy some smoke."

"Nah, I'm cool, fam."

The boy runs away.

These crab niggas got a fuckin' death wish. I finish pumping the gas and pull up to the door. Nicki comes out as soon as I park.

Chapter 17

Two months later, some of the heat on the street has died down. Everyone is back to business as usual. I think.

"I think I've made a good prognosis of this block, Tasha. We must keep all of our new workers on the probation thing until we're certain that they won't procrastinate on us." I pour myself a Bombay as we count hundred-dollar bills in the basement.

"I feel you, Jay. We've given these niggas a special immunity and benefit by putting them on." She stands up, showing her butt cheeks in her small thong with a very short skirt covering it. She walks over and hands me the blunt she just rolled. She looks at me through narrowed eyes. "What you looking at, boy?"

"Shit, your pussy is fatter than a motherfucker, Tasha."

"I don't want you, boy," she reminds me. "So quit tripping."

"Girl, you have so much potential on the body side that I didn't realize it until now," I say as I pull on the blunt. "Shake that ass, Tasha."

"Boy, you tripping."

"Nah, you tripping with all that ass and ain't gave me none yet. Shit." The liquor and the weed take over both of us. Tasha shakes her ass for me as she walks over to the basement door and locks it. The she turns around and pulls her short shirt over head to reveal perfect, erect nipples. Walking slowly up to me, she comes out of her thong, saying, "You want some of this pussy, don't you?"

"Yes."

Tasha drops to the floor, turns around and makes her ass clap together like a born stripper hoe. "What a magnificent display," I say appreciatively. "Tasha, quit playing with my emotions and come and sit down on this dick." I pull down my pants and kick them off across the room. *This is capable of happening, existing and being accomplished right now.*

Tasha walks over and grabs my dick. She bends down to run her tongue over the head to puzzle and bewilder my mind. The she stands up, grabs a firm hold of my dick and squats over me, rubbing my dick head slowly against her wet pussy. She looks me straight in the eye.

"Ooh, ooh. Shit, Tasha," I say.

"No talking, Jay. This is a bonus and a benefit in addition to our regular relationship as friends, Jay." She sticks the head into her wetness and stops there, squeezing the head with her pussy muscles as tight as she can. She lets go of her grip on my dick to savor the feeling, throwing her head back and biting her lower lip. "Yesssss . . . Uhhhh . . . Jay, you're so thick, and hard and long, baby! Shit, boy . . . . mm-mmhhhh . . . This feels so good right here."

I grab the arms of the chair and whisper in her ear, "I want this to last forever or for an indefinitely long time, Tasha."

"Me, too, baby."

Our faces show genuine lust as they engage in casual and frivolous lovemaking. A powerful emotion, plus desire, shoots through Tasha's body and she accepts the feeling without resistance. She sits down all the way on my dick. She speaks in low, indistinct tones, "Don't nut in me, baby."

Tasha puts her hand over my mouth to muffle my moans so nobody hears us. She hears footsteps coming down the stairs and slicks up very, very slowly off of me. She gives me a look that tells me it's an absolute requirement that we finish up later.

A tap on the door makes us scramble for our clothes. "Who's there?" Tasha calls.

"A.D., T.C. at the door for Jay," comes the answer.

"I'll be there. Hold up," I yell up the steps.

"Cool. Yo."

We get dressed and walk to the door that leads upstairs. Tasha turns to unlock the door. I press my body against hers and kiss the back of her neck. "That pussy is so tight, baby. I'm in love."

"Come on, boy. We got T.C. waiting outside." We stroll up the stairs hand in hand, but let go when Tasha opens the back door to see T.C. sitting on the steps.

"'Sup, Joe?" T.C. asks as he gets up from the steps to shake hands with me and throw up the rakes. "Hey, Tasha."

"What it do, T.C.?" she responds.

"I'm good, homegirl. I seen the truck back here so I stopped to holla at you, fam, for a minute."

"I got some shit to speak on. Let's bounce for a second, scud. I'll be over later, Tasha," I say.

"I bet you will," she answers. "So bring me something to eat when you come."

"Cool."

T.C. and I jump into the Bronco. I grab the CD case and put Young Buck in the CD player. "I know you gone let shine and get mine" issues from the speakers. We pull out of the alley and onto Twenty-sixth Avenue North, then make a right turn.

"What's on your mind, scud?" I ask T.C. as we cruise along.

"My nigga mario got a spot on Willow, right behind Broadway, close to Penn. I think you can make a lot of doe over there, scud. His sister lives there and she with making it a spot, so let's go holla at them real quick, fam."

"You vouch for him, dog?" I ask cautiously.

"Oh, yeah, that's my nigga. He good, scud."

"So if some shit go down, you gone put his ass down, fam?"

"Fo sho, my dude. Turn left here on Logan Avenue and keep straight," he directs.

I turn to look at him. "T.C., I'm willing to take the risks on your guy for financial profits."

T.C. smiles. "Pull over right here, fam. We don't need your truck parked in front of the spot, Joe."

We get out of the truck a block up the street and walk to the house. Two women are sitting on the porch as we walk up. "What up, T.C.?" they ask.

"Nothing," he replies. "This my nigga, Jay."

"Nice to meet you, Jay. I'm Tasha and this Rita."

"Cool," I say.

"That your truck over there?" she points to the Bronco.

"Yeah, it ain't shit, though."

She gives me a peculiar look up and down to express her interest.

"Let me go up and grab fam so we can dip, Jay," says T.C.

"Okay."

"You got a woman, Jay?" Tyson asks.

"Nah."

"Where you from?"

"Little Rock, Arkansas."

"For real." Tyson's mouth curves up like she finds my former residence amusing. Rita shows a smirk and smacks her lips to make a sharp sound. I look at both of them and think they look secretive, underhanded and very hood. I exhale a long, deep breath while I wait for T.C. to return.

"Sit down, baby. We don't bite unless you want us to, sugar," Tyson pats the sofa cushion next to her.

"I'm good."

"I think he's try to avoid us deliberately," says Rita.

"Nah, I just need the ability to see my truck, that's all, lil mama." *Shit, these two hoes are making me feel nauseated and disgusted with their asses. I need to get back to Tasha's ass and finish. I never looked at her in a sexual way before. My dick was so tight in that pussy, like a circular band worn on a finger.*

I'm still daydreaming about fucking Tasha when T.C. and Mario come downstairs. "Come on, scud, we ready,"T.C. says. "Damn, scud, you daydreaming like a motherfucker, fam." He pats my shoulder.

"My bad," I apologize.

"'Bye, Jay. Come back to see me," says Tyson.

"Take care," I answer.

We pile into the truck and head off to talk business. I pull into the downtown pay parking lot across the street from Murray's Steak House under the Civic Center. "You guys hungry?" I ask.

"Shit, yeah," answers T.C. enthusiastically.

"Well, we're going to go to Murray's and sit down and chill and eat for a second." I roll down the truck window and push the button on the machine to get a parking ticket. I find a space at the end of the first floor and park.

As we walk across the street, T.C. gives Mario a quick nod at the sight of Killer Boy, Murder Mac and Ike coming our way.

"Three today, sir?" asks the maître d'.

"Yes. No smoking, please."

"Right this way, gentlemen."

As we're being seated, The door opens up and Killer Boy, Ike and Murder Mac enter the restaurant loudly. Suddenly, feels Mario accountable for my safety. He gives T.C. a cold-blooded vertebrate look, like a snake about to attack.

"A waitress will be right with you, sir." We're seated in a booth in the back of the establishment.

I say thank-you and the maître d' bustles off to attend other customers. "It's evident that some kind of situation can increase or intensify quickly," I say as I follow to where Mario's eyes are focused.

"Nah, scud. That's them Family Cartel cats and them Shotgun Crip niggas over there at the other side of the room," Mario replies. "We good, though, 'cause I've got my .45 Colt on me, scud. Them niggas has been at war with them slob cats, dog. Me and Murder Mac go way back, fam, and Ike. So we straight, Jay."

"Who are the other two?" I ask.

"Rich. I don't know the other dude."

A waitress comes up and asks, "Gentlemen, would you like to order any drinks? My name is Vanessa and I'm your server today. Ooh, how are you doing, Mr. Baker?"

"Fine. And you, sweetie?"

"I'm okay, I guess."

"Let's get a bottle of Ace and three double shots of Bombay," I tell her.

"Coming right up, Mr. Baker." She leaves quickly to retrieve the orders.

"Now, let's get down to the matter at hand, shall we, fellas?"

"This is the guy I was telling you about," T.C. says, indicating Mario.

I'm in a state of perplexity and uncertainly as I look at Mario across the table from me. I'm not sure where he fits into the picture.

Vanessa comes back and sets down the bottle of Ace in a bucket of ice, then places a double shot of Bombay in front of each of us. "Are you guys ready to order?"

"We will all have the steak and shrimp dinner, thank you, Vanessa." She departs for the kitchen.

"Jay, he's my other half," explains T.C. "He's the reason that I've been flipping them bricks the way I have."

"Look, fam, the quality of product that you have is the best that my people have had in a long time, and it's made my money grow," says Mario. "I don't hit my shit, fam."

"I have no doubt about that, scud, but I need a considerable amount to make moves the way I need to. Feel me. It's questionable and I'm uncertain about you. Why or what makes me know you're straight, scud?"

Mario picks up his Bombay and takes a sip. He sits back, very quiescent.

Vanessa returns with our food. "Enjoy, fellas," I say. "Now you're part of the squad, but I will be taking preparatory measures before I give you a stock of necessary supplies. I have one stipulation."

"What's that?"

"Bring me Murder Mac."

"Why?"

"I need to establish the truth about something." T.C. sends a curious look my way. "This is a very practical matter with my people," I explain. "Do this, and it will show your bravery and resourcefulness to me."

"Done," says Mario. "That's what I do, scud. I roam in stealth at night in search of my prey, fam. This will be done without delay for you, Jay."

"This steak is the bomb, yo," says T.C.

"I'm full, scud. Let's bounce," I say. I throw up my hand to call Vanessa with the check.

"Will that be all, sir?"

"Yes, Vanessa."

"Here's your check, Mr. Baker. Four hundred twenty-six dollars and thirty-eight cents." I lay six hundred dollars on the table. She picks up the check and the money. "Thank you, Mr. Baker."

"Don't mind it. You're my special server."

As we rise from the table, Mario says, "I won't charge you no fee for this one 'cause he's not a soldier of low rank, and that will shatter Family Cartel's stronghold on the South Side."

"This was likely to happen sooner or later," chimes in T.C., "by how many slobs he shot a couple months ago."

"Good. It's settled then," I say. "But bring him to me alive. Take him to this address on the North Side, and call me when you're on your way."

"I got you, fam," replies Mario.

Now I can find out what my brother needs to know and kill Murder Mac in the process. I got a killer, a gangster, and I'm the dope dealer/killer. My squad is complete now.

We walk across the street to the truck. My cell phone vibrates as we reach the parking garage. Nicki shows up on the screen. We all get into the Bronco and shut the doors. I start the truck, then flip open my cell phone. "Hey, love," I say.

"Where are you at, boo?" Nicki asks in an arrogant and influential manner. I pull up to the booth to pay for parking.

I'm evasive. "Just finishing up some things."

"It's almost time for us to go to the movies, Jay," she pouts.

"I'm on my way right now, baby. Can you iron my black Sean Jean long sleeve shirt and pants, ma?"

"I got you," she says. "Just come on! I miss you, baby, and I want you to fuck me before we leave."

"Now, that's daddy's little girl that I know. Give me about twenty minutes, Nicki."

"Hurry up," she says.

"Baby, pull the BMW out of the garage for me."

"I already did."

"One."

I flip the phone closed and look at Mario in the rearview mirror. *I might have to lay his ass down.*

"Hey, T.C., let's get dropped off at Tyrell's house, fam. I got to do something real quick over there, fam." He gives me an address on Thirtieth Avenue and Fourth Street North.

Chapter 18

I drop T. C. and Mario off, then head to Twenty-ninth and Jefferson Avenue North. It's one of my houses, where Nicki lives. I pull in front of the house and see Drake coming out the front door, smiling from ear to ear until he sees me parked behind his Lexus coupe. *This nigga is a born trick if I ever seen one.* I put an "I know" smile on my face as Drake walks up to the truck window to speak with me.

"What up, Jay? Shit, big timer."

I open up the door to get out. Drake moves out of the way just in time.

"Damn that BMW 74 is colder than a motherfucker right there, son," says Drake. "It's cool, yo. When you gone get out this late model truck, Jay?" He doesn't realize the BMW is mine.

"I have, scud." I walk over to the BMW and get inside and offer Drake to come check it out.

"Man, I got money to get, yo," Drake says. "I'll holla at you, son."

I get out of the BMW and walk to the front door. I can feel Drake staring a hole through the back of my head.

A painful emotion caused by a sense of guilt and unworthiness comes over Drake. He knows I'm going to be with the woman he wants. "Fuck Jay," he says as he pulls off. *That nigga is about to have a violent surprise and an emotional upset fucking with that bitch.*

I walk into the bedroom and feel a sense of complete disorder with Nicki. She's bent over in the closet, picking out a set of Jimmy Choo heels to wear. "Oh, hey, baby, I didn't know you were here," she says. I give her a questioning look and she opens up her robe to try to seduce me into sexual intercourse. My close examination of her body is interrupted by the doorbell.

"I'll get it, Nicki, you get dressed." As I walk to the front door, I begin to feel like this is a fraudulent business deal, and I begin to analyze it more. Betty strolls out of the kitchen at the same time.

"Hi, Mom," I say. "I'll get it, Mom."

"No, have a seat, Jay. I got it."

I sit down and wrinkle my face in anger at the thought of the public disgrace, outrage, and shame this could bring to my image if Drake is fucking Nicki, too.

"It's Tony, Jay," Betty announces.

"Scud, what's the deal," Tony says, breaking into my train of thought. "Shit, yo." He sits down and Betty returns to the kitchen to finish cooking.

"You guys hungry?" shouts Betty.

"We good," I tell her.

Tony studies me closely. "Scud, you look like you want to simultaneously discharge your firearm, son. You know, give lead showers, fam."

I give him a weary smile. "I'm good, fam. So what's the deal, Ton?"

"What you got available for me to purchase?" Tony asks as he leans back on the couch.

"My nigga, you know for you, I'm offering goods at a lowered price for you, dog. I got three bricks right now for you for eighteen thousand a brick, scud."

"I'll take all of them right now," Tony says as he pulls out a bag of purple haze and sets it on the coffee table in front of me. "Jay, I knew it would be very beneficial to fuck with you, fam."

"Pull your car into the back, scud," I say.

Tony gets up from the couch and stops by the kitchen to say, "Betty, you can roll up if you want to. It's on the coffee table."

"Okay, baby. Nicki, help me out," Betty shouts.

"I'll do it, Mom," Nicki shouts back.

I walk down to the basement to put three bricks in a school back-pack. I walk back up through the kitchen, tucking a .44 Magnum in the back of my pants. "Be careful, baby," says Betty.

"I'm good, Mom."

Tony pulls into the backyard backwards as I walk out of the door. I open up the car door and Tony says, "Never put the Lil D brown sugar before the white cream, baby boy, 'cause that hard white will get you straight cash."

I throw the backpack on the back seat with the triple beam scale and sit down and shut the door. "Scud, let's blow one back here 'cause you know Mom don't let us blow in the crib, yo."

"That's what I need, too, fam." He dips two Moore squares and passes one to me.

"Roll up your window, Tony, to keep the smoke in the car. You know it's two state troopers that stay next door, and they're gay. We don't need no attention right now, either, scud."

In the house, Nicki yells, "Mom, this some fire shit. Come smell it real quick." Before Betty comes into the room, Nicki stashes three grams into a piece of paper to smoke later with premos. *I'm good now with the zone I took out of them keys at work,* she thinks as she licks the blunt closed.

Betty walks into the living room and sits down on the couch be-side Nicki. She can tell her daughter's been smoking crack by the look in her eyes, but says nothing because Nicki said she quit and Betty doesn't feel like arguing right now. "Fire up, Nicki," she says.

Nicki takes the lighter out of her back pocket and lights the blunt. She takes a heavy pull off of it without coughing. She pulls in a lot of smoke, then exhales slowly. Betty reaches for the blunt, takes a small pull, then says, between puffs, "You know how especially fond I am of Jay, but I know Drake is Marc's

friend and you mess with him, too. But I like Jay, Nicki. I think he treats you like a lady and is very respectful towards you. And me, for that matter." She passes the blunt back to Nicki.

"Well, ma, that might be a seemingly contradictory statement that may nonetheless be true."

Betty puts on a theatrical performance for Nicki as she gets up to go check the food. She uses motions and gestures rather than speech. Nicki thinks about what will happen if Jay finds out about all of her secrets. An unpleasant, hurting feeling arises from inside. She puts out the blunt and walks to the back door to see if Jay is still back there.

"Mom, I didn't know Tony was back there," she says.

"Yeah, that's who left the sack to smoke," says Betty.

"Damn, I forgot to iron my baby's clothes. Excuse me, Mom, for a second, please."

Tony and I are getting into a serious discussion. "Look, Joe, I met this nigga named Mario today. Do you know of him?"

"Look, fam, I know the lil nigga, and let me be the first one to tell you he's not truthful, and he's not trustworthy to be fuckin' with you, son, on no level. Look, he be with some niggas named T.C. and Tyrell. All them niggas do is gangbang and jack."

"E.B.K., son, on any cat who fucks with me. I do or die 24/7 and I'm ready to blast when I have to."

"I feel you, scud, but watch that lil sneaky ass nigga, Joe."

"Now let me go so I can do me."

"Reach under your seat," says Tony. "There's sixty thousand dollars there, so I'm six thousand with you, Joe."

"No doubt." I grab the grocery bag and head for the house. "Hit me up later, Ton, so we can take care of something."

"I got you fam."

I'm greeted by the pleasant smell of fried chicken as I walk back into the house. "Mom, that smells so good!"

Betty smiles. "You want a piece, baby?"

"Just one, if it's okay."

"Sure, it's okay, son-in-law." She hands me a leg and I take a bite.

"Mmmmmm. Now that's very good."

Betty gestures toward a chair. "Sit down for a second, baby." It's clear she wants to talk about something. I'm just finishing my chicken leg when Sean appears in the doorway.

"Jay," he says, "smoke with me and I'll match you."

"Okay. Let me speak to Mom first."

Betty waves me off. "Nah, baby, go ahead and I'll talk to you later."

"You sure, Mom?"

"Yes," she answers. "Don't smoke it all before I get through cooking, now."

I walk into the living room and motion to Sean to light up his blunt and roll one out of the bag on the table. Then I open up the basement door and go downstairs to put the money away. When I come back upstairs, I find Nicki, Sean and L.G. puffing away on three blunts. "Come over and sit down, baby." Nicki pats the cushion on the couch beside her.

I pull the .44 Magnum out from behind my back and lay it on the coffee table. "I got some Belvedere in my truck," I say as I sit down.

"I'll grab it," L.G. says with a grin. I toss him my keys. "I'll be right back." He hits the alarm on the truck, opens up the driver's side door, and hears my cell phone vibrating in the console. He looks at the caller ID and sees Pookie on the screen. A sly smile comes over his face as he grabs the vodka off the back seat. He heads back to the house without activating the Bronco's alarm.

"I need to take a nap, Nicki, real quick," I tell her.

"Okay, go in my room and shut the door, baby."

"Wake me in a couple of hours, then we can dip, baby." I walk to the bedroom, high on wet.

L.G. sees me enter the bedroom. "Shit, girl, that nigga frosty, caked the fuck up." He turns excitedly to Sean. "That damn BMW out there got dark blue candy paint on it, limo tint like the president's car, twenty-four-inch Dub X-wangs on it, with low-profile Falken tires.

Nicki, that shit alone cost a fuckin' grip, don't it, Sean?" He passes Nicki the keys to the truck and reaches for the blunt.

"Hell, yeah," says Sean. "But you forgot the custom leather seats made out of Prada with his initials on them, Alpine CD player, the TV screen that comes out, plus two TVs in the headrests. To top it all off, he got six twelve-inch Memphis Competition subs back there."

"Nicki, let's go for a ride," says L.G. "It's in your name, and he sleeping. Come on, Nicki, let's go floss. That punk-ass coupe Drake got can't fuck with the 745."

"You need to leave that trick-ass nigga alone anyway. He got too many kids already. Shit," says Sean.

"But that nigga buys me any and everything I want when I want it," Nicki protests. She crosses her legs to get more comfortable on the couch.

"Little sister, I've heard on the street how that nigga Jay's doing it, and let me tell you, Drake ain't in his fuckin' league. Yes, true enough, Nicki, that nigga Drake got money. But look, he rents that Lexus and every other luxury car he drives. Now compare that to owning a 745 plus a '89 Ford Bronco tricked out with custom shit, too," says L.G.

"Listen, to top it off," he continues, "he pays Mom's mortgage, and gives us weed, too. Look at your twenty-carat chain with diamonds in it. It's clear that he is trying to provide a sumptuous environment and lifestyle for you and us, and that's clear, sis."

"I can see the crazy desire in your eyes every time you see him or someone says his name around you, Nicki," says Sean.

Nicki makes a sudden forward movement to put out the blunt. "Listen," she says. "My feelings for Jay are growing very abundantly and faster than I wanted them to, I must admit. When we are together, I feel an intense affectionate concern for him."

"You love him, don't you?" asks Betty.

"Yes, Mom, I do. He's beautiful, enjoyable, and delightful, all at the same time."

"Well, then make it official, baby. Go with your heart," says Betty. "He's been living here with us for about two months now, and I love him like a son already, Nicki. He's so sweet to me."

"You guys have me feeling very emotional right now," says Nicki. "Let's go take a ride and floss my man's shit."

"I thought you was never going to say that," says L.G. "I'm fucked up and ready to roll."

"Nicki, drive that boy's car with care," warns Betty.

"I will, Mom."

I had shut the door to make them think I was sleeping. Now I hear Nicki coming toward the bedroom. "L.G., start up the car. I'm going to look in on my baby real quick." She opens the door and finds me laid across the bed on my stomach. She leans over and plants a soft kiss on my jaw, then leaves the room.

The nerve of this bitch. I'm about to roll over onto my back when the bedroom door opens again. Nicki comes back to put the keys to the truck on the dresser and the .44 Mag under the pillow next to me. She walks out of the house to the BMW and they leave.

Chapter 19

"You're a lackey, fam," says Big John.

"What's that supposed to mean, scud?" asks Scab as he sits on his bottom bunk in the Anoka County Jail.

"A footman, a servile follower," answers Big John, his jail mate. "Look, people who know you smoke dope know you're capable of being read." He closes the door for more privacy. "Shit, you're the lowest of importance and in rank to your people, and the smallest in magnitude to them. It seems to me that you have or had potential to do more, but didn't have the chance to manifest it. Now, I haven't known you but for a couple of months or so, but to me it seems you need to help yourself out and give up your current particular trade."

Scab gives John a suggestive and cunning look. "This must be an instructional speech?"

Big John produces sounds of mirth and derision at the question. In a cheerful, rhythmic manner of speaking, he replies, "5-K-1."

"You're talking motorkey to me, fam," Scab says.

"Wait 'til someone goes to the magistrate before you, then you'll see shit is real with the F.E.D.S.," John says knowingly.

Police Officer Jackson speaks at the door. "Eric Beale. Visitor."

Scab puts on his jumpsuit and shoes and heads to the door. Awaiting Eric are Rory Henderson (Red Beard), Patty Jensen and Tracy Hays from the narcotics unit, Special Agent Randall Wright of the FBI, as well as Agents Dan Lyons and Adam Crown and U.S. Attorney Larry Kline. All are sitting around a big table talking. C.O. Jackson opens the door for Eric to enter.

"Have a seat, Eric Beale," says Kline.

"What's this about?" asks Scab.

"Well, for starters, you're facing federal charges of one count of possession of three-and-a-half grams of crack with the intent to distribute, one count of conspiracy, murder, and being part of organized crime." Kline sets one folder down and picks up another one. "You're facing some serious time here, Eric."

"I didn't do nothing," Scab protests. "I don't know what you're talking about."

"Look," says Kline, "you can either take the deal of a lifetime or go to a U.S. prison for the rest of your life. Now, I understand, from looking through your background, that you're a career criminal who has ties to the Shotgun Crips in this area. You have a brother named David Thompson, a.k.a. Tank, right?"

"Yeah, why?"

"Don't ask questions. Just answer. Clear?"

"Yes."

Turning through the files, Kline stops and pulls out photos of various people and places them on the table in front of Scab: Chuck Pettis, a.k.a., Fat Cuz; Oliver Dexter, a.k.a., O.G. Big Bear; Clayton Downs, FBI; Kevin Jenkins, a.k.a. Crooked; Benny Thompson, a.k.a., Biggie; and Tyrell Young and T.C. He sits quietly for a while so Scab can analyze the photos. "Does Reggie Powers and the rest of the 30s Bloods know who you are?" he asks.

"No," replies Scab.

"Now we know you're not who we want, but you can give us the people we want in exchange for immunity. Understand?"

"Yes."

"Look at these photos here, Eric. Do you recognize anybody?"

"Yes, all of them except the white guy."

"Eric, that's federal agent Clayton Downs. He was killed on the North Side with a C.I."

Shit, a fuckin' fed. I'm not going down for this shit.

Kline notices the look that crosses Scab's face and leans toward him, interested. "What can you tell me about that?" he asks.

"I know who shot them, but I don't know the other dude, though," says Scab.

"Tell us who and what you know."

All of the police officers get out pens and pads, ready to take notes. Scab swallows and says, "Killer Boy is one of the shooters."

"Is this the man?" asks Adam Crown as he pulls out a photo of Killer Boy and sets it down on the table in front of Scab.

"Yes."

"I know him. He's from California," says Crown. "His real name is Dorance Weeks. I have a file on him right here."

"How did you come onto this information?" asks Agent Randall Wright.

"Me, Tank, Foolish and Killer Boy was over at Foolish's house chilling and stuff. Killer Boy told us he smoked a couple of people up the street in a white Yukon. To be exact, he said three people. He gave Foolish a Colt .45 Mag and an AK-47 to sell for him, too. I took that as them was the murder weapons," Scab says slyly.

Kline and Lyons look at each other at the same time. *Not only does he know who did the shooting, but the exact weapons used.*

"Where are the weapons now?"

"I don't know, but I can find out," Scab says helpfully.

"Good. Now, who's Foolish?"

"A G.D. we kick it with."

"I know who Foolish is, sir," Henderson speaks up. "Carlos Moore is his name. I've busted him a couple of times and I know where to find him, sir."

"We need to find him and get those weapons out of his possession like yesterday," says Lyons.

"Done," replies Henderson.

"Now, do you know how to contact Killer Boy?"

"Through Cookie, Foolish's girl. They mess around on the low."

"What is he driving?

"A black Grand National."

"Can you tell us why he shot and killed three people?"

"It's war between the Bloods and Crips right now," Scab explains. "Rich has put hits out on Ghost, Lil D, and all the heads of the 30s gang. It's kill on sight. Every Blood body they drop, they get paid for it."

"I know who Ghost Baker and Derrick Johnson are," replies Lyons. "Do you know this man?" He points to the photo of Biggie.

"Yes."

"How?"

"He's Rich's main man. He distributes all of the work to the Crips and handles the picking up of the money."

"Can you locate him?"

"Yes, he's been holed up in one of Flip's houses. Where, I don't know exactly right now, but I can find out." Scab points to the photo of Tyrell Young. "They be together."

"Who?" asks Kline.

"T.Y. and Biggie for some reason I don't know."

"It seems to me we have to locate Freddy Jones to find those two," says Lyons.

The U.S. Attorney points to the photo of Oliver Dexter. "Who killed this man and don't lie, or our deal is off. I have to know the truth, Eric."

"My brother, Tank, with a Tech-9. Biggie was the driver and Spook was with them in the back seat. It was the hit that got Tank put on with stripes." "We appreciate your honesty, Eric," says Lyons. "It takes a very big man to do what you're doing."

Shit, this guy won't live twenty-fours after his release, thinks Crow. *He knows too much for his own good. I have to capitalize on this one.* He glances around the room. *He said it was a woman coming out of the liquor store with him at the time.*

Lyons points at the photo of Fat Cuz, a.k.a. Chuck Pettis. "I don't know who shot him," Scab says.

Thank God he doesn't know, thinks Henderson. *What kind of man gives up his brother on a fuckin' platter for murder? A damn crackhead, that's who!*

"Do you have any questions, Patty and Tracy?" asks the U.S. Attorney.

They shake their heads. "No thank you, sir."

"Well, Mr. Beale, we have to look into the info you've given us today. We'll be in touch with your lawyer to let him know what our deal is. You will have to go see the magistrate this week to confirm all of this information. We can get you out and on the street next week, so sit tight. We'll be in touch."

Scab gets up from his seat with a smile on his face, thinking about getting out of the county jail. He heads back to his unit.

Big John, Stunna, Boo, and Chello sit at the table playing spades when Scab walks back through the door and heads straight to his cell. "Big John, you got some info on that nigga Scab yet, P?" asks Stunna.

"Nah, P, but I'm working on it, believe that."

"Shit, from the way you fucked them hood rich niggas, you should be out by now. Plus, you give up some murders too, fam, in the Chi."

"I know, Boo. Don't trip. You gave up Monk and the rest of the Royal Family, so you can't talk, fool."

"I know, P. That nigga floss too fuckin' much. It's his fault I'm in this motherfucker, showing bust-downs keys of dope and shit, you know."

Chello slams down the ace of spades and hollers, "You set, homie!"

"Shit, Stunna. You didn't make your books, P."

"Man, fuck you, skud."

"You owe me anyway, Big John, so pay the bill, yo."

Stunna gets up from the table to go into Bud's room. "Come up to my room to get paid, P," says Big John. "I'll grab it, fam, then come by your cell, Chello."

"Cool."

"We pass through hoes, pass them like Newports. Feel me."

"Come on, scud, let's go holla at Scab for a second, Joe, to see what we can find out, Big John."

They arrive at the cell to find Scab smiling and making soup.

"What up, P?" asks Boo.

"Chilling. About to make me a butt naked," replies Scab.

"Who came to see you, homie?" asks Boo.

"My lawyer. He cool, too," says Scab. "He saying I got a good chance of beating all of the charges but the possession charge."

Boo sits down on the bottom bunk next to Big John while Scab stands by the sink, putting hot water on the soup in the bowl, then puts a lid over it.

"Man, G, them public pretenders be playing with your life, fam. I was facing forty years until I came to my senses, yo. That nigga, Greedy, set me the fuck up, G. They popped me with nine hard and 9 mm, G. Plus, I'm a career offender. That nigga started this whole conspiracy shit, trying to look like the big man to his bitch with our shit. That bitch-ass nigga gets popped with a brick hard, one soft and a Mac-11. Then he gives me and the whole clique up. So I had to save myself, G," says Big John.

"I feel you," replies Boo. "That nigga Monk kept three bricks at the spot in the 63s and shit, you know. But that nigga bought a bullet from some hoe and the dog bit some other bitch. The police came out to investigate and found one hundred thousand dollars-plus in the spot. I told that nigga to move the money, but no, he knew every fuckin' thing, skud. Look at me now, in a federal holding cell, about to go do some time. But not as much as he is, though. I'm getting a 5-K-1 and a Rule 35, so I'm good, skud."

"Yo, fam, get me and Chello's shit," he says to Big John.

"My bad, G." Big John gets up off the bunk and opens up his locker to get ten soups, four bags of Cheetos and four cans of tuna. "Here, G."

Chello takes his and says, "Good looking, scud. I'll holla, fam." He goes to his own cell.

Scab walks over to the bottom bunk and sits down. "What the fuck are you tell me all of this shit for, Big John?"

"Look, G. All of these cats in this jail jump on cases to get their time cut down. I mean a lot of these niggas, too. The only niggas you don't have to worry about is the ones who are going to trial, you. Them are the ones we prey on, scud. We hear that nigga Smoke and Lil Holster and Spider are going to try to put all of the shit on you, fam."

"I'm good, fam. I don't even know them like that, yo. My people will look out for me, 'cause you know murder is a business, G."

"You're speeding, Scab. I just hope you don't crash alone, 'cause to me it looks like you got a fifty-fifty chance."

Big John walks out of the cell to make a call on the phone outside the cell door to his lawyer about Eric Beale.

Chapter 20

It's 6:30 p.m. Julz and Carl P. are sitting inside a white van down the block from Foolish's house. With them are Red Beard, DEA Agent James Horn, Dan Lyons of the FBI and Angela Jones, ATF. They're about to purchase eighteen ounces of cocaine and two .45 Glocks.

"Put this small tape recorder in our pocket so we can hear what's being said in there Julz," says Red Beard.

"We do this, we get our charges dropped, right?" says Carl.

"Yes, like it never happened," says Lyons. He picks up his Nextel and says, "People, look alive! It's a go, so be alert."

Carl and Julz exit the white van and get into a four-door Pontiac Grand Prix and head down the street to park in front of Foolish's home. As they get out of the car, Julz says, "Damn, this tape recorder shit is crazy, Carl. You know Foolish like to play a lot and shit, fam."

"I know, but we here now, so I got you, bro."

They're standing outside the front door, and it's fifteen seconds to show time. Foolish looks out the window and sees them standing there. He opens the door and reaches his hand out for Carl to shake it. "What's good, fam?" asks Foolish.

"You, scud," replies Julz as they enter the living room.

"Sit down, fam. Do you want a beer?" Foolish asks hospitably.

"Nah. A shot of that Yack, fam, will do."

"Cookie, get us some glasses, baby. Shit, where you two niggas been at, yo?"

"We been grinding, skud. Making moves, fam."

"Where my doe at, Julz? To me it looks like you ain't got none on you, Joe."

Julz rises and pulls his shirt up to show rows of money taped to his body. He starts throwing knots of money wrapped in rubber bands at Foolish's feet.

"There's thirteen thousand right there for you, fam."

Foolish gets out of his chair and picks up the money off of the floor. "Let me get Cookie to count this doe real quick," he says. He meets Cookie coming out of the kitchen with the glasses. "I'll take them from you, baby. Count this for me. There should be thirteen thousand. When you're done, bring me that bag off the dresser in the downstairs bedroom."

"I got you," she says.

"It's good we put that bug on the inside of that tape record for back up," says Lyons in the back of the white van. "I didn't hear Julz press the record button, so when we hear they see the dope, move in on my signal."

"That will blow their cover, sir," says Red Beard.

"That's just a minor glitch to our plan, Mr. Henderson."

Foolish passes out the glasses and the bottle. "Here, pour your own poison," he says.

"I need me a stiff drink, too, scud," says Carl. "Man, where Tank at, Foolish?"

Foolish shakes his head. "I don't know. That nigga he on so much shit, you know. Smoking all them damn sticks and shit. It's hard to catch the scud sober." He continues, "I got some triple slacks to blow, dog, want to try one?"

"Yeah. What kind you got?"

"Red Playboy Bunnies, Blue number one stunnas, green Mario Brothers, any kind you want. Here, try these free on me." Foolish reaches over to Carl and drops two Red Playboys in his band.

"Here, baby. Everything is everything," Cookie says as she drops a black backpack on the floor beside Foolish and walks out of the room.

"Here, scud. Check this shit out." Julz gets up to grab the bag off of the floor. The front and back doors fly off their hinges.

"DEA. Get down! Police. Get down! Search warrant."

Foolish drops the backpack back on the floor. DEA agents come through the doors in all-black riot gear, automatic weapons pointed at all three of them. "Lie face down on the floor now. Get down!" One of the masked agents walks over to Foolish and slaps him with the butt of an AR-15 and forces him to the floor. Other agents sweep the rest of the house.

"One female in the bedroom," shouts one of the agents.

"Leave her back there for now. Cuff these three here and sit them over there in the corner facing the wall."

"Roger that, sir."

"Code four. People, this house is clean of anyone else. Radio out for them to bring in the dog. Now, what do we have here, people?"

One of the agents picks up the backpack. "It's not mine," say Julz and Carl simultaneously.

"Somebody has a lot of explaining to do."

Agent Lyons, Red Beard and Angela Jones walk through the door. Red Beard has hold of the K-9. "I'll start downstairs to sweep from the bottom up," he says.

"Okay. We'll search up here until you get up here," says Lyons. "Have they been patted down yet?"

"No, I don't think so, sir."

A masked James Horn and two other agents stand the three of them up against the wall. The tape recorder falls out of Julz's pocket to the floor in front of Foolish's feet. Foolish glares at Julz with the look of death, but doesn't say anything.

"They're clean."

"Sit them back down facing the wall."

An agent shouts, "More guns and drugs!" Lyons and Horn walk back to where Cookie is looking on from her bedroom.

"Take her back with the rest of them," says Lyons. Angela Jones pats Cookie down, then walks her into the living room. She returns as Horn says, "There must at least two hundred thousand Ex pills right there, plus ten keys of powder cocaine and six more guns! The bottom dresser drawer is full of money."

"I'll take the guns as evidence," says Jones.

"Let me go to the van, Angela, and get some property bags for the cocaine," says Horn.

Red Beard comes up empty-handed from downstairs, the K-9 in tow. "Anything down there, Red?" asks one of the masked DEA agents.

"Nah, let me try my luck up here."

Lyons comes out of the bedroom and picks up the backpack and looks over at Foolish with an "I know you're going to talk" face. "Take them outside to the squad cars so this officer can sweep the area with the K-9," he orders.

Three agents escort Foolish to the back of the van. Cookie is put into the back of Angela's unmarked car. Carl and Julz are let go out in front.

Red Beard notices the small recorder on the living room floor and picks it up and hands it to Agent Lyons. "You just got them boys killed, sir," he says.

"Things happen, officer," Lyons says indifferently. "Like my partner getting killed." He walks toward the van holding Foolish. "Open up the door. I need to speak with him."

The doors open and Foolish says, "I know they set me up, pig."

"That is not the most important thing you need to be worried about, son," Lyons replies evenly. "You're in so deep that whatever you do will only keep you from getting life, Carlos Murphy. You have some info that I need."

"Fuck you, bitch-ass pig!" Foolish snarls.

"Now, look, Mr. Murphy, I'm the only one here who will help you out. We know that you work for Rich and we know that this isn't your merchandise. So if you keep up this tough-guy role, you're never going to see the light or your pretty woman again." Agent Lyons gets into the van and sits beside Foolish now. "Listen, I need to know where and who has the Colt .45 and the AK-47 you had in your possession."

Foolish thinks for a second, then says, "Deal for me."

"We'll talk later about your deal. Right now I need to know!"

Foolish is stubborn. "Let my woman go right now, not later." Agent Lyons steps out of the van and waves ATF Agent Angela Jones over to him.

"Yes?" says Angela.

"Let his lady friend go without charges when they're done inside the house," Lyons instructs.

"Yes, sir."

Lyons turns back to Foolish. "Now that's settled, tell me what I need to know."

"Mario," says Foolish.

"Excuse me?" Lyons asks.

"Mario. That's his name."

"Where's he located?"

"Twenty-sixth and Bryant. I don't know the exact address."

Agent Lyons leans on the van's bumper to hear more clearly. "I sold them to him," Foolish says. "He's part of 26 Mafia, a clique of G.D.s."

"Now, where can we find Killer Boy?"

"Ask Cookie," Foolish replies. "They think I don't know they fuck around. She can help you out with that."

"This information will help you out a whole lot, Mr. Murphy, as long as you cooperate with me, son. I will make sure to tell Homicide that you told me how to find Killer Boy. They will take you down to processing, then sign you out to work for me, so stay cool and don't talk to anyone but me," Lyons warns.

"Cool. You got a card?"

"Yes, here. Take him to the station," Lyons orders. He walks over to

Angela's car, where Cookie is crying in the back seat.

"Am I going to jail? I didn't do nothing," she wails.

"Miss Lowe, no, you're not going to jail. Yes, you did do something, but your man, Mr. Murphy, covered your ass. Now, stop crying for a second to help Mr. Murphy out." He hands her a handkerchief. Cookie sniffs a couple more times and regains her composure.

Agent Lyons puts his foot on the edge of the floor board and takes off his shades to give Cookie his "so serious" look, eye to eye. "Can you get me Killer Boy?" he asks bluntly.

Cookie stalls for about thirty seconds, then swallows and asks why. "Listen, young lady, this is a very important matter. If you don't want to face federal cocaine and gun charges, I advise you to answer my questions very truthfully."

She sighs. "Yes."

"How do you contact him?"

"Cell phone."

"What's the number?"

She rattles off a number with a 612 area code. "It's the only number I have for him," she says.

"I need you to call him for me later, so don't leave the house when all of the agents leave," Lyons says.

"I won't," she promises.

"I and some of the other agents will come back to get you."

ATF Agent Jones walks up. "We're done on the inside of the house, sir. We're ready to go process all of the evidence from today's raid, Mr. Lyons."

"I'm done here. Step out of the car, Miss Lowe, so I can take off the cuffs." Cookie gets out of the back seat looking like a runway model in high heels, apple bottom jeans, and cut-off baby phat shirt.

"Turn around, ma'am," says Lyons. He sticks the key into the lock and unlocks the cuffs. Cookie turns around to face him.

"Thank you, sir," she says.

"No problem, Miss Lowe." Cookie walks back toward the house with a hooker strut shaking her ass. Agent Lyons pays close attention to every bounce of her jeans. Agent Jones clears her throat to bring Lyons back to reality. He puts on his shades and walks over to the curb to Red Beard. "Meet me down at the Federal Building in an hour," he says, not giving Henderson a chance to respond.

He's becoming a real pain in the ass. Red Beard walks over to his cruiser with one hundred thousand dollars taped to his stomach. He found it in the basement during his search.

Nicki comes home after a few hours of rolling around town with L.G. and Sean. Coming through the front door, she notices how quiet the house is. *I'm glad I dropped L.G. and Sean at the 200 Club.* She walks through the house to the basement door and goes downstairs. *Now I can blow me a few premos real quick.*

Pulling out the purple haze that she stashed in her bra earlier today, she walks over to a stack of Jay' clothes on the floor by the hot water heater. She bends down, picks up a pair of Levis jeans and searches the right pocket. She pulls out a zip-lock bag of cocaine powder and a pack of blunts. She opens the baggy to get a small amount on her pinky finger and inhales it into her right nostril. She sits down very quickly on the pile of Jay's clothes and savors the feeling. *This shit makes my pussy so fuckin' wet. I need some of that nine and a half Jay got up in my bed after this.*

Nicki cracks open a blunt with her fingernail and empties its contents on the floor, setting the blunt down on the floor to break the purp down into the blunt slowly. Reaching into the bag to scoop powder out with a spoon lying beside a pair of boxers on the floor, she puts at least a gram and a half of cocaine powder into the blunt. She picks up the premo blunt to fold and lick the edges and rolls it closed.

Picking up the rest of the purp, she puts the bag of powder back into the Levis pocket. She picks the rolled blunt off of the floor, then lies back on the pile of clothes, digging through her pocket for the lighter. She pulls out the red Bic, then walks over to the open window and lights the end of the blunt. The cocaine in it sizzles at the touch of heat. She inhales the smoke slowly and holds it until her eyes water.

The cocaine begins to take effect; she begins to feel numb. Her pussy throbs for attention. She blows out the smoke, feeling very light-headed from the large amount of cocaine she put in the blunt, as well as the high-grade weed. *Damn, this blunt reeks, but it's so damn good, too.*

Chapter 21

Rich, Lacy, Lil D, Maniac and Red Beard all sit around a table in Rich's safe home in St. Paul discussing the events that have occurred in the last few months.

"Man, I knew that dope fiend ass-nigga Scab was goin to fold," says Lil D. "I knew I should-a have smoked both of their asses, scud."

"We need to have someone on the inside kill him by choking him or suffocating his ass before the feds let out, people," says Red Beard. "That Agent Dan Lyons is on his own mission, so we have to be careful how we take him out."

"Shit, all of they asses need to get their tongues cut out. Fuck Killer Boy, Foolish, and Scab. Them niggas is dead," Rich says. He nods to Maniac.

"Pass me the blunt, Lacy," Lil D says.

"Now, with Julz P. and Carl P. knowing Foolish knows they set him up, it won't be a problem for me to put some work on them and put them into federal custody," Red Beard suggests.

"Nah, homie, let the streets take care of the two," replies Lacy.

"I've lost a lot of money in this raid over at Foolish's house," Rich says, then pushes his chair back and walks over behind Red Beard.

"Listen, with all of the killings that has happened, all of your guys are hot right now," the double-dealing cop says. "Biggie has the feds looking for him for a gun charge they're going to pin on him when they catch up with him. Plus Biggie, Spook and Tank , if caught, will be charged with the murder of O.G. Big Bear."

At the mention of O.G. Big Bear, Lil D looks up with fire in his eyes. "What do you mean for the murder of O.G. Big Bear, cop?"

"Scab told the U.S. Attorney that Tank put in the work," answers Red.

"I didn't know that shit, Blood."

"Hold on, Lil D, don't start that Blood shit in my house, cuz."

"Fuck you, crab," retorts Lil D. "That's my big homie from Cali, nigga."

Maniac pulls out two Desert Eagles from under the table and points both of them at Lil D's face at point-blank range. "What you say, slob?" he demands.

"Chill, people," Red says. "I'm a cop, remember, fellas? And we have more business to discuss now." He stands up to show his badge.

"You work for me, pig, so keep your fuckin' mouth shut," says Rich.

"Get down or lay down, slob. What's your choice?" asks Maniac.

Lacy puts a hand on Lil D's arm. "Lil D, chill, baby."

"I'm good," Lil D says. "But me and you ain't, crab," he says to Maniac.

"My pleasure, slob," Maniac replies.

The room falls silent, but only for a second. A tap on the door breaks the tension.

"Come on in, Flip," says Rich. "Have a seat, cuz."

"The first thing we need to take care of is this fed killing, people," says Red Beard. "That's what's putting so much heat on both of your gangs right now. I suggest you kill Killer Boy now, not later, people. Cut all ties that can fuck you."

"I can get him set up, cuz, to be put down," Rich says with a smirk on his face.

"Damn, you gone smoke cuz, big homie?" asks Flip.

"Nah. You gone do it, cuz," Rich says, continuing to smirk.

"Me? Why me?"

"He trusts you a lot, so it'll be very easy for you to play the role."

"What about them two niggas, Biggie and T.C., cuz?" Flip asks.

"I got them, fam. Don't trip," replies Lil D. "Just let me know where they are, son."

"At my loft downtown, cuz," Rich tells him.

"I'll go see Foolish at Anoka County Jail to see where he's going to stand on this case, Rich. If he made a deal with Dan Lyons, I'll know," Red Beard says.

"I'll get Do-Right and Murder Mac to smoke Tank and Spook, cuz," Rich decides.

Red Beard stands up. "Look, we need to find out who bought those guns from Foolish so we can put them on Killer Boy, people. I'll be at the station early tomorrow, so call me when one of you knows something."

"Bitch, you listen to me, cop!" Maniac bursts out angrily. "I'm here to take care of my business for the big homies in Cali, cuz, so don't *ever* try to tell me what to do! Feel me? I only need to know who killed Fat Cuz, cop."

Lil D smiles and looks at Maniac. *If only you knew, crab. But that can wait for now. I don't want start anything else before we handle this situation that can put all of us into a federal prison, Mr. Maniac.*

Red Beard looks at his watch. "It's eight o'clock and I have to be somewhere, people. So if there isn't anything else, I'm out."

"Yes, there's one more thing, cop," says Lil D. "Does C. O. Jackson still work at Anoka?"

"Yes, he does," Red Beard replies.

"Well, do your homework on him," Lil D replies.

Red Beard scratches his head, then nods toward Lil D. "Well, let's get this shit taken care of, people. I'm out." The door closes behind him.

Everyone else gets up to leave. "Hold on for one second, Lil D. I need to holler at you, cuz," Rich says. He walks over and puts his right hand on Lil D's shoulder, pushing him back down into the chair. "Shut the door behind you, Lacy baby."

"I'll be upstairs, Lil D," she says.

Rich pulls out the chair beside Lil D and sits down. "Lil D, I know you and Ghost smoked Fat Cuz over South, cuz. Now you can either give me Ghost on a platter, or both of you gone die soon, cuz."

"I, I, I . . ."

Rich cuts him off in mid-sentence. "I know, so save what you're about to say. By killing Ghost, that makes you number one over there, cuz."

Lil D gives him a confused look, pretending to be surprised about the proposition.

T.C., Mario and Tyrell roll down the street and know they all have rapacious desires to ball out of control. They also know I can make it happen. As the gray Chevy Caprice turns another avenue, Mario smacks Murder Mac in the eye with the AK-47. "Nigga, you're our guarantee for ghetto fame, scud, when we hand you over to Jay, fam." Murder Mac's face expresses pain and contempt.

T.C. pulls over behind my Bronco and gets out of the car. Tyrell puts the Colt .45 into Murder Mac's side and shows no sorrow anguish toward the handcuffed Family Cartel member.

"Now, when Jay comes out of this house, I want you to tell him what you told me, scud," says Mario. "When I take the duct tape off of your mouth, no screaming or you're dead, hear me?" Murder Mac nods.

I walk out of the house with T.C.. We open up the car doors and sit down in the front seat one by one. "Looks like the preliminary work is done," I remark, taking in the bleeding body seated between Mario and Tyrell. I tell T.C. to drive to a house on Glenwood Avenue. "My nigga's over there, waiting on us right now."

T.C. pulls off to head over to the spot. I turn forward, flip open my phone and dial Tasha's number. "Where you at?" she asks.

"Hold up, baby. I need you to bring me six cups of coffee over to the Glenwood spot right now," I tell her.

"I'm on my way."

"Okay. One. Look, fellas, I'm going to give you guy's three bricks apiece for a starter kit, Mario and Tyrell." They laugh in hearty satisfaction. T.C. parks in front of an empty house. Mario sits in the backseat with a look of discontent on his face. I have so many possessions of such quality, things he has a strong desire to acquire for himself.

"I'll be right back, T.C.," I say. "Pull in the back."

"Yeah, fam."

I get out of the car and disappear through the front door. As the Chevy pulls through the dark alleyway, Murder Mac starts to sweat. He pisses his pants as they park. Being threatened with extinction, he desires to make an attempt to make a deal when the duct tape comes off.

Big Chief and Tre Duce come out of the back door. They walk toward the Chevy, holding enormous .357 Magnums. They shine at their sides, even in the darkness. They open up the back door of the car.

"Who ar —"

Big Chief cuts Mario off with the wave of his hand. "We got this from here, fam," he says. "Jay will be out soon."

Mario steps out of the Chevy, pulling on Murder Mac to stand up. Tre Duce puts the .357 to Murder's back and walks him to the house. Big Chief checks out the AK-47 in Mario's hands. Back in the house, he locks the door behind him, not knowing if he can trust Mario walking Murder Mac down the basement stairs into a soundproof room.

"Sit his crab ass down right here in this fuckin' chair and take off his shoes and put his feet into this bucket," says Black Mike. He snatches the gray duct tape off of Murder's mouth, removing half of his mustache with it.

"Look, Big Chief, I got info you need to know," Murder says eagerly.

"I bet you do, crab," Big Chief replies. "Put them chains around his ass, too, blood," he says, pointing to a pile of metal on the floor. Tre Duce grabs the chains and wraps them around Murder with a purpose, a goal in mind.

Big Chief comes over with bottles of raw acid. The four of them en-circle Murder now to see how much pain he can endure before he dies. "Don't kill me, please, man. Please don't do it, Black," Murder pleads.

"Why shouldn't we?" I ask.

"I can tell you about Lil D's and Rich's plan to kill Ghost and the rest of you all," he replies desperately. With that statement, he grabs the complete attention of all four of us.

"What you say about the big homie, crab?" Tre Duce says as he squats down and puts some epoxy on the bottom of Murder's bare feet and glues them to the bucket.

"Talk, nigga," Black Mike says. He thinks about Lil D and Rich hav-ing the same capabilities and status and feels a chill.

"Me, Rich, Killer Boy and I was at Murray's chilling, talking about how the Bloods are going to fall," begins Murder.

My phone rings. "Let me get this," I say, holding up the palm of my hand. "Yeah, pull into the back and give that to the two dudes in the Chevy with T.C., then smash out. But tell them the bill is sixty thousand for both of them and tell them I'll holla. One." I turn back to Murder Mac. "Now you can go on, crab."

"That nigga Lil D been giving you guys up for a top spot on the hood when Ghost gets killed," he says, sweat running down his face. "That bitch Lacy been sleeping with the Shotgun Crips and giving up info on you niggas on a regular, too. Rich has a special importance placed upon putting you cats down. "

Guided by experience rather than theory, I rely on observation. I look closely at Murder Mac. "How do we know you're on the money with this, crab?"

"I've known about the plan ever since we ate at Murray's, no lie."

"You seem very persuasive," I say.

"It's the truth." He begins to babble excitedly. "Look, if Rich and Lil D both have a position of superiority, who can stop them? Rich put Fat Cuz and Cougie and Trap on you guys that night, Jay, but they didn't know you was going to be with Ghost that night."

"Fuck that shit. You killed my boys in the park, fam. We're the only succession of rulers from the Blood family line, crab," says Big Chief. Impatient, he pours the acid into the bucket.

Murder Mac screams as the acid melts his feet up to his ankles. He passes out. Tre Duce slaps him awake. The stench of burning flesh flows into the air. "Blood, light that blunt in your ear, Black," says Big Chief. He turns to me.

"Fam, either he has deliberate deceptiveness about his story or he's telling the truth, blood."

"I don't doubt his ass one bit, but we got to prove it, blood. Lil D is a real killer, fam. Not the kind to play with," I say.

"Let's kill this nigga and get the fuck out of here," Black Mike says between puffs of the blunt.

"I'll be upstairs," I say, and walk out of the basement.

Black Mike pulls out his .50-caliber pistol and puts it to the back of Murder Mac's head. He pulls the trigger, ending his life and putting his brains all over the plastic on the walls.

Big Chief surveys the mess then says, "Fam, I'm-a drop off and you two clean up here."

"Cool, blood. We got this right here," says Black Mike.

"Don't nobody tell what this dead crab said, blood," Big Chief cautions.

"We good on that shit, blood."

"Blood, if that shit is true, we'll let Pit Bull take care of that shit. You know, Pit Bull and Ghost go way back, before Lil D, so he'll take care of that," I tell Big Chief when he joins me upstairs. "One, lil homies," I call down the basement stairs.

Chapter 22

"Yeah, this Murder Mac. I'm busy right now, so holla at me. Leave your game at the beep."

Damn. I've been trying to get at this nigga ever since last night, cuz. Where the fuck this nigga at? Do-Right shuts his cell phone and walks up to Tank's door. He knocks and waits for someone to answer.

All of the good times me and Tank has had together, and now I got to be the one to lay him down. Shit, this just part of the game we play.

The door opens. Spook looks like he's been up all night smoking chem. "What it do, cuz?" he asks.

"I'm good, Spook. Where Tank at?"

"He went to get some dip, homie. Come on in. We got Stacey and Tamika in the back, butt naked and higher than a motherfucker off of ex and dip, homie."

"Not Jamal's old girl, Tamika? Move, let me see for myself, cuz."

Spook closes the door, then follows Do-Right to the back room.

"Damn, cuz it's only about eleven a.m. and you two niggas is on fuckin' party mode already!" Do-Right exclaims.

"Who that?" asks Tamika as her lips kiss Stacey's clit.

"Me, baby. Do-Right."

"Take off your clothes and come 'cum' with us," she says invitingly.

I might as well make one last memory with my guys before I smoke they ass.

Stacey walks over and unbuttons Do-Right's pants while he pulls out a silenced 10 mm and lays it on the dresser by the door.

"Shit, fam. That's your 2009 Cadillac XLR-V, black with black paint, twenty-four-inch ASANTI$s on it! It's a drop-top, too. You getting paid, cuz?" Spook says as he picks up the pistol. "Cuz, this here a nice piece of work you got." He points the strap at Do-Right. "Hoes, you can go now."

"But, baby, can we have some fun with him first?" Stacey asks.

Spook ignores her.

"Look, cuz, don't shoot me," says Do-Right. "I don't know what's on your mind, but we fam." He rises from the bed with his hands in the air, stark naked. He pleads for his life. "Please, please don't kill me, cuz."

"Sit yo bitch-ass down, cuz. Stacey, go get yo toys, the big ones we play with."

Tamika gets up and retrieves a black shoe box from under the bed. She opens the box and pulls out two twelve-inch dildos, two twelve-inch strap-ons and places them on the bed. Do-Right's eyes widen at the sight.

Tank, Flip, Biggie, and T.C. walk into the room. "'Sup, cuz?" Tank asks. "You come to kill me and Spook, huh?"

"Nah, cuz. I was going to let you two cats leave town and say I killed both of you, cuz." *Damn that nigga Flip for flipping on me. Shit. I don't know how I'm going to get out of this situation.*

Tank pulls a Tech-9 from behind his back. T.C. pulls out a camcorder and shuts the door. "Cuz," drawls Tank, "you about to perform, since you act like a hoe."

"I wonder how you hid your skirt, cuz," says Spook. "Get yo ass on all fours, yo."

"Cuz, don't do this shit to me, Spook. We been boys for too long, cuz. This Do-Right, baby."

"Strap up, girls," Spook orders. "Nigga, accept all of the pain in silence. You was going to fuck us, so now it's you getting fucked. Cut up the music, Tank, so the neighbors don't hear this hoe-ass nigga. T.C., as soon as Tamika penetrate his ass, start recording. And, nigga, you better perform for the camera."

Staccy walks up to the edge of the bed. "Suck my dick, nigga," she commands. As soon as Do-Right deep throats Stacey's twelve-inch, Tamika puts the head of her strap inside him without KY Jelly. She shoves the whole thing inside him, busting his ass wide open. "Aaaaahhh!!!" shouts Do-Right with six inches of plastic down his throat.

Flip, Tank and Spook hit the floor laughing. "Kill me, cuz. Shoot me, nigga," Do-Right yells as he comes up for air. Tamika smacks his ass, pounding the blood out. "Take this dick, baby," she says. "Take all of it."

"Cuz, you slept on my loyalty to my niggas," says Flip. "These are the niggas I eat with, sleep with, and ride with, cuz. You musta forgot that shit, nigga. "I had to let my man know last night about this shit Rich is on, cuz." He lights up a blunt. "Throw that shit, baby," he says to Tamika.

"You like this dick, don't you?" she says to Do-Right.

He answers feebly, "Yes."

"I can't hear you, baby," says Tamika, pushing harder now and holding his hips. Do-Right decides he'd better play along.

"Yessss, baby. Fuck me. Ahhh. . . yessss . . . right there."

Stacey pushes the dildo far enough down his throat to make him gag and spit all over the bed. "Don't take my dick out your mouth until you cum, baby," she says.

Spook waves for Tamika to pull out. The door opens and two fags walk in, Diamond and Delishis, just released from the state penitentiary in St. Cloud. Delishis pulls down his pants, displaying a hard fourteen inches. He slides into Do-Right with ease, filling him to the rim.

Stacey pulls out and sits on the floor by the head of the bed while Diamond strokes himself. "Open wide, for Diamond," she says. Do-Right raises his head and looks at the size of Diamond *Shit, not a real man now.* He looks back and sees Delishis long-stroking him. He licks the head of Meli's dick, hoping to end some of the pain Delishis is inflicting in his stomach. "Mmmmm . . . aahhhhh," he pretends.

Damn, that nigga is taking some serious dick. Tamika fingers herself as she stands by the bed. She holds one cheek open for Delishis.

"I'm about to nut. I'm about to nu –" Diamond busts off into Do-Right's mouth. "Drink every drop, baby, for Diamond. Don't waste a drop now." Do-Right chokes down every drop.

"Cuz, you're a real porn star now," says Tank.

Delishis pumps faster and faster, giving Do-Right extreme pain and banging the headboard against the wall. Do-Right keeps talking, hoping Delishis will leave him alone. "Mmmmhhh … yesss… knock that ass, daddy. Nut in me, please. Harder, harder, fuck me."

"I'm cumming, I'm cumming!" shouts Delishis. "This is some tight boy pussy! Ahhhh…." He pulls out of Do-Right slowly. "Don't kill him, Spook. Let me have him, please?"

"Your job is done here, sump. I still need his ass."

Do-Right falls flat on his stomach. He's in so much pain he's ready to fall out.

"I'll have this on the Internet by three o'clock," says T.C. "Cuz, smile. You're a star."

Tank walks over to the head of the bed and shakes his head, pointing the Tech-9 at Do-Right's face. "I know you was a bitch, nigga. How you like your dick, bitch?"

"Leave me alone, cuz," pleads Do-Right.

"Now, let's go find Maniac to put Plan Number Two into effect," says Flip. "Tamika, we're going to need you, bitch, to fuck and suck this nigga to get him to put his guard down. Your head game is fierce, bitch."

"Thank you for the compliment, baby," Tamika smiles. "I'll do whatever you want me to."

"Tie this nigga's ass the fuck up 'til we need this nigga to call Rich to say he did the job on us," says Spook. "By the way, where are your keys at, boy Crip?"

"In my front pants pocket," mumbles Do-Right.

"We'll hit you niggas on the hip later tonight, cuz." Flip, Biggie and T.C. leave.

"Tamika, you and Stacey pull the car into the garage, then dip. Leave the keys on the hood, baby, and keep your phone on you, okay? Tank, throw me that bat over there by you." Spook shows the bat to Do-Right. "Look this is for you, nigga. Tank, tape his mouth." Tank obliges. Whop, whop. Spook slams both of Do-Right's knees with the bat, breaking them.

"Now you can't get out of that bed until we need you to, slob lover. In the bed with Lil D. I should have known."

Down the block, parked behind a dark green Ford Taurus, Lil D and Rich observe Flip, T.C. and Biggie leave in a 2007 white Mercedes Benz CLS63 AMG. As the trio pulls away from Tank's house, Lil D and Rich follow them in a red 2008 Chevrolet Corvette 206 with tinted windows.

"I didn't see Do-Right come out of the house, Lil D," says Tank.

"I know, but we got to stay on these fools for now. Call his phone, Tank."

"The voice mail comes on, homie. I can't believe that nigga Flip. He gone die very, very slow for this shit. Betraying me, the Big Homie! I'm Shotgun Crip, the Shot Caller, the Made Man. Feel me."

"Sho 'nuff," says Lil D. "Call Killer Boy."

"Nah, I'll call Maniac to put him up on what's going on now. I'm glad we followed Do-Right this morning, Lil D."

"Shit, they're getting on the freeway now, heading toward Brooklyn Park. Let me focus on the road, Tank, before you make me lose them."

"Not in this car. You can't lose them. Catch that light, Lil D! It's about to turn red."

Lil D punches the pedal and the Corvette flies down the shoulder to merge into the freeway.

"I'll call homie when they get to where they're going," says Rich.

I need to call my dick, 'cause I'm so damn lonely and that fuckin' cop haven't called me or come by yet. So I'm leaving this fuckin' house for a while now. Cookie dials Killer Boy's cell phone number. "Hello?" he answers.

"Hey, baby, what you doing?" she asks.

"About to get some dro," he answers. "Want to go?"

"Uh huh. Come pick me up. I miss you, baby. Mama needs her fix, and I need to talk to you."

"I'll be there about now — I'm right outside the back door in my new 2009 Mercedes-Benz G-550 truck, baby."

"Oh, let me lock up and I'll be right out, love." Cookie hangs up the phone, grabs her purse and walks out the door.

Damn, that cop said that I was not staying here, and I'm still here. Foolish dials his home number. "You've reached Cookie and Foolish. We're not home at the moment, so leave us a message." He slams the phone down. He's frustrated that Carl P. and Julz set him up.

Scab walks down the stairs and notices Foolish walking his way. He calls Foolish's name and breaks into his thoughts. "Foolish, when you get here, scud? Don't matter. Let's go sit in the back over there so we can holla."

As they walk to the table, Foolish glances at Scab. *Where has this nigga been? This shit don't look right. He knew the deal. He was there with Killer Boy that morning.* "What's the deal with you, fam? You sold me out, too, huh?"

Scab has the look of a confident politician, but his response gives him away. "No, fam." He bites his fingernails and looks around to see if anyone can hear their conversation. "But I know how to get us out of this shit, though."

Before Scab can begin to impart his wisdom, however, a Breaking

News sign flashes on the TV screen. A reporter appears on-camera. "I'm sorry to interrupt your regular television show. I'm Cassandra Clark, and I'm at the scene live."

The inmates crowd around the TV to look and listen to the broadcast. "Today, a child was talking to a friend at this bus stop and noticed a foul smell coming from this trash can right here on this corner Blood was seeping from under the trashcan, and when the child looked closer, he could see fingers hanging out of the opening of the garbage can. He told his mother, and she called 911. The police are on the scene, waiting for Homicide to come and take over the investigation as we speak. There is a body inside the trashcan. How long it's been there, we don't know, but we're here to keep you posted. It appears to be a black male. As the investigation develops, new information, we'll be here to give it to you. I'm Cassandra Clark, Channel 11 News."

"Shit, fam, Spook a cold-hearted motherfuckin' Crip, scud," says Flip as he makes an exit on Boone Avenue. "That was some unexplained shit that I didn't know about, cuz, did you, T.C.?"

"Yeah. Cuz called me last night after you talked to him, Flip. Them two sumps are his cousins. They did that kind of shit in the joint, fam, to niggas. Make a right on Clavall Avenue, cuz. It's the fourth house on the left."

"Damn. He shoulda have just killed Do-Right, not let some fags rape him and film it, too."

"Look, cuz. The only reason they are alive right now is because of me," Flip says as puts the car into park in the driveway.

"He looked like a true sump porn star, you know, like this wasn't the first time he took dick up the ass. To me, it looked like he was enjoying himself the whole time, cuz. Moaning and shit like a real bitch, cuz," says Biggie with a frown on his face at what he just witnessed.

"Whose spot is this?"

"My uncle Steve's," says Biggie. "I'll hit you up tonight to swoop me up, loc."

"Cool, Biggie. Do that."

"Here, take this .380 with the extended clip," Biggie says. "Good looking out, T.C." He disappears through the front door. Flip looks over at T.C. "Cuz, this shit done got real deep now." He starts the Benz and they pull off.

Chapter 23

"They pulling into the KFC drive-thru, so pull up in the space beside the ordering machine and park. We can drop their asses right now and hit Hwy. 100 to swoop the fuck out of here, Lil D," says Rich.

"That's what the fuck I'm talking about, homie." Lil D parks, checks his Mossberg pump.

"Will that be all for you today, sir?" the girl at the drive-thru window asks.

"Yes, shorty. Damn, cuz, Do-Right looks fucked up on this video here," says T.C.

Before Flip can take his foot off the brake to coast forward a few inches, boom, boom! Tank's shotgun blows the front half of his face off through T.C.'s window. Boom, boom, boom. Lil D hits T.C. two to the back of his head as he turns to see who's shooting Flip. The third bullet tears through his spine and his chest to rest on Flip's bloody body. The Benz slowly rolls forward into a parking bumper.

"We up, Lil D," says Rich. "Let's bounce."

The tires on the Corvette burn as they fly out of the parking lot.

I hope them niggas didn't tell the rest of the homies what's up with me and Lil D, Rich thinks. "Shit, nigga, you got slob on my blue khaki suit," he says, coming out of a daze.

"Chill with all of that shit, crab," says Lil D. "You in as deep as me, Rich, so quit with all the disrespect."

"Drop me off over North so I can go get my 2002 Chrysler Prowler out of the garage so I can move around," says Rich.

"Cool," says Lil D. "You can drop these heaters while I dump this stolen car."

"Have you heard from Ghost yet?"

"Nah. I'll let you know when he gets back. Make sure Maniac handles his business, Rich. Now, not later, 'cause our lives is on the line on this shit, fam."

⚜

"Baby, lunch was good and it was on time, too, 'cause that weed gave me the munchies like a motherfucker."

"I got you, Cookie," Killer Boy says as he opens up the passenger side door.

"A gentleman, too," purrs Cookie. "How did I get so lucky?"

"You're special, baby. Any true man, whether he bang or a regular dude, should know a real woman's worth."

As he sits down behind the steering wheel of the Benz truck, Killer sees a suspicious, slow-cruising blue 2009 Hurst/Hemi Challenger Series 4 SRT8 go by. It gives him a strange feeling.

"You okay, baby?" Cookie asks. "You look bothered." Killer pulls off from the Best Steak House and wonders where he's seen that car before.

"Did he see us, Larry?"

"No, I don't think so. The tint on this car is so dark, nobody can see inside to see us." "

"I told you she would do our job for us," says Dan.

"We'll wait until they get to Cookie' house before we box him in," Larry says to Adam Crown on the Nextel.

"Copy that."

"I have to put a bullet into his head myself for killing my brother, Dan. He has to die for that shit," Larry says.

"He's at the light," Lyons tells Burgess and Crown. "I'm going to fall back so you two can take my spot. Don't lose him."

"Copy that, sir."

Agents Crown and Burgess pull in between Killer Boy and Agent Lyons to head the tail, driving a silver Chrysler 300. Looking over at Agent Crown, Burgess smiles as they enter the freeway. "What has you so bright?" asks Crown.

"One of ours has fallen and justice will prevail. That always makes me get in the right mind, you know, Crown."

"You brought the throw-aways with you, right?"

"Yes, I got the .40 Glock and a twenty-one-shot Ruger from a bust last year. We good, Crown."

The Benz truck up ahead swerves a little. Inside, Killer Boy says, "Oooh, shit that feels so good, Cookie. You keep that up and I'm going to crash on the freeway, baby!"

"Nothing feels better than you, baby," she says. She squeezes Killer's balls to make him harder, then she sucks him hard and slow, stroking him to bust off in her mouth. Feeling him harden, she pulls up just enough for her tongue to circle the head. Killer spits nut all over her face. "Yes, baby," she exults. "Let it go on momma!" She props her mouth around Killer to the suck the rest out. The truck weaves to the left a little.

"Baby, please stop before I wreck," says Killer. "I thought I would never say no shit like that to you."

Four car lengths back, Crown asks, "What are they doing in there?"

"Let me guess, Crown," Burgess replies. "If I was him, I'd be doing the same thing. She's a very pretty woman."

"I know. I've seen her, too. He better get all of his rocks off today, because later all bets are off."

Up ahead, Cookie asks, "Where are we going?"

"To see a movie. You with that, baby, and maybe some shopping, since you've been so good?"

"Yes, I'm with that." A smile creeps across her face at how easy it was to whip Killer on the pussy and head. She leans back into the seat, wiping her face.

"Homicide, Sgt. Ted Jenkins speaking. How can I help you?"

"The two suspects who killed O.G. Big Bear are at Thirty-fourth and Oliver Avenue North right now."

"Who am I speaking to?" asks Jenkins.

"Look, Tank and Spook is there right now." Click.

"That should take care of them two cats. Now I can finish taking me a hot bath. Tamika, put that phone on the charger and come back over. Do your thing on me, baby, okay?"

Standing up at his desk, Sgt. Jenkins pushes the line to get Lt. John Franco on the phone. "Hey, Ted, how are you?" Franco asks.

"Sir, I know where the suspects are at this moment."

"What suspects are we talking about?"

"In the O.G. Big Bear killing. I just got off of the phone with an anonymous caller who gave me the information. I'll dispatch some uniformed officers to post up near the location in case the suspects try to leave soon," Jenkins says.

"You do that, sergeant. I'll get the warrant and a task force to go take them down. I'm on my way to survey the house. We will be on Channel 10, sergeant."

"Okay, sir."

"Foolish, let me holla at you for a second real quick, fam," Spider says, standing at Foolish's door with some Bloods behind him, looking grimy.

"One second, fam. What they want with me, Scab?"

"I don't know Scud. I got locked up at one of their spots over South."

"Go up to your room," Foolish says. "I'll be up in a few, fam."

"Cool. Don't put me out there, Foolish."

"I got you, scud."

Scab leaves and Big George, Spider, Lil Holster and Smoke walk in. "That you man, Foolish?" asks Big George.

"Nah, I fucks with his people. Why?"

"That nigga got homies in this shit and he snitchin' to the peoples, too."

"What that got to do with me, homie?" Foolish asks.

"Nothing, now that it's not your boy," replies Smoke.

They all stroll out the same way they came in, leaving Foolish to think about all of the shit Scab just told him about his meeting with the peoples. Spider comes back and sits down on the bunk beside Foolish. "Want to drink some hooch with me, scud?" he asks.

"Yeah, I do need some of that," Foolish says.

Spider takes the cap off of the bottle and takes a gulp, then passes it to Foolish. "Fuck it," he says. "We know he's Tank's brother, but we don't know how much he knows about shit he shouldn't know. Feel me."

"I do, scud," Foolish answers. "But he ain't told me shit yet, fam. Give me some time to work on him, Spider."

"Nah, that's okay," Spider says. "We got this, son. His time is up, yo. The clock is about to stop ticking for homie real soon." Spider rises to leave and turns around at the door. "Keep the drink. It's on me. One."

He's on his fucking own. I got nothing to do with that shit there. Them Bloods is about so deep in this quad. Foolish takes the last sip of hooch and lies down to sleep it off.

"They're at the mall, so stay alert, people," says Larry Kline on his Nextel to the other agents.

"Copy, sir."

"We cannot lose them in this mall, Dan," Larry says urgently.

"We won't sir. He doesn't know we know he did the shooting, sir. We impounded the Grand National from the Benz dealer he traded it to. Plus, Cookie knows better than to open her mouth. She was the one found in the room with the drugs and guns and she's on tape counting the money for Foolish. We got her bringing the backpack into the living room of the house we raided, sir."

Lil D leaves the Corvette on the corner and walks toward Pit Bull's spot. He drops the brown gloves on the pavement along the way. Before he can push the buzzer, Pit Bull buzzes the door open. Looking up, Lil D sees multiple security cameras on the building that weren't there before. Walking through the building, he notes new doors and locks on every apartment. *What the fuck happened here?*

Pit Bull steps out the door. "Blood, my nigga. What brings you through here, fam?"

"Shit, damn," Lil D replies. "To holler at my nigga."

"Come on in, fam."

As he shuts the door, Lil D looks at all of the TV monitors in the living room. Locking the door by remote, Pit Bull walks over to the monitors and points to two that are focused on Lake Street and Bloomington Avenue. "They will never sneak up on me no more, Blood," he says solemnly.

Sitting down, Lil D asks, "Who?"

"Them peoples, scud. I got hit, Blood, by that motherfucker Red Beard and the FEDS.," Pit Bull says as he lights a fresh-dipped Moore.

"I see I'm just in time, homie," Lil D responds.

"Fo sho, my nigga. Go to the freezer and get your own."

As he walks toward the ice bar, Lil D gets on point. Then, smelling the piss burning in the other room, he relaxes at the scent of love in the air.

"Lil D, man, remember when you and Ghost come through to talk about that nigga Crooked?"

"Yeah, scud. Why?"

Look them two low-down bitches that was with that snitch, was the law.

Lil D sits down on the couch across from Pit Bull. There's a lost look on his face as he lights and pulls on the dip.

"They almost had me, too, but I put all that was left into the spots in the building." Standing up to walk to the window, Pit Bull pulls out two .44 Magnums from two holsters.

Lil D's heart starts to beat a hundred miles an hour and sweat starts to pour down his Jug into his lap. "I got these two for them two bitches," Pit Bull says.

"Damn, Pit Bull, it's hotter than motherfucker in here, fam."

"You wet, Blood. Take off that leather coat, yo."

"Shit, I forgot I had it on, scud."

Pit Bull looks out the window and pulls on the Moore. "Blood, I'm almost through with this hustlin' shit, dog. That was close."

Lil D walks over to stand next to Pit Bull. "What you looking at, fam?"

"My 2008 Lexus IS7. I just bought that yesterday. That's right, blood. I need to floss a little bit, dog, you know.

"But real talk, dog. That nigga, Tank's brother Scab was in the raid over here, too, so I need to move my operation from here. I can't have them crabs creep up on me."

"I feel you, son."

"Fuck that for right now, Lil D. What's hood with the killer, yo?"

"Doing me dog, you know. Pit Bull, you got a bucket around I can use, fam, for a while?"

"Yeah, in the back, dog. My 1993 Acura NSX is on deck. Don't do no bullshit in it, though, fam. I need that whip, yo. I knew you didn't just stop by, Lil D."

"You know me like a book, blood."

"We go way back son, like two 79 'lacks, you know."

The buzzer rings. Pit Bull walks over to the TV monitors and smiles. "Look, dog, I got me some pussy coming in, so here's the keys and make sure you bring me my hoodie back, Lil D."

"Damn. She fine, blood. I never seen her before, scud."

"I know. So holla."

Pit Bull opens the door for Lil D to leave and buzzes Pinky to enter the building at the same time. "One. And good looking out, Pit Bull."

What is this nigga on now? I can smell gunpowder on this nigga and I seen the blood on his hands, too. That nigga started sweating bullets when I pulled out my Mags. I have to watch blood closer. He bugging.

"Hey, daddy," Pinky speaks to Pit Bull as he comes down the hallway, breaking his train of thought.

"What up, baby?" Pit Bull asks, moving out of the way so Pinky can enter the apartment.

"You, sexy. That's what's up," she replies, dropping her leather trench coat and revealing nothing but skin under it. Pit Bull closes the door just as quickly as he opened it.

"Blood, that lick we pulled with Lil D put us on for real, Big Chief. We got to blow two crabs away, plus one for a bonus on the way to the hood, dog."

"Yeah, that was some s'more shit right there, son."

"Broad daylight. Damn! That nigga Lil D don't give a fuck like us."

"Live how you eat, dog, is the motto. Damn, we riding Mercedes Benzes and shit now, dog, 'cause of that nigga Lil D. Damn."

"But if we have to lay that nigga down, we have to do it, Big Chief."

"Pass me the vial so I can dip me one more before we go holler at Black Mike, yo."

Tre Duce and Big Chief sit outside of the house and talk in Big Chief's white and tan Mercedes Benz SL 550.

"What's taking them two wet heads so long to get out of the Benz? Damn."

"Them niggas getting wet out there."

"Damn."

"I know, K.C. They don't know you want to holla at them, big homie."

"Let them take their time, blood. I ain't in no rush, you. Fire up some of that purp over there."

"Roll up your own shit, big homie."

"Them two shorties done come up since the last time I was here, Rob."

"Yeah, they cutthroat, willing to do what it takes."

"Where the blunts at, Mike?"

"Oh, my bad. In the freezer, blood, to stay fresh."

K.C. walks through the living room to the kitchen. "This pad is straight, Mike. Looks like a woman decorated for you." He walks back to the living room and Big Chief and Tre Duce walk through the front door.

"K.C. Big homie!" shouts Big Chief.

Chapter 24

"Baby, it's getting late," says Killer to Cookie.

"Let's just go up into Victoria's Secret real quick so I can get a little something for your eyes only," she says softly.

"You got that, baby. But let me pick out something for you to model later."

Cookie smiles at the clerk as she walks through the door and strolls over to a blue negligee with fishnet stockings on a display mannequin. She points to it and Killer smiles. She approaches the clerk and says, "Can I get —" Before she can finish her sentence, Killer grabs her arm.

"Look, baby. See that white guy over there trying to look normal on the bench outside the door?"

"Yeah, why?"

"That's the fuckin' feds from Cali."

"You cool, right?" she asks, looking concerned.

"Here, take this money and the truck keys and I'll get at you later. Don't worry about me, baby. I've been feeling funny all day. Every time I looked to our backside with my peripheral vision, I could see someone following us through the mall, but I played it off."

He kisses Cookie on the lips and loosens his leather coat to give access to the Two Face Uzis inside. As he makes his way to the mall exit, Cookie says, "I love you, baby. Be careful."

Looking casual as a regular, Killer sits down beside Crown and pulls out one of the Uzis. He shoves it into his side. He grabs one of Crown's arms to conceal the Mag under it. Speaking in very low tones with murder leaking from his voice, Killer says, "I'm leaving out this bitch with you as my shield or you die right now, fuzz."

"Look, son, you won't make it out of here no matter what you do," Crown says none too confidently. "I have agents all over this mall waiting for the chance to put a bullet in your head. Give yourself up right now and I can help you, Dorance."

"Our cover has been blown, sir," Burgess says to Kline on his Nextel.

"I see that. Copy."

"What do you want to do, sir?"

"Play by play, we take him down when it's clear."

"Roger that, sir."

"Get up and no funny shit, cop, or I put some of these Teflons into your vest."

Cookie walks out of Victoria's Secret holding her bags and winks at Killer. She heads toward the elevator. Killer puts one of his massive hands on the back of Crown's neck and leads him toward the escalator. He looks back over his shoulder and notices a figure with his hand tucked under his coat, looking very intent. At the top of the escalator, Killer squeezes Crown's neck hard, like a melon, and it pops. He lets off six shots into Crown's side and throws him over the side of the escalator. Screams issue from the floor below.

Randall, Dan and Burgess pull out their weapons to shoot, but there are too many innocent people near to get a straight shot off. Down on one knee, Randall takes a shot before Killer slides down the side of the railing to escape. As he reaches the bottom of the escalator, Killer looks up into the agent's eyes and says, "Ain't no love in this garden block of life."

"Shit, Crown's dead, Randall," says Dan as he looks over the railing at a motionless body. Call for EMS now, Burgess."

"We can't let him get away now. You two take pursuit and I'll cross over from the east side to cut him from the closest exit, says Randall.

Mall security runs through the food court and meets Killer at the corner. "Freeze, sir. Stop and put down your weapon now." People stand frozen in shop doors, watching the confrontation.

Killer sprays the spot where the security guards stand pointing their weapons at him. He hits three and wounds one. Dan and Burgess close in on his position, their guns raised in combat mode. "Stop, Dorance. FBI. Put down your weapon."

Killer snatches a passing woman to shield himself from shooting. "Fuck you, cop." He backs up, knowing he has to keep moving to avoid capture. He looks at his shoulder and notices a spot of blood forming on his leather coat. *Shit, I'm hit.*

"Let the woman go and surrender."

Killer backs up toward the railing and looks over at the blown-up cartoon balloons below them. Randall approaches from Killer's blind side, creeping low to avoid drawing his attention. His finger is on the trigger, waiting for a clean shot. Burgess moves counter clockwise to trap the suspect. "Nowhere to go. Release the woman," Dan shouts.

Sweat drips from Killer's face. His heart races and his shoulder starts to ache from the wound. Shoving the woman toward Burgess, he lets off a bundle of shots, hitting him in the stomach. He jumps backwards over the railing, landing on the balloons that break his fall.

"I'm hit, sir," shouts Burgess. "It's a stomach wound. I'll be fine. Get the bastard, will you?"

"Help is on the way," a security guard tells Dan.

Dan looks over the railing and shakes his head. *This guy is so unpredictable!*

Stopping just long enough to make sure the woman isn't hit, Randall runs toward the elevator. He presses the button in a frenzy. *Come on, come on, you goddamn elevator!*

Running toward the front exit, Killer stops short as he sees the Bloomington police enter the mall. Thinking fast as they approach with caution, he plays the victim. He closes his coat to conceal the Uzis. "They're shooting over there, officer, and I'm hit!"

"There is medical help outside, sir," says one cop. Killer Boy casually strolls out the two double glass doors and looks for a cab to hail. Dan and Randall exit the elevator, running toward the front exit. They stop to ask one of the officers, "Have you seen a big black male wearing a black leather coat? He's wounded."

"Yes," says the last officer to see Killer. "He went through those doors over there."

"Is this cab taken?" asks Killer as he opens the back door and tosses a stack of C-notes in the cabbie's lap.

"No, sir," replies the cabbie with a smile. "It's your cab now. Where to?"

Killer gives him an address and slumps down into the seat as Dan and Randall burst through the mall's front doors with the Bloomington Police on their heels. The cab driver makes a left out of the lot to avoid the police who want to keep his bonus.

Randall stops the car behind the cab and searches it. He bangs it on the back fender as he realizes Killer's not in it.

The cab driver exits onto Highway 77 North and looks into the rearview mirror to find Killer Boy calm. He sees the shoulder wound, but minds his own business and says nothing.

"Stop every fucking thing with wheels on this property now, and block every possible exit. Now, people!" Dan shouts. He looks at Randall with revenge in his eyes.

"You touch ours, we touch yours," Randall says.

"No more playing games, Randall, with these gangbangers. Hear me."

"Yes, sir."

"It's 8:45 p.m., Judge Sinclair."

"Stand by, sergeant. I'm getting the warrant to go into the house as we speak. It's a go. Take them down and I'm on my way."

"Copy that, sir. People, we have the warrant secure to go into the house and apprehend the suspects. These two are armed and very dangerous. They may be under the influence of some kind of drug, so move with caution. Officer Jones will hit the door with the battering ram. Officer Covington will ram the back door. We move at the same time on my call. I want everybody on Channel 3, people. Let's move to surround the house. Let the task force go inside to clear the house."

"You thought you were the dick motherfucker, huh?" Tank says as he walks through the door and cuts the light on Do-Right. Puffing on a lovely, he sits down in the chair at looks at his watch. "It's almost show time, nigga. The homies will be back soon to knock your fuckin' brains out, cuz."

Do-Right looks away from Tank and sees a figure through the window that he doesn't recognize peeking through the window sill. *The police. I'm saved.* He relaxes a little at the thought of leaving alive. He lies back and closes his eyes for a second. Bap, bap, bap. Tank hits Do-Right's already broken knees with the bat that was on the floor beside the bed. Muted screams escape from Do-Right's throat, muffled by the duct tape over his mouth. Tears of pain flood his face.

Tank laughs and drops the bat to the floor, then slaps Do-Right with the 10 mm pistol. It makes a deep cut over his left eye and leaks blood into it. He stands over him. "You're a slob now, homie, so bleed, nigga. You pretty motherfucker, yo." He spits into Do Right's face. "Bitch nigga, want to smoke with me, cuz? Here, loc." He smashes the lit end of the Moore on top of Do-Right's head. "Yeah," laughs Tank. "Sizzle, nigga." He holds his head still to inflict more pain.

Tank sees a shadow outside the window and moves over to inspect the outside of the house. Just as he reaches the window, one of the task force officers lifts his head to look through the glass. On instinct, Tank shoots the officer as soon as his face comes into view. Tat, tat, tat. The silver 10 mm spits through the glass and kills the officer on contact.

Tank runs toward the living room, shouting, "Cops, cuz! Spook, we got company. Heat up, loc!"

Spook grabs the AK-47 off of the couch and posts behind the chair. He waits for the door to fly open. Tank pops a clip into the HK and posts up in the kitchen by the back door.

"Man down. Move in now! I repeat, man down. Move in now!"

On command, both doors fly open. The officers take heavy fire from Spook and Tank, who sends the task force running backwards for cover. "Officer Covington's hit, sir, and he's in direct gunfire."

Spook creeps closer, like a Vietnam vet. He lets off a few more shots.

"Somebody help me! I can't move my legs!" shouts Covington, who's lying on the back steps on his back with the battering ram on top of him. Sensing wounded prey, Tank crouches down low and makes his way to the doorway. Stopping behind the kitchen counter to aim, he lets off one shot, hitting Officer Covington under his chin when he looks up to spot Tank's position. The top of Covington's head blows off.

Automatic gunfire hits the house at random. Tank and Spook move upstairs to avoid being hit and reload their weapons. They shut the door behind them, ready for war.

"Sir, we have a hostage situation in there."

"Move, people, move!"

Officers enter the house, cautiously surveying the kitchen and living room for threats. "Sweep the bottom floor for the hostage now."

"I have him, sir, but he can't walk." An officer carries Do-Right out to safety while the rest of the task force focuses on the upstairs. One by one, they climb the stairs, each one covering the others' backs, ready for surprises.

"Here, put on this bullet-proof vest," says Spook. "If we go, we go out hard, cuz." He slides the dresser in front of the door.

"Fuck!" yells Tank in frustration. "Who gave us the fuck up, loc?"

"That's not important right now, Tank," Spook says calmly. "When that door pop open, shoot to kill."

"We might make it out alive, loc," Tank says hopefully.

"I don't think so, Tank. We trapped, but we got heat for they ass. Ain't nothing but killers in real niggas. Feel me, loc?"

"Yeah, son, I got you, Spook."

The window shatters from a smoke bomb thrown through it. Spook grabs a shirt, picks up the bomb, and throws it back out the window.

"Come out now with your hands up. This is Sgt. Jenkins from Homicide, and you won't be hurt. This is your last warning, fellas."

Feeling superior off of the dip, Tank lets off ten shots through the door. He makes the task force re-think its approach to the situation. "Men, let's go back to the streets to come up with a better strategy. They have the upper hand on us right now with the strength of the special ammunition they're using on us."

Lt. Cummins arrives on the scene. "How's it looking, people?" Sgt. Bell of the task force steps up.

"We've lost two of our men so far, and they are using armor-piercing bullets, sir. We came out to regroup. They had a hostage we rescued, sir."

"Where is he?"

"Leaving with the EMS."

"Listen, get the neighbors on both sides out of their houses so we can put snipers close to the room where they're holed up."

"Yes, sir."

"Call the station and get us some more weapons for the task force to even the odds, Sgt. Jenkins."

"On it, sir."

Cummins takes the bullhorn and starts speaking. "David Thompson and Mike Sooden, I'm going to throw a cell phone through the window for you to talk to me, so don't shoot, okay?"

"Do what you want, cop," says Spook. "Ain't shit to talk about."

He turns to Tank. "We killed some cops, loc. We won't go for no mind game on this. It's capital murder, loc." He sits on the floor out of sniper range. He watches the door.

A cell phone flies through the window, wrapped in cushioning. It rolls on the floor near Tank's feet. They look at each other and think, *This is how it ends.* The phone rings and Tank and Spook look at each other like, "You answer it."

"Fuck it, loc, I'll answer it," Spook says. He grabs the Nextel and takes the cushion off. It stops ringing. "He'll call back," says Cummins.

Spook presses the talk button. The phone explodes in their faces. The C4 pack inside the phone blows both of them into pieces. Every window in the house shatters. Glass blows into the neighbor's house onto the snipers.

"Move in, people. Clean up and make sure no one else is in the house."

Chapter 25

"Cuz, have you pushed homie's wig back?"

"Look, loc, let me do me. I don't answer to you, cuz, so get my fuckin' doe ready for cleaning up after your ass."

Wiggling out of the embrace Tamika has on his body, Rich sits straight up. "Nigga, as long as I have to put doe into your pocket, you answer to me, cuz." He hangs up abruptly on Maniac, slides out bed and starts the shower. As he waits for the water to heat, he contemplates murder.

Who the fuck this slumming ass nigga think he's talking to? Rich chews this over as he sits outside of the house on Clavall, waiting for Biggie to come out. He sips Crown Royal whiskey and smokes a dip stick, waiting patiently for the kill.

Inside the house, the sun shines through Biggie's window, blinding him as he rolls over to look outside. *Damn, I slept all night long and didn't call Flip back yet. Them niggas might think I punked out on them. Let me hit cuz up to see what's the deal.* He picks up the cell phone on the dresser. It's nine in the morning. *It's too early to be calling them right now.*

He lies back down on the bed and visualizes the vicious manner that Spook violated Do-Right the other night. The thoughts bring Biggie back to his feet to grip the .380 from under his pillow. He's alert now, and wakeful about his surroundings. He steps to the window and looks bout, but notices nothing out of the ordinary. He relaxes in the chair by the window.

Maniac makes a prophetic sign after he puts on his Dish One employee's uniform and prepares for the onslaught that's about to happen to his opponent for his opprobrium to the Shotgun Crips. He exits the white van wearing a tool belt and carrying a notepad. He heads toward the front door feeling very optimistic about the situation. He looks attentively back and forth, up and down the block, thinking about any obstacle that lies ahead.

He rings the doorbell once and stands back to be in view of the person who answers the door. He smiles.

"I got it, baby," Nikki yells from the kitchen where she's making a pot of coffee. She closes her robe and makes her way to the front door. Who can be at the door at this time of the morning? The doorbell rings again. "I'm coming, hold on." She looks through the peephole and smiles to herself. "Who is it?" she asks.

"Dish One, ma'am. I'm here to update some equipment you have," responds Maniac.

He's very cute for a Dish network worker. She answers, "One moment," and opens her robe slightly to show off the top of her nipples before she opens the door. She greets him with elegance, showing passion and sensibility.

"Good morning, ma'am."

"Yes, it is, Mr. Dish Man." Her voice is full of promise and insinuation.

Maniac is embarrassed to feel a child-like blush spread across his face. He finds himself staring at 36DDs pointing straight in his face.

"Are you sure you're qualified, worthy of choice to handle your job?" Nikki coaxes him.

Guided by experience rather than theory, Maniac responds. He relies on observation or experiment. He moves to the side so he can enter the house.

"What's your name?" she asks.

"Mike," Maniac answers as Nikki closes the door, opens up her robe completely and drops it to the floor. Turning around, he sees a naked Nikki standing behind him. *She's very persuasive, that's for sure, with a flawless body and huge tits and ass on her.*

He drops the tool belt to the floor after setting the notepad down on the couch. He approaches Nikki with an obliging look of lust on his face and an erection showing through his pants. He walks toward Nikki, stopping in front of her. "Turn around, baby, for me," he says.

Obediently, Nikki turns around. Getting closer, Maniac gently pushes on her naked ass cheeks with his erection to confuse her mind. Thinking about his obligation, he pulls out a hunting knife and grabs the back of her neck. He presses the blade into her kidney slowly, then releases the back of her neck to cover her mouth as she tries to scream. "Shut up, bitch. Now listen to me, freak. Where is he, and don't play games now."

Nikki cries quietly from the pain and points up the stairs.

"Who else is here?" Maniac asks as he slides the blade deeper into her kidney. Nikki shakes her head from side to side, about to faint. "Good girl." He shoves the knife all the way into her body with emphasis on showing no empathy toward her feelings. "Now you're obsolete to me, ma."

Maniac lays the corpse face down on the couch and picks up the tool belt. He retrieves two snub nose pistols with silencers on them. He looks back at Nikki as he creeps up the stairs. *She's very pretty, but so slow to understand the murder game.*

He stops at the top of the stairs and hears the shower running down the hall and music playing. He walks into the bathroom and sees the .380 lying on the toilet where Biggie had put it close by, just in case he needed to grab it quick and defend himself. Maniac stands in the doorway, listening.

Biggie's phone starts to ring. He looks at the caller ID through the clear shower curtain and says, "Yes, Lacy." He reaches for the phone and sees Maniac standing in the doorway with two pistols pointed at him. Maniac smirks at the .380 and the phone on the toilet. Biggie follows his gaze and says, "Do it, cuz. You get one chance to live." He covers his private parts and contemplates his next move.

Tat, tat, tat. Three shots through the shower curtain leave his face leaking in the shower water. Two to the head killed him instantly; one went into his abdomen. He slouches down in the shower, dead. Maniac opens up the shower curtain to empty the rest of the shells into his victim, then flees the scene, wiping anything he may have touched on the way in.

He stops to pick up his tool belt and straps it back on, then heads out of the house. He gets into the van and drives off. "E.B.K.," Maniac whispers as he leaves.

"You have a call from a federal correctional institution. Press 7 to decline the call or press 5 to accept."

Tamika presses 5 and a deep voice comes over the phone. "Who this?"

"Nigga, you calling my house, Detrick, remember?"

"Yeah, ma. My bad, shorty. Where my dude at?"

"Downstairs."

"You miss me?"

"I sure do, daddy."

"What you miss about me, ma?"

"Your big-ass dick and the way you used to fuck me with it, big daddy. I'll always be your bitch, baby, and I'll be to see you tomorrow with your – you know."

"Chill, baby. What you doing right now?"

"Playing with my pussy. Ooohhh . . . yeahhhh . . . Baby, your voice makes me feel so freaky, daddy." She lies back on the bed spread-eagle and flicks on her clit.

"Let me hear your sexy morning voice, bitch," he urges her on.

"Let me get my rabbit, baby, so you can get the full effect."

Downstairs, hand over the receiver, Rich is getting horny again. He thinks about being up inside Tamika and his dick gets hard. *This bitch should be a real hoe. Shit.*

"Mmmmm," Tamika moans as she slurps the dildo.

"Yeah, baby, suck that dick for daddy. I want to hear everything," says the voice on the phone. She stands up by the edge of the bed and positions herself above the rabbit to sit down on it. She releases soft moans of ecstasy into the phone. "Uhh . . . ooooo . . . Yessss . . . Fill my pussy up, daddy."

"Do that shit, ma."

Rich gently hangs up the phone and creeps up the stairs to join the fun. As he reaches the bedroom door, a text message vibrates his cell phone. "Get me my doe, nigga." He texts back, "We good on that shit, loc." The message makes him feel hot, like he stepped into a ninety-five-degree heat wave. He calms back down at the sight of Tamika fucking herself. He pulls down his khakis and walks out of them. He stands next to the bed and smiles and strokes himself harder.

Sweat drips down Tamika's Jug. Her eyes are closed as she shoves the rabbit all the way to the end into her moist, wet, swollen pussy lips. She senses some pressure and opens her eyes to see a rock-hard Rich standing beside the bed, pre-cum spilling onto her thigh. Sex fills the air.

She pulls the rabbit out of her pussy lips slowly, with erotic moans of pleasure escaping her mouth. She arches her back to savor the release of the rabbit. She looks very seductive, licking her lips and gripping the rabbit with her pussy muscles as she pulls the head of it out of her body. She sets it down on the bed and grabs Rich's swollen dick. She puts the head of it into her mouth and plays with it with her tongue ring. She hears Detrick say he'll call later. The phone goes dead in her ear.

She grips Rich's dick with both hands and circles the head with her tongue, moving inch by inch down her throat. Rich takes photos with his cell phone to send to Detrick to view in the joint. It takes her by surprise, but she says, "Lay down, daddy." She guides Rich to lie on his back, then reaches for some heated massage oil to apply to his hard dick to elevate the sensation. She squeezes some of the oil in the palm of her hand and strokes his dick. He feels a sense of pleasure and relaxes fully to explore the experience that awaits him.

He runs his hands through her long, wavy hair and pushes her head further and further down his dick. "It's so fuckin' good, ma," he says. She slides her lips gently up and down his shaft, pressing softly to arouse him more. She gets up on all fours, pussy dripping cum, swollen and hot. "Play with my ass, daddy, please."

He places a firm hand on each one of her cheeks and spreads them open. He slides his right middle finger in and out of her ass. "Whose dick is this?" she asks.

"Yours, bitch," he answers.

"Who's your bitch, daddy?"

"You are."

She pushes back against his finger and rotates her ass in a circular motion. "Daddy, I'm about to make you cum. I can feel it." She begins deep throating him, long and slow, pulling on his shaft. He cums like a volcano, filling up her mouth. She sucks every drop down like a vanilla milk shake.

"Baby," Rich says, "I need to lay down before you kill me with that head of yours."

She smiles, walks to the bathroom, and gets into the shower.

Maniac gets out of the van on Fourth and Logan Avenue North, leaving the keys on the seat for a potential car theft to occur. He walks over to a 2009 Aston Martin DB9 coupe. As he reaches into his pocket to pull out the keys, he looks up the block and sees an unmarked police car parked not too far away. He looks to see if the car is occupied and decides to walk to Norma's to get a bite to eat.

As he approaches the car, he notices two police officers inside with a camera taking photos of the neighborhood. Turning to the left, one of the officers looks Maniac straight in the face and snaps a shot of him. Maniac flips him off and mugs as he strolls about his business.

Agent Dan Lyons and Executive Agent Randall Wright sit in the car, focused on the situation at hand, finding Killer Boy. "The cab driver said that he let him out on this corner, but didn't see where he went, Dan," says Wright.

"Randall, he's made us look very unprofessional. That's what has us in this unfortunate predicament now, sir."

"We deny him the basic necessities of the game now to trap him up, Dan."

"That's probable, sir. We can't fail at this attempt."

"There are other agencies looking for him as well. Dan, we have to find him and kill him before some other agency finds him and locks him up."

Wright puts down the camera and Lyons starts the car. They cruise to Sixth Street and park to survey the neighborhood more. They watch the early-morning fiends get their fixes from the young drug dealers on the block. "Mark, these kids look to be getting younger and younger each year."

"Yeah, I know. But there's nothing we can do about that. It's up to their parents to instill morals and self-respect into them, sir." He grabs the camera and points it at a man walking down the sidewalk. He looks very much like Killer Boy. Mark snaps photos of the man, trying to place the face in the Rolodex he keeps in his head. "Let's go get this film developed, Randall."

They pull away from the scene, sensing Killer Boy's nearness.

Chapter 26

Lil D is having second thoughts about getting caught up in the cat-and-mouse game he and Lacy have started with Ghost and Rich. It's cost many people their lives.

Sitting in the Lazy Boy and drinking Hennessy and Coke, Lacy watches Lil D's thirty-two-inch flat screen TV and comes up with one last plan to be on the safe side. She contemplates sharing her thoughts with Lil D.

"What's on your mind, Killer B?" asks Lil D.

"Shit, nigga, let me think for a second on some shit," she replies. "Yo. Look, the only two people who can put us out there are Rich and Maniac, right?"

Lil D grabs the remote beside him and begins to channel surf. "Yeah, so what's your angle, Lacy?"

Lacy comes over to sit beside him on the couch. She picks up a blunt, puts some heat to it and takes a long puff to get an instant head rush. She coughs, chokes and starts to gag, her eyes red. She reaches for the glass Lil D's drinking out of to soothe her throat. Lil D pats her back and rubs his hand up her blouse without rejection. An erection comes up. Noticing, Lacy rubs it through his boxers, then leans him back onto the couch to get a better view as she pulls it out through the boxer legs. She strokes him slowly.

"Now, back to what I was saying, nigga." She sips the Hennessy and drops her mouth over his shaft as she explains her plan in between licks and sucks. She deep throats his pipe, stopping to let the warmth consume him. Stroking slowly and softly pulling her mouth up for air, her head is right above his dick. "We need to knock them off real quick, Lil D. The way I see it is to close all ties to them. The shit me, you and my sister did can get us killed, boo." She closes her eyes, moving her head to the strokes she gives hm.

"I don't know, Lacy. They two smart crabs," Lil D says. "Oooowww . . . ooowww . . ." That's all Lil D can say after Lacy applies her mouth to his dick with a couple of ice cubes tucked in her cheek. She swirls the ice cubes around in her mouth to drive him crazy. He grabs the back of her head, pushing her face down as far as he can. He feels very arrogant at the sight of Lacy busting him down so good. He picks up the pace of fucking her mouth, busting off a thick load down her throat and screaming, "Shiiiittt, biitchhhh!" She sucks down every bit of juice before sitting up.

Panting, Lil D says, "How that sound, me running from a confrontation, ma?" He looks Lacy in the eyes. "Let's finish what we started, shorty." He stands up and scans the room for the artillery he has arranged for his safety. He smiles to himself as he looks at his arsenal.

Across the street sits a black Ford Expedition. Pit Bull, Big Chief, Tre Duce, and K.C. are posted inside, watching through the open window with high-powered binoculars and a high-tech listening device that gives them a helpful advantage over the situation.

"Blood, how could he betray the hood like that, fam?" asks Pit Bull incredulously.

"I told you what Murder Mac told us before we merked his crab ass, scud," says Big Chief. "Where to, big homie?" They pull away from the house and head down the block to a parked black '91 Jeep Wagoneer 4 x 4. Pit Bull gets out of the Expedition and nods to them as they pull off. He pulls out a Nextel and dials K.C. He speaks into the phone in a low and very calm voice. "Yes, homie. It's one hundred percent. He on it as we speak." He hangs up the phone and sits back with a blank look on his face.

"Where to, big homie?" asks Big Chief as he drives down Highway

7, headed toward 169.

"That crab-lover broke the covenant, fam, and for that, his cranium has to be split. But not before we know the whole story, blood."

"I feel you on that shit, C.K. Big homie, his credibility is dead fo sho, dog," replies Tre Duce.

"Take me to the hood to blow some dip with my dogs, yo."

"Cool, blood. No problem there," answers Big Chief.

Handcuffed to the hot water heater in the basement of Du-Low's house, Shaunna is breathless at the thought of the shit that is to come. Just thinking about the brutal way she is about to die for fucking with the enemy makes her stomach turn flips. Not eating in four days adds to the pressure.

The basement door opens and a burly Du-low comes down the stairs and stands in front of Shaunna. "Bitch, you know this is business and not personal, don't you?" She shakes her head up and down in answer. "Now, look, hoe, when I get the call, you might get butchered the fuck up for your role in trying to set up the big dog."

He walks to the light switch and cuts the light to let light come through the window. "I haven't got the go-ahead to do shit to you yet. Not until we snatch up Lacy and Lil D's low-down asses, so chill, hoe."

Shaunna tries to remain quiet and undisturbed by the news she's just heard of her fate. She calculates her next move to try to save her life and comes up blank.

Du-low turns and walks back upstairs to finish playing NSA Live 2009 with Dirk. "Du-low!" Shaunna calls out, stopping him in mid-step.

"What, bitch?"

"Want to have some fun with me?" she says enticingly. "I know you want to fuck me, big daddy," she says desperately.

Du-low comes back down the stairs, grabbing his dick. Shaunna moans low, to arouse him. Du-low stands in front of Shaunna, then kneels to feel her big breasts. He loosens the buttons on her shirt to expose her 38DDs. He places the 9 mm Ruger on the floor, not thinking she can see it. He licks her erect nipples and sucks them roughly.

"Yes, baby, I like that. Don't stop," Shaunna says. "Baby, uncuff one of my hands so I can lay flat on my back to fuck you." She knows Du-low is thinking with his dick and not his brain, and tries to capitalize off of his vulnerability. "Baby, get some of this sweet pussy," she croons.

Du-low appears to be getting hornier by the minute. Suddenly his Nextel vibrates. He stands up to answer it. "Yeah. One," he says. He bends down to pick up the pistol. "Change of plans, ma." He strolls over to turn the lights on.

Damn, this nigga fucked up my plan, Shaunna has time to think. Du-low stands behind her. He smirks and places the Ruger to the back of her head. Boom. One to the head leaves her slumped on the water heater. "Bitch, you thought I was a trick, huh. Now look at you."

"Come on, blood. Let's finish up this bet, dog," shouts Dirk from the living room.

Rich and the lil homies shoot dice in a dark alley. The only light is from the street light on the corner. "Yeah, cuz, point!" shouts Rich as he picks up the bet from the concrete."

"Fuck, can a nigga get fooled, loc." Jug drops five Gs on the pavement. "You fooled, cuz."

"What's that, cuz?" asks Rich.

"Five stacks, big homie, and roll 'til you crap." Jug drops the bet on the pavement and shakes the dice. All eyes are on the dice as he releases them. One flips over and shows a one. The other spins before stopping on a one also. "Snake eyes, cuz. Good looking out, big homie," he says as he picks up his doe. "I'm up, cuz. I got to dip, big homie."

"Cool, cuz. 'Cause I got bricks to get off, lil homie. Did all you cats drop that doe on Dread over there to re-up, locs?"

"Yeah, you good, loc," replies Dread.

Rich walks over toward the 1970 Chevelle SS 454 where Maniac is posted in the passenger seat, chilling and talking to Will on the phone. Rich looks down the street at the headlights of an approaching car. *Who's that in that whip?* He pauses to see.

"He did what, O.G.? Snitched Spook and Tank out to the people? Fo sho, I'll make sure to bring him there, O.G."

A 2009 Bentley Continental GTC driven by a woman pulls up behind them. Rich reaches for his baby Desert Eagles, then relaxes when Will's face comes into view. "Cuz, what you doing over here, rolling up on me like this?" Rich asks. Will signals for him to get into the car. Rich sits down in the back seat and shuts the door with all eyes on him as they pull away.

"What it do, cuz? Shit, Will, what's the deal, my nigga?"

"Kathy, pull up there and park, baby, for a second," Will. He turns around to face Rich. "Lil homie, I got four hundred bricks of pure raw to off as a tester for you so you quit fucking with them Jamaicans." He grabs a plastic back off of the floor and hands it to Rich. "Here's a tester for you to see how pure my shit is. A whole brick on me, cuz. I need to know if you're in or out right now."

With the look of a tractable person all over his smiling face, Rich says, "I'm with you, cuz."

"It's 8:30 right now, cuz. Meet me at this address to pick up the shit at ten o'clock sharp. Don't be late, and bring Maniac with you."

"Cool, cuz. I got you." Rich opens the plastic bag to put some of the coke in one pink nail and rubs it on his gums for effect. They go numb almost instantly. "Damn, cuz, this is some fire shit. I see how you roll so tight, cuz."

Will looks at his watch. "I have to make moves, homie, I'll see you later." He opens the door to dip Rich, who puts the package into his Pelle Pell leather and shouts, "Shotgun Crip!" He strolls down the street, watching the back of the Bentley as it makes a left turn and disappears.

Maniac looks at Rich as he comes closer and he gets angrier by the second. *He broke the code too many times, and on top of all the other shit, he's a rat.*

Rich opens the door, tosses the brick in the back seat and breaks Maniac's train of thought.. They pull off. "We got somewhere to be later, cuz," says Rich.

"I'm with you."

The phone rings twice before Lil D answers, "Bounty hunters."

"Dog, I need you to meet me somewhere tonight to look out for me, scud," says Pit Bull. He's sitting outside of Lil D's place in a Jeep that Lil D doesn't recognize.

"Where you at, Pit Bull?"

"In the hood. Why?"

"I need to put on my war shit, you know, and drop off this bitch, too."

"Cool. Meet me at Seventeenth and Pleasant Avenue at 10 p.m. I'll be outside. One."

Down the street, Ghost and Black Mike watch from the opposite side of the street, waiting to follow Lil D. "She don't know her sister's ass is dead, blood," says Mike.

"I know, Black" Ghost replies. "She thinks shit all good. I never left town, blood. I just kicked back to see shit, you know?"

"I feel you, dog."

"Is Jay already there, scud?"

"Yeah, Ghost. He on point with K.C., Big Chief, Tre Duce and one of his folks."

Ghost smiles with grim satisfaction. "Them niggas with their grimy asses don't even know they all fixing to die together tonight, Black."

"Fuck them cats, Big Chief. They was trying to knock off my big brother," I say. "But the craziest thing about it is that I didn't want to fuck with Lil D the first time I met him."

"Well, look, Jay, that nigga is a real motherfuckin' killer if you ever seen one, scud," says Big Chief. He walks over to the window of the house on Pleasant to look out.

"When 10 p.m. comes, we become their makers' blood, so be on point, dog," says Tre Duce, dipping a Moore.

"Fam, the game is cold. Not fair to those who don't play by the rules," says C.K. as he loads two HKs.

"Who spot is this, fam?" asks Mario with a deadly smirk on his face as he notices the sound-proofed walls. He grips a silver AK-47.

"Don't worry about whose spot it is," I say. "Just do your part. I brought you with me to drop bodies, gangsta, so don't trip."

"I got you, Jay."

"Shhhh," says Big Chief, holding up his hand. "I see headlights outside. Somebody is coming up to the door now. I don't know who this is, blood."

I get up and walk to the window to take a look. "Man, that's my other brother! Open up the door, fam."

Will walks through the door with Do-Right following stiffly after him on crutches. They go straight to the back room without acknowledging any of us. I'm confused and I waste no time following them.

Lil D drops Lacy off at Ghost's house and dips off to meet Pit Bull at the spot. He's ready to hold him down one time with Two Face Mac-11s lying next to him on the front seat.

I shut the door behind me and give Will a puzzled look. "I can't explain it to you right now, Jay. But listen, go back out there and tell them when a black Chevelle SS pulls up, to let me know. Then come back here and stay put until I say so."

I nod and return to the living room. I see Big Chief looking out the window. "What that, scud?" I ask.

"Two niggas in a old school," he says.

"Go to the back room and tell my brother to come out, yo."

Rich shifts the two Uzis around as he gets out of the car. He glances over toward Maniac as they walk in silence to the door. They hit the first step and the door opens. Will stands there holding a blunt in his mouth. "Loc," he says. "You ten minutes early." They walk through the door. Before it's shut all the way, Will nods at Maniac, who pulls out two .45 Colts and puts them to Rich's head.

"You a snitch, cuz, and I can't fuck with your kind, loc," says Maniac.

Rich opens his mouth. "Don't even speak, nigga," Do-Right says as he comes over to disarm Rich. His eyes blaze and it's clear he's thinking about being raped.

"Take him in the back, duct tape his mouth and tie his ass the fuck up until the rest of them cutthroats get here," Will orders. He and Do-Right walk upstairs.

"Tell them to come out and wait on Lil D and Lacy," shouts Do-Right from the top of the stairs. He watches Maniac walk Rich to the basement with a smile on his face.

K.C. remembers who Will is now, and his smile grows larger at the sight before him. "Come on, blood, we up next, scud. They should be here soon, dog." He looks out the window and sees Pit Bull's Jeep parked outside.

"We good to go, fam?" asks Tre Duce.

"Fo sho, killer. The O.G.s got this shit under control."

Pit Bull looks into his rearview mirror and sees a red Mustang GT creep up behind him and park. Lil D jumps out of the Mustang and walks over to Pit Bull to give him dap. "What business you got over here, blood?" he asks.

"This nigga that K.C. knows got some bricks he's try to get off for cheap, and I want in," says Pit Bull. "Feel me."

"Yeah, so let's go in and buck these niggas, Pit Bull."

"That's the plan, you know," Pit Bull says agreeably. "You strapped, blood?"

"Two Face Mac-11s on me to spray, homie. Come on, let's get money, fam," Lil D says eagerly.

"Let me get my extended clip out of the glove box real quick." Pit Bull opens the Jeep door and leans down to open the glove box. He sees two people in black hoodies on the other side of the Jeep wink at him. He shuts the door and inserts the clip into the 10 mm. "Come on, blood. Let's drop these out-of-town fools."

Lil D puts his hands inside his hoodie and follows Pit Bull. As they walk toward the house, Mario and I pop up from the other side of the Jeep and place our weapons to each side of Lil D's head and pull his hands out of his pockets. Pit Bull raises Lil D's hoodie and snatches the Two Face Mac-11s. "You won't be needing these no more, nigga," he says evenly.

"You set me up, Pit Bull," Lil D says incredulously.

"Nah, you been playing both sides, blood."

Mario puts the AK hard into Lil D's gut. "Take that nigga to the basement with the other trash, fam," Pit Bull orders.

Ghost calls into the house to talk to Lacy. "I'll be right out," she says. "Give me a second to lock up."

"Cool, lil sis," he says, then hangs up. He turns to Black Mike. "When she come out to the car, knock her ass out and put her into the trunk, blood."

"Got it, Ghost."

The trunk latch pops open on the 2009 white Charger. Mike gets out to open the door for Lacy. As she starts to sit down, he strikes her on the back of her head, knocking her out cold. He places her in the trunk and Ghost pulls off.